# You Must Be Jo King

*Not so much a diary, more a way of life!*

Moira Murphy

The Book Guild Ltd

First published in Great Britain in 2017 by
The Book Guild Ltd
9 Priory Business Park
Wistow Road, Kibworth
Leicestershire, LE8 0RX
Freephone: 0800 999 2982
www.bookguild.co.uk
Email: info@bookguild.co.uk
Twitter: @bookguild

Typeset in Minion Pro

Printed and bound in Great Britain by 4edge Limited

ISBN 978 1912083 114

British Library Cataloguing in Publication Data.
A catalogue record for this book is available from the British Library.

Printed on FSC accredited paper

*To Eddie,*
*For keeping the faith*
*–x–*


*And,*
*To the rest of the Gang,*
*With Love*
*–x–*

# 1

## IT'S LIFE AS WE KNOW IT

Life. Some people manage it. Excel in it. Pirouette in ballet shoes around it. Amanda, the managing director's ex PA was one. Amanda was never late, never flustered, never a hair out of place, no chipped nail varnish, no discernible knicker line, wouldn't be seen dead hauling up a bra strap and heaven forbid that a dog's hair should come anywhere near her, oh-just-grabbed-it-in-sales, Armani jacket. No, childless and dogless, Amanda merely levitated in Chanel and cool detachment, an inch or two above us lesser mortals, until, that is, the day she drifted off and into the passenger seat of some high-flying city-type's Porsche.

Being one of the lesser mortals and surviving in some parallel universe to Amanda is me. Sadly, no city-type with a Porsche is waiting in the wings to whisk me off, or if he is I haven't noticed, distracted as I am by demanding kids and picking up dog poo and giving myself a pat on the back if it gets to lunchtime and I haven't had a breakdown. Me, I couldn't even manage to hang onto George and his Qashqai.

Me, is approaching forty and about to be divorced; George, my ex, having upped and left ten months ago to live with 'soul

1

mate' Fran. Now, although I realise it's possible I should have been a bit more devastated by this than is actually the case, the fact remains, I'm not. Peeved, yes, devastated, no. Peeved because while George is living the life of Riley, I now have sole responsibility for Lucy, fourteen next birthday, and Josh, nearly thirteen, who would gladly shop each other to the local mad-machete man without a seconds thought and, just to make absolutely sure my mental capacities are stretched to breaking point, I also now have Millie, a cross-bred Springer Spaniel who, it has since transpired, George brought home for the kids as a distraction to his leaving. His plan has worked because the dog is driving us, well me anyhow, to distraction and, although my previous knowledge and experience of dogs is non-existent, the appellation 'Springer' in Millie's case seems more than apt; spring-loaded is possibly nearer the mark. God only knows what she was crossed with because it seems George didn't bother to find that out.

So there we are and, although I had never really given George much credit for forward thinking, he was definitely on the ball the day he shipped out. Oh, yes! He was well out of it him and his excuses. I can hear him now:

"I mean let's face it, Jo, you were never there for me, always gadding about doing God knows what."

"God knows what! Do you mean looking after the kids, cleaning the house, going to work, doing your accounts and looking out for my mother? While you were where? It'll come to me in a minute. Oh, yes, you were having it off with fantastic Fran."

"Oh there you go, sarcastic as ever. Let's face it, Jo, apart from the kids, you and I just had nothing in common anymore."

Of course we have a common denominator now, we both live with bitches; mine being Millie the four-legged variety; his being Fran.

Fran runs a Man Power Recruitment agency, George has a

small building business which often needs to recruit short term labour. Fran had 'business luncheoned' George to within an inch of his life, promising discounted rates should he use her agency.

Now, it had been one thing George getting fat on all the business lunches Fran was providing, as well as being fed all the egotistical claptrap she was doling out, but bringing it home to me had been another matter. I did not want to hear it. He had stalked me with silly Fran sagas until I wanted to string him up.

The kettle would be boiling, the toast would be burning, the kids would be late for school and Josh would be unable to find his other trainer yet George would follow me around, prattling on about Fran starting up an agency for school leavers. I would be late for work. He would be hanging onto the open car door preventing me from moving off because he had forgotten to tell me that Fran, some years ago, had had the wit to save a man's finger that had been severed with an electric saw so that it was able to be sewn back on.

It was Fran this and Fran that. Fran had impressed him with her A level in English Literature, told him she had read Shelley and Keats. I reminded him of my A Level in Art, but he said that didn't count. One day I found him pouring over Google trying to find out who the hell Shelley and Keats were.

So it seemed Fran had been after my husband from the word go and he had been seduced by the attractions of her 'company' in more ways than one. There had been no point in confronting George, he hadn't realised it yet, the subtly had eluded him. Of course combine the intuition women possess in spadeful with a wife's well-tuned antennae and it certainly hadn't escaped me.

He had said it was time he changed his image. This was delusional, George had no image. Yet, the stuff which had constituted no image – Velcro fastening trainers, shell suits, anoraks – etc began filling quite a few black bags for charity while

3

the trendy new gear which was to forge him an image replaced it on the empty shelves; all neatly piled in varying shades of blues and greys and all because Fran had told him blues and greys brought out the colour of his eyes. He began growing his hair longer because Fran had said he had a passing resemblance to Michael Hutchence. I said the resemblance was not so much passing as completely missed unless we were talking after Hutchence had hung himself, in which case, I could see where she was coming from. Instead of making his usual remark about sarcasm being the lowest form of wit, he had shook his head and walked away. It was clear Fran was making her presence felt;

> *Let's face it, George. Why have a wife who is not aware of your existence unless there's a spider in the bath or the grass needs cutting or the garden hose needs to be looped around that orange plastic thing on the back wall. Do not be told the grass is never greener on the other side. It is! Leave this life of drudgery to that simpleton you call your wife, she's used to it. It could be her middle name. Joanne 'Drudgery' Charlton. It suits her, don't you think? Has a certain ring to it.*

Of course it goes without saying that I had been curious to meet this Fran, in fact, it had become something of an obsession. I had devised scenarios in my mind which usually took the form of finding the two of them in the usual compromising situation, whereupon I would stand over them, aloof, superior, and dignified while they grovel for their underwear and my forgiveness.

Of course it also goes without saying that the drama of the imagined scenarios bore absolutely no resemblance whatsoever to the banal reality.

But, enough of that for now because today the kids and I had a doctor's appointment to get to and as appointments in our house were never arrived at without some degree of underlying panic; this was no exception. I was up-ending cushions because my car keys had to be somewhere. I was trying to get the kids to get a move on; trying to make myself heard over the noise of Lucy singing, 'Don'cha wish your girlfriend was hot like me', into her karaoke and Josh shouting triumphantly over all the people he'd managed to kill with the control button of his Xbox, while at the same time listening to my mother who was talking to me through the phone which was jammed between my shoulder and my cheek.

"… and you will need to watch out for the buses when you're out and about today, Joanne, because they've been painting them different colours. I mean why do we need Shocking Pink and Lime Green buses? What's wrong with just red? The Number 21 is now Canary Yellow with palm trees up the doors and parrots fluttering around the outside of the top deck. It's all very silly. Sadie said it's like mounting a fairground ride. Anyway, Joanne, forewarned is forearmed…"

I'd hardly been on a bus in ten years.

"… Oh, and by the way, Joanne, if a bus driver with an odd looking eye comes to see you, don't let him in. Oh, there's the doorbell. I hope it isn't those Jehovah's Witnesses again. Like I told them last time, I have enough on my plate trying to keep up with the Catholic Church without taking anything else on. I'll have to go, Joanne. Speak to you later, bye for now."

And off she went leaving me to wonder why on earth a bus driver with a dodgy eye would be coming to see me.

My mother is eighty-three. Apart from me and the kids, God, her best friend Sadie and my ex George (who, it has to be said, she is still very fond of) my mother's favourite people are Fiona Bruce, David Dimbleby, Alan Carr (as in, 'Alan Carr-chattiman, was on Loose, Woman today, Joanne, such a pleasant boy'), Father McCaffrey from St. Augustine's Church and Ant and Dec. Ant and Dec by virtue of the fact that Dec has a brother who is a priest.

Then the dog passed me, frothing at the mouth.

"Guess where I found *these*?" said Josh, jangling the car keys in my face. "They were only in the fruit bowl, innit."

I took the keys. "Please don't say innit, Josh, you do not live with gangsters."

"There's a tube of shower gel chewed to bits on the bathroom floor," said Lucy, coming downstairs. So the dog didn't have rabies. Just my luck. I grabbed the dog by the collar and pushed her into the kitchen. I filled her water bowl and I threw her a pig's ear (there was a time when, if I thought of pig's ears, which wasn't often it has to be said, I just assumed they were to be found on a pig, yet now, I keep a supply of them, roasted, in my kitchen cupboards! Sometimes I wonder what my life has become). I gave the dog strict instructions to chew the pig's ear and to leave the kitchen chair legs alone. Wishful thinking I know, but I live in hope.

I waited in the hall until the kids were sure they had all the technology they would need for a visit to a doctor's surgery, then I herded them out of the front door and into the car and we set off.

I say set off, although that's not strictly true because ten minutes later we were still on the drive, the car wouldn't start.

I had turned the ignition key and got a high-pitched whining noise. I'd turned it again and got the same noise.

"You'll flood the carburettor accelerating like that," warned a man's voice from over the front fence, "sounds to me like the battery's flat." I looked in the direction of the voice and saw a red face with a ginger beard and the body of a fading pink Camellia. "You'll need to leave it for a few minutes, give it time to settle."

I wound down the window, gave the man a smile of acknowledgement, took his advice and waited. Then from behind the fence the man nodded his indication for me to try the engine again. I did and with a bit of a splutter it grudgingly started up. The man started to move off but not before nodding his acknowledgment that this minor miracle was entirely down to his intervention.

I mouthed a thank you to God, made a mental 'note-to-self' (an expression picked up from my boss Ian which he accompanies with crooked fingers of exclamation marks), to remember to book the car in for a service with Mick the Mechanic; then we were off.

"Can I play One Direction?" asked Lucy, plugging in her MP3 player while ejecting Robbie Williams before I'd had time to answer, "and can we talk about my birthday please, because I've done sleepovers, pizzas and movies for the last three birthdays and this year I want something different?"

"How different?" I asked.

"A proper party with a DJ. I mean I will be fourteen!"

"Well if she's having a party," piped up Josh from the back seat, "I want a season ticket."

"Well if he can have a season ticket, I can definitely have a party."

"I haven't said yes to anything yet. Where do you suppose I'd get money for all of that?" I asked.

"Well, Dad might cough it up, innit," said Josh.

Cough! He'd probably choke on that, I thought.

Okay, so the house was mortgage free, courtesy of my father's legacy, I had my part-time job in Human Resources, there was no problem with George and his child maintenance and he usually called every other Friday to give the kids pocket money or to take them bowling or to the pictures which was actually more than he had done when they all lived in the same house; it just never seemed enough.

"It's a bit premature to be talking about your birthdays (there was exactly a year between Lucy and Josh), we've loads of time yet and please don't say innit, Josh."

"Well, *she* says, 'talk to the hand' and she gets away with that!"

"You are sooo juvenile, Josh," said Lucy.

"Takes one to know one," said Josh.

And on it went.

Now, although it might not be everyone's idea of a morning out, and sad as it may seem, I was actually quite looking forward to my visit to the doctor's. Perhaps if I'd had something seriously wrong I might have had to rethink that, but, as it is, I pictured the scenario in my mind's eye. I would sit between Lucy and Josh, first to keep them apart and second to inhibit some total stranger's determination to regale me with their illness. I would flick through an out of date magazine to see which celeb had lost weight then put it on again, or I might just think the thoughts I usually don't have the time to think.

# 2

## DR WATSON, I PRESUME

Although the carburettor had flooded and the roadwork lights were against us and the traffic seemed busier than usual, probably due to half-term holidays, surprisingly, for us, we arrived at the surgery with some time to spare.

Beryl the receptionist looked up from her computer screen, mopped her face and the back of her neck with a tissue, mumbled something about 'damned hot flushes' and with a sigh asked us to take a seat. It seemed Dr Khan, who we were meant to see, had been called out to an emergency and, call me cynical, but Beryl's sigh sounded suspiciously as though she was hoping our condition was serious enough to warrant the late finish which was obviously on the cards due to the backlog of patients now waiting to see the new locum: Dr Watson. This was *the* Dr Watson, who was responsible for turning my neighbour Janice, and most of her colleagues from the local bingo hall, into drooling hypochondriacs.

I looked around. The only empty seats were in the row that backed onto the back wall and which faced the rest of the waiting room. This was the row normally avoided by people who had an aversion to stage fright, but having no choice, I motioned to Lucy and Josh and the three of us sat down, divided from the rest of the waiting room by a magazine table and an arrangement of imitation plants.

My back itched. I sat on my hands trying to ignore the itching while wondering what I wouldn't give for a coat hanger and some privacy when a little boy, sitting in a corner amongst a scattering of toys, pointed to the Fat Controller on a Thomas the Tank Engine picture and called out loudly to his mother, "Look Mam, it's the fuckin' troller."

To which his mother, without looking up from the magazine she was flicking through, drawled, "I've told you not to say fuckin', Levi."

I smiled, different interpretations put onto things always made me smile. I had gone round singing, Give Pete a chance, for ages before someone pointed out that it was Give Peace a Chance. And Buddy Holly's cupid hadn't shot his dart, he'd shot his dog.

I looked at the Fat Controller. There was something about him that reminded me of my boss, Ian; something about the moon face and the dark suits and waistcoats. Ian always wore dark suits and waistcoats to work, to give the illusion, I suppose, of less bulk around his middle. It didn't work. Of course it was in stark contrast from wearing armour and wielding a pike as a Roundhead at the weekends and besieging towns in pretend battles. I mean, why would anyone want to do that?

I watched as Levi scored a direct hit with a Mega block, clattering it off the head of a naked Barbie doll which was straddling the wheel of an Action Man truck. Poor Barbie, where was Ken when she needed him and where were her designer outfits and make-up? There was a time when she would have been the proud possessor of a cute little camouflage number with nipped in waist and thigh high boots, just the ticket for riding around in an army truck. Strange as it may seem, I felt a kind of affinity with that doll. After all, Barbie was a cast-off, dumped, usurped and pulled from pillar to post by belligerent kids.

It seemed we were in for a long wait. I was occupied trying to ignore the itching when a Sunday supplement on one of the magazine tables caught my eye. A digitally enhanced – very digitally enhanced – picture of Delia Smith was on the front cover. What's she been up to I wondered? I was just about to reach for the magazine when a man suddenly appeared between me and the cheese plants and demanded I tell him where Robin Hood kept his horse. For a split-second I thought, hell, why me? But then I mentally took that back because being my mother's child I knew I should have been thinking, there but for the grace of God go I, but still.

Before I had time to switch my thoughts from why Delia Smith was front page news to the whereabouts of Robin Hood's horse, a woman hurried from the reception desk where she had been registering her appointment and took hold of the man's arm. Throwing apologies in my direction she persuaded the man into a seat; one away from Lucy. Once seated, the man, who we now knew as Trevor, stretched across the empty seat and leaning his elbows onto Lucy's knee, prodded at my arm with his fingertips while insisting I tell him where Robin Hood kept his horse. Lucy stiffened. Trevor's uninhibited use of her knee had rendered her immobile. It was obvious Trevor had no concept of stage fright whereas Lucy and I had an acutely overdeveloped concept of it. I smiled at Trevor. A bit forced admittedly, but which I hoped might extend a smidgen of empathy and quietly suggested that perhaps the horse was kept in a stable in Sherwood Forest.

Trevor jumped up excitedly, clapped his hands and said that was exactly the right answer. I thought, thank God for that. Grinning happily, again he sat down. Lucy wilted thankfully into her seat and, although watching Trevor suspiciously through a curtain of her straw blonde hair (the colour of which, along with her height and her pale blue eyes, she had inherited from her father), warily retrieved her magazine.

Seconds later, Trevor once more sprung to his feet, this time holding an imaginary microphone and with his free hand waving about him, started to sing, very loudly and only vaguely in tune, to his audience, which was me and Lucy, and, bearing in mind it was now May: *I'm dreaming of a White Christmas...*

After the first verse he stopped singing, went down on one knee and with his arms outstretched and ignoring his carer's pleas in get back into his seat, in a very pronounced American accent said, "I'd like to take this op-por-toonity to wish you awl, a very merry Christmas and a happy noo year," then back into song mode, whereupon, as Trevor hung onto the last note, his carer unceremoniously popped a pink marshmallow into his mouth while tugging at his elbow and whispering something into his ear. She managed to get him back into his seat, albeit tentatively, when Beryl from reception came over and hunkered down in front of him. She seemed to assume Trevor was deaf because she said slowly, deliberately and actually, quite loudly, that although he was a very good singer, he needed to keep his voice down, as the patients would not be able to hear their names being called over the loudspeaker system.

Poor Trevor, assuming he was being told off, immediately burst into tears. He leaned over the spare seat, grabbed Lucy's bare arm and sobbed onto it. Lucy nearly fainted.

His carer, managing to tug Trevor off Lucy's arm, comforted him with the promise of more marshmallows. She then proceeded to lead him out of the waiting room to calm down outside. On the way out, she gave Lucy one of her apologetic smiles and a Pampers wet-one to wipe the icing sugar and tears off her arm.

Just as I was thinking that this anticipated quiet little sojourn could have gone better, the tannoy system called for us to go to room eight.

I nudged Josh to life, who up till then had had his eyes closed, listening to music from headphones lurking somewhere within his mop of thick auburn curls, which he had inherited from me and which he hated. I put my arm around Lucy's waist to keep her upright and along we trooped to room eight.

"Ah, Joanne, Lucy, Josh," Dr Watson, stood to greet us. There was a discernible intake of breath from the much perked up Lucy as the doctor held out his hand to shake each of ours. He treated us to his Brad Pitt smile as he indicated the chairs. My neighbour Janice, wasn't wrong. He leaned back in his chair, his tie was loose and the top two buttons of his shirt were undone. He held the tip and the end of a pen between his forefingers and half rotated it back and forth. I got the same little flutter, in an otherwise dormant erogenous zone, that I'd had years ago when, after waiting for ages at the stage door, Adam Ant appeared, toting his pistol and demanding I Stand and Deliver. I would have. With pleasure. But my mother, who would have been hard pressed to accept her daughter's street-cred, having had her assets plundered by a Dandy Highwayman, was waiting round the corner with fish and chips.

I knew the smile I gave Dr Watson was pathetically sycophantic but I didn't care.

"And what can I do for you?" he said, smiling a collective smile at the three of us.

Oo-er doctor, I thought. Quite a bit, I shouldn't wonder. But I said, "Well doctor," hoping not to sound too flirty because a: I was with the children and b: flirty and red, itchy spots didn't seem to go together somehow, although it has to be said they were marginally better than say piles or genital warts but anyway you couldn't really be flirty with a doctor, it would be like flirting with the priest; you just wouldn't, "it seems the three of us have come down with some sort of mystery complaint, we're covered in red, itchy spots."

"And are there any symptoms accompanying the spots?" he wanted to know.

I shook my head, "No, only the spots."

"Like-er, yes there is, Mam."

I looked blankly at my daughter.

"Yes, Lucy, go on," said Dr Watson.

"Well actually, I sometimes feel quite sick and when I do I get black spots floating in my eyes and then I feel like fainting and my ears go all funny."

Josh sniggered behind his hand.

I looked at Lucy. My God. Surely it's not possible my daughter is practically taking her last breath and I hadn't even noticed!

"Well, we certainly need to check *this* out," said Dr Watson, probably hoping like hell his medical encyclopaedia was where he'd left it. "Is it okay if your mother and brother stay or would you rather they left the room?"

"I'm sure she'd rather have us stay, wouldn't you, Lucy?" I said, before she had time to answer.

She looked at me sulkily, before nodding.

"O-kay," said Dr Watson pushing back his chair and walking round his desk towards her. He looked into her eyes (and I don't suppose for a minute he missed the look of adoration looking back). He checked her ears. He sounded her chest. He pressed her fingernails and watched the colour come back. He looked at the back of her throat. Then he smiled dazzlingly, reassuringly, yet obviously not without some relief and said he was pleased to report he could not find anything for her to worry about.

"Now," he said, "let me see those spots."

He looked at the spots on each of us before asking if we had any pets; a cat or a dog, perhaps? I said we had a dog. He wondered if the dog had been scratching more than usual

14

because he thought our problem might be insect bites and that the dog might have fleas. He went on to say that fleas were not fussy who they lived off and he suspected they were biting us (I thought that could have been phrased slightly better). He then suggested we see the vet who, he was sure, would recommend some treatment for both the dog and our home which should sort the problem out. However, if, after using the treatment the problem persists, we were not to hesitate to make another appointment to see him.

I stared into the space above his head.

*Another appointment! I think what you really mean to say is, Mrs Charlton, you no doubt find me overwhelmingly attractive, feel free to look, join the queue, but please do not allow yourself any illusions because I actually wouldn't touch your flea-bitten body with the soggy end of a bargepole.*

I mumbled a thank you without making eye contact and ushered the children outside.

"OH-MY-GOD!" said Lucy through clenched teeth. "That was just sooo embarrassing!" She couldn't possibly fall in love with Dr Watson when he knew she had been bitten by fleas!

Josh bent over, clutched his stomach and rocked with feigned laughter, "Fleas! Just wait till your mates hear about this, Luce, especially Danny Miller." He then mimicked his sister with his hand on his head, "Doctor, doctor, there are black things floating in my eyes, do you think they could be – FLEAS?" He then fell about laughing.

"Mam! Tell him!" Lucy screeched.

"That is *enough*, Josh! And don't you dare breathe a word of this to Danny Miller or anyone else, do you hear me?"

I bundled them into the car, Lucy again in the front and Josh in the back, it was safer that way.

Josh chanted, "Lucy wanted love-bites but just got flea-bites."

"When we get home," said Lucy, menacingly, "you are sooo dead."

I started the car. So it's all down to the dog! I might have known it. The dog that is as alien to me as ET. The dog I just know was never intended to be part of my destiny. I have had my palm read, I have had tarot card readings; no mention of any dog. This is the dog I was lumbered with because George, in his misplaced wisdom, thought it would distract the kids, while a week later he, metaphorically speaking, swung out of town. This is the dog that has chewed everything it could lay its paws on: potted plants, dishcloths, fluffy slippers, cuddly toys, old trainers, new trainers, Josh's cricket bat, Lucy's tennis racquet, kitchen chair legs, school books, rubber gloves, you name it and, if complete destruction was impeded in some way, dog's teeth marks will show evidence of intent. I now have open shelves in my kitchen, not by design, but because the dog has chewed the doors. The dog is fed Pedigree Chum and Winalot mixer yet she eats soap, Blu tack, cotton wool, shower gel and drinks out of the toilet. And if she can lick Harpic from under the rim, it's party time. It seems Ambre Solaire is also something of a delicacy because if I am disillusioned enough to think sunbathing might be an option, I am licked clean before I get anywhere near the sun-lounger. And, if I don't manage to grab the post as it comes through the door, I end up piecing it together like a jigsaw and reading it through Sellotape. All this not for much longer though, because while I was looking for my car keys this morning, I came across the vacuum cleaner nozzle which has been missing for ages and which has rendered the dog even more dispensable. She is now no longer required as a nozzle substitute for picking up toast crumbs and Bombay Mix, so, bye-bye, dog, I would like to say it has been nice knowing you, but it hasn't.

# 3

## FANTASTIC FRAN

"Well can I then?" Lucy asked, distractedly, as she scanned the street for any familiar face or better still, any familiar outfit she could put a shop name and price tag to.

"Can you what, Lucy?"

"Can I have a proper DJ party for my birthday?"

"Like I said, Lucy, we'll discuss that nearer the time. It will really depend on the money situation so please don't pester."

"That probably means no!" She sunk deeper into her seat.

The roads were busy. The lights were on red. Josh vibrated in the back seat to the inane noise from his iPod.

"We'll never get home at this rate," Lucy pouted. "Will you tell Josh to stop kicking the back of my seat, it's soh annoying."

"Josh, stop kicking the back of Lucy's seat."

"Whaa?" He stripped out his earplugs.

"I said, stop kicking the back of Lucy's seat."

"I'm not."

"He is, Mam. You're such a nerd, Josh."

"Lucy, don't speak to your brother like that!"

"Well he is a nerd."

"I'll be a nerd all right, when I tell Danny Miller you've got fleas."

"Mam! Tell him!"

"You've been told about that, Josh. I don't want have to tell you again. Now for goodness sake, stop it, both of you. You're like a couple of three year olds."

"He's like a three year old."

"You are, you mean."

"ENOUGH."

Josh replaced his earplugs and Lucy sulked. I drummed the steering wheel as the traffic stagnated and I thought of George and Fran living their flea-free life and I thought of the day I eventually got to meet Fran.

It was a Thursday. Wednesday was the day I would normally spend in the yard doing the books, but Josh had needed an urgent dental appointment that day which meant I'd had to swop days. This was something I had forgotten to mention to George. Well that is, I might have mentioned it to George, if he had hung around long enough. Anyway, on this particular Thursday, with my head down and my fingers banging the keyboard and amid the sounds of cement mixers mixing and Stihl saws sawing, I detected the light, clip-clopping of stiletto heels. I stopped and listened, it being intriguing, as the dragging of cement-laden hob-nailed boots was more the norm around a builder's yard. Then, as the footsteps got close enough to be at the other side of the door, a cooing, "Is that Georgie Porgy?" signalled the arrival of Fran who, as she playfully popped her head round the door, went the colour of her magenta shoes and matching handbag when she realised that today, her Georgie Porgy was in fact, his wife.

Well there you go. Life's full of little cow pats; Fran expecting to find her Georgie Porgy at the other side of the desk and me expecting to find Fran positively, absolutely, fabulously fantastic; yet here she was, a stick thin, straight backed, spectacled woman in a pin-striped business suit.

You know when you have that dream, the one when you've stood at the bus stop, chatted to fellow travellers, gotten onto the bus, paid your fare and looked down to find you're still wearing your nightie? (And it's an Ann Summers see-thru creation, obviously someone else's, and you've no knickers on.) Well that was the feeling I had while smiling fixedly at Fran and while frantically wishing I had made more of an effort with my make-up, my clothes, my hair, my nails, my shoes, possibly even had a leg wax.

I was wearing slightly balding-on-the-backside, grey velour jogging bottoms with a matching zip-up top, which had definitely seen better days, but which, at 7.30 that morning had seemed like a good idea, all things considered. The considerations being that I would be spending the day in George's builder's yard in what was laughingly called the office. This was really just a grubby, portable cabin-type thing where the only human contact I could expect would be in the form of old Mick, who sweeps the yard and cleans out the cement mixers and who sometimes grunts a greeting in my direction and who should have retired years ago but who keeps turning up and getting paid anyway, and Billy, who takes the deliveries, and who is so shy he can't even manage eye contact.

But, the impromptu arrival of Fran, in her seductress get-up, not quite as fantastic as one had imagined, but nonetheless a thousand times more resplendent than me at that particular moment, hoisted me and my sleepy morning ensemble into the category of candidate for Trinnie and Susannah:

*Ooh Susannah! Just look at her arse in those pants, like ferrets in a sack. And those tits, wobbling around inside that revolting top! She could be mistaken for something bovine, an escapee from a farmyard, yet this is one of our own species! Can you believe it? Well I'm sorry, but if I looked like that, it would be back to the bottle for me (Champers of course, dahling. Oh and vintage).*

Of course there was nothing else for it but to offer the

Preying Mantis a cup of tea while we soaked up each other's discomfort, under the umbrella of feigned, friendly chit-chat.

I gave Fran her tea. She gave me a benevolent smile. What on earth do you talk about to the woman you suspect wants to bed your husband? Perhaps I could ask her if she'd been up to anything exciting lately, but thought better of it. Knowing what I knew of Fran, there was every possibility she had thwarted an Al Qaeda attempt to blow up the local library and if she tried to tell me about it, I would seriously lose the will to live.

So instead I said, "I was just thinking, what a pain it is having to do these accounts, life's too short to balance a spreadsheet. Don't you agree?"

Fran spoke through a fixed smile which she probably kept in a drawer and which went on with her make-up.

"Well as I have a scholarship in bookkeeping and commerce, it's something I don't mind doing at all really."

"Of course you have. Silly me. George *has* to have mentioned that somewhere along the line. Well, I really must speak to George, if only he would get someone in to do the accounts, that would mean I could stay well clear of this place and good riddance, I say."

Well wouldn't you just know it. Fran knew of a student from Croatia who was in her final year at university studying for a degree in accountancy: Bernica Sarola. Fran said Bernica would be delighted to do George's books as the money would help stretch her student grant and of course, it would also provide *me* with me time and, more time to spend with the children.

Me time *and* children time. Oh well every silver lining has a cloud. Still, as I was never one to look a gift horse in the mouth, even one in the shape of Fran, who of course had her own agenda for keeping me out of the way, I considered the advantages of this idea in about three seconds flat. I really begrudged the one day of the week I spent in the yard doing the books and to be free of it would mean I could do something for myself.

For a split second I could have kissed Fran. Well perhaps not. But I thanked her and although I have to admit the front I was putting on was nothing short of multi-faceted, it was an almost-ran in the face of the blatant duplicity which Fran exhibited when she touched my arm benignly and said, "Sisterhood, Joanne, sisterhood."

And I just knew Fran meant that most sincerely: from the heart of her bottom.

# 4

## SWINGERS AND THE PTA

"Mam!" Lucy pinged her seatbelt open. "Stop the car! There's Chloe. I've got some mega news about Zara and Scott. I'll get the bus home."

"Sorry Lucy, but you heard what Dr Watson said, I'll need to go to the vet's when we get home, and either you come with me, or else I will need to know you're in the house."

She bounced her legs, "Pleeese, Mam, ten minutes, that's all. Five then."

I looked at my watch, "Okay, you can have ten minutes."

I pulled over. The car was hardly parked when Lucy all but fell out of it. She ran to Chloe and they immediately started gossiping and giggling. They nudged each other and looked at a passing paperboy who blushed.

Then Josh said, "Mam, you know that bloke in the doctor's, him who was playing for the away team. Whatsisname. Trevor?"

"That's not nice, Josh!"

"Well anyway, you know him, Mam? I think he could be one of the teachers at my school."

"That's not funny Josh."

"It's not meant to be," he said, as he replaced his earplugs, slouched further down in the seat and shut his eyes.

I studied Josh for a few seconds not really sure what I was looking for. Was being part of a dysfunctional family beginning to tell? But he looked like he always did so I opened the glove compartment to look for some mints and a change of CD.

Josh was nodding in Eminem mode in the back seat. I weighed up the possibilities: James Blunt, Oasis or Coldplay? I fingered James Blunt (figuratively speaking) but Josh, suddenly springing to life, begged me not to play James Blunt. He said he'd had all the hell he could take for one day, what with missing his rugby practice and having fleas; so I settled on Coldplay.

"I heard a great poem the other day, Mam, d'ya want to hear it?"

"Hmmm," I said, suspecting it wasn't going to be one of Emily Bronte's, "go on then."

"Cousin Billy had a five foot willie and he showed it to the woman next door. She thought it was a snake so she hit it with a rake and now it's only two foot four."

"Oh, for goodness sake, Josh."

He replaced his headphones, laughing. I let him have his moment. I didn't tell him that had done the rounds when I was at school.

A paperback I'd stuffed in with the CDs fell out. It was something my mother had bought from Oxfam; a Barbara Cartland. I scanned the pages. Nothing wrong with a bit of romance I thought, while also thinking that in reality, what was romance but the product of an over indulgent imagination?

While pondering the concept of romance, I looked from the pages of the book to a woman crossing the road with exactly the same prodding way of walking as had Fran in her three inch stilettos. Fran of Green Fables I remembered calling her, the wit of which totally eluded George, who sulked because he said I was making fun of Fran, which of course I was. George said

Fran was a clever woman who didn't deserve to be made fun of. Really! In order to win George over, she could quite easily have dispensed with the Fantastic Fran scenarios and the providing of 'me' time for keeping me out of the way. All she needed to have done when she'd first clapped eyes on him, was to tell him she was an out and out 'swinger' and she could have saved herself all that bother.

He had met his soul mate. They were kindred spirits, birds of a feather. He Tarzan. She Jane. Swinging on a vine of perversion through a jungle of debauchery, while I was dumped on the forest floor like something excreted from a primate's bottom. Of course I had suspected it long before he had sheepishly suggested the three of us – as in me, him and Fran – might go to one of the clubs Fran enjoyed. George said according to Fran, everyone was welcomed – singles, couples, threesomes, foursomes – it didn't matter, as everyone joined in. Sometimes there may be twenty or more people engaged in the various activities. One big happy family really. He was obviously having trouble forming the word orgy. A bit of an enigma was George. Although a closet sexual deviant, once out of the bedroom or presumably the swingers, dubious establishments, he became very straight-laced, no smutty jokes, innuendo or articulation of the word orgy for Georgie.

So, could he tell Fran we were up for it? Up for it! Of course I wasn't up for it! After years of marriage had it really never occurred to George that I wanted romance. I wanted scented rose petals scattered over a bed of white linen. I wanted to be caressed by soft, sensuous music. I wanted to look up at a ceiling draped in shadows of dancing lace, bestowed by an opalescent moon twinkling its way through flimsy lace curtains. I wanted the sensibility of ecstasy that had made Marianne Dashwood lose her senses when carried through the storm by Willoughby. I wanted to languish in a leafy glade, dressed in my best sprigged muslin and peer coyly from beneath my parasol into the eyes of Mr Darcy in thigh high boots and a frockcoat, and, if he came in the guise of Colin Firth, then so much the better. I wanted to be persuaded, as had Anne Elliott to sail into the sunset with Captain Wentworth.

Was that too much to ask? Had it really not dawned on George that I hated being hauled into position with one hand while he held onto his pocket Karma Sutra with the other. Or, tied to the bedpost with stupid fur handcuffs which were miles too big and which I could have gotten out of quite easily but went along with because it was usually the first time I'd been off my feet all day?

George had been my first boyfriend who, in retrospect, seemed to have walked me from the school disco, been invited for Sunday tea and stayed for twenty years. And although our courtship could never be construed as love's young dream, he would be, according to my mother, a good provider. So a good provider was what I had settled for. And because I had settled for that and although my pride had taken a bit of a bashing when he had up sticks and left, my world hadn't exactly come to an end. In fact I kind of mentally wished him luck. Of course I would never have admitted that to George, opting instead to play the injured party and providing him with a first class ticket when he was on one of his guilt trips, which Fran ripped to shreds before he could wonder where his passport was.

Yes, romance was certainly in short supply in my neck of the woods and, come to think of it, things didn't seem any better for other people if last quarters PTA meeting was anything to go by.

Going to the pub after last quarter's PTA meeting wasn't something I would normally do; it wasn't really my scene, and for the first half hour or so I remembered why. Okay, Cillit Bang is fine for cleaning grease off a hob and yes it's irritating when partners leave towels on the bathroom floor, or who put empty milk bottles back in the fridge, or who put trousers in the wash with tissue in the pockets so that the whole wash needs de-fluffing; but the semi's of Britain's Got Talent was on...

I was planning my exit but then, as glasses emptied then refilled and amid giggles and flushed faces, Margery, who works on school dinners, said she was mortified when she had found some lad's mags that her Jim had stashed behind the tank. 'Readers' Wives' some of them were called, she said, and she shuddered as she wondered what sort of perverts could possibly take disgusting photos of their wives and send them into a dirty magazine. It seemed to me it was probably the same sort of perverts who bought the dirty magazines and stashed them behind the tank. Margery shuddered again and said these people were walking among us in the streets, sitting next to us on the bus, eating at the next table in McDonald's!

Then mousey little Sally Stevens, who works in Mahmood's corner shop, giggled, looked around furtively then whispered that what got her husband Pete going, were suspenders, a peep-thru bra, high heels, long gloves and a whip. I really struggled with that image as I'd only ever seen Sally in a zipped up fleece, fingerless gloves and a fur-trimmed Trapper hat (Mahmood's corner shop was like a fridge), and before the wine had taken effect Sally had been over the moon with bi-carb and vinegar for de-scaling kettles. Perhaps the wine was having an effect on me. I found myself quite fancying the idea of high heels and suspenders and using a whip on George certainly had its appeal, yet, although I was no stranger to perversity having being married to George for years, it had nevertheless felt curiously odd when Sally said the only place Pete could find his size of fish-net stockings and suspenders was at John Lewis!

I decided I wasn't really in such a hurry to leave after all when Linda Holmes, the school secretary, said she never ceased to be amazed how she had conceived of her twins as her Derek had worked nights all their married life and was always shattered. She said he had once slumped on top of her while right in the middle of you-know-what, and she'd thought he was dead until he started snoring like a train.

Belinda Evans, dazzlingly amoral in her shocking pink lurex boob-tube, leather pants and orange spray tan, whose daughter Symphony was suspended from school for refusing to wear school uniform (a case which Belinda intended to take to the European Court of Human Rights), said she never ceased to be amazed by the promises she was able to extract from her Dave in moments of post-coital euphoria. So bring it on! she said.

And there was me thinking post-coital euphoria meant getting it over and done with.

I stuffed the Barbara Cartland and the notion of romance back into the glove compartment then I tooted for Lucy. I pointed to my watch in a time's-up gesture. She produced some pleading facial contortions before putting up two fingers which I optimistically took as a mime pleading for two minutes more. I got out of the car and insisted she said goodbye to Chloe and Emma. Her original ten minutes had turned into twenty and I needed to get home to ring the vet.

She pleaded to be allowed more time; said she could easily walk home. I refused.

"That's like, so-not-fair!" she huffed as she flopped into the car.

# 5

## PLEAS AND FLEAS

At home Lucy stomped upstairs to sulk while Josh went into the garage to practice his snooker. I looked for the Yellow Pages and wondered why in God's name I found it impossible to remember a number I rang practically every other week.

The dog scratched manically while at the same time furiously wagging her tail. It was obvious she was expecting the usual pat on the head by way of a greeting but I thought of the fleas and held my hand just above her head and did a sort of flapping gesture, like a pat but without actual contact.

The Yellow Pages was in the hall under Josh's trainers, keeping the mud off the floor. I wiped it down, found the number and waited while it rang out. I bounced my legs in a sort of Lucy-type plea, hoping anyone other than Mavis Moffatt would answer.

"Apollo Veterinary Centre. Mavis Moffatt speaking. How can I help you today?"

Damn. "Oh, hello, it's Joanne Charlton, here," previous to this I had suggested that Mavis Moffatt might like to call me Joanne or Jo, it sounded much more friendly but she insisted on calling me Mrs Charlton, so I called her *Ms* Moffatt.

"Yes, Mrs Charlton and what can we tell Mr Robinson Millie has been up to *this* time?"

*This* time! Snooty cow. I'll have you know it is we, the owners of idiot dogs like Millie, who pay your wages, madam.

"Well, I've just come from the doctor's and it seems Millie may have fleas."

"You took Millie to the doctor's, Mrs Charlton!?"

"No of course not, Ms Moffatt. *We* went to the doctor's, my children and myself, and it seems Millie may have fleas. Anyway, can I bring her in to see Mr Robinson?"

"Oh now that's not such a good idea, is it? We can't have our other patients catching Millie's fleas, can we? Are you sure it's fleas, did you read up on it?"

I'd read Bridget Jones's Diary, for the second time and a Gracia magazine from cover to cover, both zilch in the flea department.

"You've lost me there, Ms Moffatt."

"Yes of course I have," she patronised. "Well, Mrs Charlton, do you remember the 'puppy pack' duffle bag you were given when you first registered Millie with us? Because, in that bag, as well as free samples of food and treats, a puppy feeding bowl, a rag-pull and a CD of noises, was a pamphlet of information on the pests and diseases puppy may be susceptible to."

"CD Noises?"

"Yes a CD of the noises puppy needs to get used to, washing machine, vacuum cleaner, ticking clock etc. Obviously poor Millie has had to learn the hard way."

Hell's bloody bells, whatever next! And anyway who has a ticking clock these days? I vaguely remembered Josh delving into the bag and pulling out the interesting bits; the free food, the dog-pull etc, the rest must have been binned.

"Have you any idea of Millie's weight, Mrs Charlton?"

"No, sorry."

"No, of course not. Okay, I'm looking at her records on

screen now, so let me see. When she was first registered with us she was 5kg. Then, three weeks later, when you noticed the string coming out of her bottom which turned out to be the mast and rigging from a Lego ship, she was 8.5kg. Three weeks after that when you noticed a pirate brandishing a musket also trying to make an unsuccessful exit, she was 10.5kg. Then there was the pipe-cleaner angel from the Christmas tree which needed to be removed and then the lollipop stick wedged in the roof of her mouth then, when she had the cassette tape wound round her tonsils and needed an overnight stay, she was up to 18.5kg. We can assume she hasn't gained that much in a few weeks, so the treatment I can give you will be fine. You will also need a spray to use in every room in the house, the directions are on the container. Has Millie been in contact with any other animals?"

I mentioned Bobby the cat from next door which Millie seems to have an odd relationship with. He jumps the fence every morning around seven, just as Millie is let out to pee. He allows her to pull him by the collar, zig-zagging around the lawn, then after about five minutes, he turns onto his belly, digs his claws into the ground forcing Millie to free him, then he scales the fence, back into his own garden.

"Well," said Ms Moffatt, "that could be where Millie has caught the fleas. Cats are notorious flea carriers as they play around with mice and birds. It might be as well for you to have a chat with the owner of the cat, it probably needs to be treated as well. That will be £40 to pay. I leave at 3pm today so if I'm not here when you come in, someone will explain the procedure, it's really very simple, nothing for you to worry about. Is that all today, Mrs Charlton?"

"Yes, Ms Moffatt, thank you. Hopefully the procedure will be explained in words of one syllable. Bye for now."

I made a mental note to get there after 3pm.

At 3.30pm I collected the flea treatments from Trudy which now also included a spray for the cat. The bill had jumped to

£55. There was definitely some satisfaction in knowing how much George will sooo regret lumbering me with this dog when he gets these bills. Trudy also had a recommendation from Mr Robinson which was that I should be cleaning and flossing Millie's teeth morning and night at least twice a week.

Mr Robinson is obviously a mad-man.

£55! On the way home I vaguely wondered if it would be possible to get onto a veterinary access course with an A level in art.

Janice's front door was slightly open and I called into the hall. She called back from the kitchen in her one octave drawl, "Hi, Jo, you comin' in?"

"Better not, Jan. I've left the kids in the house and you know what they're like. I came in half an hour ago and the place was in chaos. The dog was charging around trying to kill a bluebottle and the kids were doing the same trying to kill each other."

She flip-flopped along the hall wearing a 'too shagged to shag' tee shirt and cropped leggings, and drying her hands on a towel which looked as though it might have been used to clean Kev's bike.

"Tell me abow it. My two were exactly the same at tha' age, but I'll tell you this, it's downhill all the way."

I groaned. "Bloody hell! Anyway, the thing is, Jan, we've just been to the doctor's and... oh, by the way, you were right about Dr Watson, he is positively *dripping* sex appeal. He could make my reflexes jump anytime."

"Tell me abow it. Just thinking about him makes my varicose veins throb," she said.

We laughed. Well I did and Jan did her silent shoulder shaking.

"Anyway, the thing is, Jan, we've been driven mad with this itching and..." she butted in.

"Itching! Tell me abow it. A while back righ', after tea on a Friday and after Kev had dropped the kids off at Cubs and

Brownies, Kev righ', usually fancied a bit of the other. Well, all weekend afterwards, I was driven mad with this itching."

She gave a furtive look behind to make sure no-one was listening, which seemed a bit odd as there was no-one else in the house, then, pushing up her not insignificant chest, Les Dawson fashion, she mouthed, "Down there. Well," she continued, "I tried everything in the chemist shop, righ'. Nothing worked. I had to go to Dr Khan in the end, and he prescribed cream for us both to use, but Kev, righ', said he might as well be a bloody eunuch as he couldn't feel a thing with us both slippery as eels. Guess what the problem turned out to be?"

I shrugged and wondered if I'd ever be able to look Kev in the eye again.

"He had just started work at that fibre glass factory, righ', and that damned stuff gets everywhere."

"Oh, right," I said, nodding sagely, while thinking this seemed like an awful lot of information for a Tuesday tea time on a front doorstep.

"Well, Jan, the thing is, it seems Millie could have fleas and, as I would hate Bobby to catch them while they're messing around in the garden, I've been to the vet for a spray for you to use on him. Just a precautionary measure of course."

I pushed the spray into Jan's hand and, walking backwards down the path, I called, "The instructions are on the container, dead easy."

And I heard her calling down the hall, "Frig-gin' fleas! Bobby, get your arse here now, righ.'"

# 6

## THE IMPORTANCE OF
## NOT BEING ERNEST

"Why are you vacuuming the bath, Mam?"

"There's a spider in it and I'm taking no chances. I tried flushing it down the plughole, but it ran up sides."

"That is soh shocking! How would you like it if you were a spider and someone suddenly sucked you up in a vacuum?"

"If I were a spider, Lucy, I'd probably expect it."

Then the phone rang and the spider was forgotten because, as there was no one else inhabiting the planet other than Lucy and her friends, it was obvious she expected the call to be for her. She bounded downstairs and grabbed the phone. I waited at the top of the stairs in the unlikely event that it was for me.

"Like-er-no Gran. I don't know if the school bus has changed colour or has paisley patterns on it. I don't look at it really. I just get on and sit and chat with my friends then I get off. I'll ask Josh when he comes out of the toilet, he might know. I'll get Mam for you. *MAM,*" she yelled, up the stairs, "Gran's on the phone. Speak to you later then, Gran. Luv you, bye."

Oops! I had forgotten to ring my mother.

"Hi, Mam."

"I was waiting for you to ring, Joanne."

"Yes, Mam, sorry. I had to go to the vet's and then I forgot."

"Well what did the doctor say about the spots?"

"He said Millie has fleas."

"Oh! Well perhaps I won't call round for a while. Guess what, Joanne? They've changed the colour of the bus that goes to the precinct."

"Yes, Mam, you said. But what was that about a bus driver with a dodgy eye coming here?"

"Oh yes, that's right, I knew there was something I needed to tell you. Well, when I waited for the bus to go to the precinct yesterday, along came the Number 7, but it was mauvy coloured with cats and dogs running along the sides. So I asked Ernest the driver if it still went to the precinct, and do you know what he said? He said, 'M-r-s M-orri-son,' slowly like that, as if I were senile, 'you have been going to the precinct on this bus for as long as I've been driving it. Sometimes you wear your grey coat, sometimes you wear your navy coat and sometimes, if it's warm enough, you just wear a cardigan, yet you still go to the precinct. Am I correct?' I said he was and he said, 'Well it's the same with this bus, same destination just a different colour coat. Now are you getting on or not?' Well," my mother went on, "I sat down without noticing Mrs Todd was sitting behind me until she tapped me on the shoulder and said, 'Take no notice of the miserable so-and-so, Mrs Morrison, his face is tripping him up because he had five numbers on Saturday's lottery and the dog has gone and chewed his ticket.' Oh dear, that's terrible, I said, Poor Ernest. So when we passed St Augustine's, I made a sign of the cross, and hoped Ernest hadn't taken this bit of bad luck out on the dog."

"Well what's that got to do with me, Mam?"

"Well, when I stood up to get off and while I was waiting for the bus to pull in and to make Ernest feel better, although to be honest, Joanne, he didn't deserve to feel better talking to people like that because I wasn't the only one, anyway, I told him he should call on you, as you knew all about dogs chewing things."

"Mam!"

"And do you know what he said, Joanne? he said, 'Oh I know your daughter, Mrs Morrison, she's the looker from Willow Grove whose husband buggered off with that skinny, ropey looking bird.' He said George must be mad, even though the ropey looking bird drives a soft top Mercedes. Anyway, Ernest said you were just his type as he likes his women with some meat on their bones and he got a funny look in his eye, the one that doesn't swivel about so much, although when Sadie rang the bus company to mention that that eye looked a bit suspect, they told her she had nothing to worry about, as it was fine for driving a bus with. Anyway, I didn't like the look in that eye, so if he calls on you, Joanne, don't let him in. Tell him you had to get rid of the dog and he might just go away."

It was then that the doorbell rang and Millie barked her head off.

I looked through the three-inch gap which the door chain allowed. The rain had splashed his glasses, but even so he didn't look as if he had a dodgy eye. He said he was from the Salvation Army and that he'd come to collect the envelope he'd left last week. Normally this would initiate a little surge of panic as I wondered where the envelope could be. But not today. Today I loosened the chain, smiled, opened the door wide and asked him to wait in the hall, out of the rain. He said he wished everyone who answered the door was as pleased to see him. Then my smile waned, as I hoped out of relief, I hadn't given him mixed messages. Then came the little surge of panic. Where the hell was the envelope?

It wasn't under the lamp on the hall table, or under the pot with the spider plant in it. Nor was it in the telephone book drawer among the takeaway leaflets and paint sample sheets and that handy holiday, needle and thread and safety pin folder, still in its cellophane wrapping. I shrugged, smiled and said, "Isn't it just like the thing? I'm sure it was here only this morning." It was a lie, but under his watchful gaze I felt I had to say something.

Nor was it in the other drawer among the stash of emergency greetings cards and sheets of wrapping paper and that lint roller thing and the old mobile phones and half dead batteries.

"I'm sure it's here somewhere, perhaps if you'd like to call back?" I suggested, hopefully, but he said he'd wait. I asked him if he had any spare envelopes, he said he hadn't.

I mentally asked help from St Anthony, Patron Saint of lost things, yet I kind of knew with his workload, he was hardly going to put himself out to find an envelope with nothing in it. I asked him anyway and wondered why, when I thought of St Anthony, a hunky, macho Roman soldier, he always came across as being a bit camp. It wasn't as if the plume in his helmet would have been a cerise Ostrich feather or that he was likely to have a Shih Tzu named Kylie or even that he could produce a fabulous centrepiece with some wired Delphiniums and a chunk of oasis, but there we are; camp as a crystal cocktail shaker:

*Joanne. Do you honestly expect me to drop everything to find an empty envelope when the only time you think of me is when you want a favour? Oh yes there's always plenty of promises of prayers, but do they materialise? No they do not. What about the time I showed you exactly where to look for the school hamster which went missing on the second day of the holidays when Josh was supposed to be looking after it? Poor kid was demented. You'd never have thought to look in the hem of the landing curtains, now would you? Of course not. Then, with the hamster found safe and sound, forget about St Anthony. Not a thank you prayer, kiss my saintly backside, nothing! Hamster found, good intentions lost...*

I felt inside the pockets of the coats on the coat stand and shook open an umbrella. I felt inside Josh's filthy rugby boots and got a handful of something horrible and I nearly swore, but remembered just in time I had a Salvationist in the hall. For God's sake! Surely he must have a prayer meeting or something to go to. I said I'd need to look in the kitchen. I closed the door behind me then swore then grabbed the dog and looked in her mouth and under her gums, but all I could see were traces of something blue that looked like blotting paper. Of course she'd had a week to have eaten the envelope. I called upstairs and asked the kids if they had seen it. They called back, almost in unison.

"Envelope? Whaa envelope?"

St Anthony was still twittering on in the background.

*... Still, I shouldn't complain. Poor old St Jude is the guy I feel sorry for. I mean who wants to be lumbered with lost causes? If it's lost, it's lost, accept, move on. Why beat yourself up about it? He takes the whole thing far too see-riously. Okay, back to moi. I'll expect a rosary offered up for the repose of the souls languishing in Purgatory and a Glory Be for a good intention; mine. I won't hold my breath of course, but one lives in hope. Now, seek and ye shall find. Was St Peter a fisherman? Did Jesus feed the five thousand with a loaf and five fishes? And the common denominator is...*

The envelope was stuck to the underside of the fish tank along with a red letter from BT. I looked towards heaven and mouthed a thank you then cursed almost in the same breath as I checked my purse for change, because apart from a fiver, there was only a five pence piece. I couldn't possibly give the man five pence, not when he'd come in all the rain and stood in the hall for twenty minutes and wasn't Ernest. But the fiver was for Josh's karate lesson that night. Hell and Damnation!! Did everyone's life revolve around dilemmas or were they kept exclusively for me? There was nothing else for it, I'd bribe Josh. I'll promise to take him to Pizza Hut on Saturday, that should do it. I stuffed the fiver into the envelope, stuck it down and gave it to the Salvation

Army man who held it up to the light. As he smiled his grateful thanks, a fleeting glow of unintentional munificence shrouded me. Then I had to face Josh.

He came downstairs singing to himself and swinging his karate bag which was packed and ready. He sat on the sofa to lace up his trainers. I sat with him.

"Squashy, Joshy," I said, ruffling his hair.

He ducked, "Cut the crap, Mam."

"Language, Josh! I just wondered if you fancied Pizza Hut on Saturday, that's all."

"Yeah, great," he stood up and put out his hand. "Can I have the money for my lesson now please?"

"Sorry, Joshy, but – there's a problem. You know the Salvation Army man who came to the door just now? Well, as he'd come in all the rain and wasn't the bus driver with the funny eye and as I only had your karate money in my purse – I – gave it to him."

"Whaa! You gave him my karate money!?"

"I know, Josh, sorry. But Pizza Hut on Saturday – sound good?"

He looked down at me, incredulously. "But I've practised my Fudu Dachi all week to get my yellow belt!"

"I know and I'm sorry, there just didn't seem anything else I could do. You could think of it as giving something to those less fortunate than yourself."

"I don't know anyone less fortunate than myself!"

"The Salvation Army do lots of good work, especially for the homeless, Josh."

"Huh! I would shake a tambourine and sing to the homeless for a fiver!"

I'd obviously gone wrong somewhere along the line. I knew I would. I vaguely wondered if Father McCaffrey might take him on, but decided I would be in the firing line for marrying a Non-Catholic, then getting divorced, so I decided not to bother.

Then the phone rang and Josh churlishly answered it. "Uh, hullo, Gran. Yes, Gran, I know I go to karate on a Tuesday, but my *mother* has given the money for my lesson to a Sally Army man. I don't want a bleedin' plenary indulgence, Gran! I want a yellow belt. Here's Mam... er, soz, Gran."

I took the phone from him and he got a warning look for using that tone of voice to his grandmother.

"Joanne," said my mother, "I got so waylaid earlier talking about Ernest that I forgot to ask if you know how I can contact Esther Ranzen, because I think Esther should know about the dangers of the Big Slipper from the 'Home Comforts' booklet. Poor Mrs Chisholm from number 5 had been sat watching Emmerdale with her two feet in her Big Slipper, like the lady in the booklet, when the doorbell rang. Mrs Chisholm got up to answer the door, got tangled up in the Big Slipper and ended up in casualty with a badly sprained ankle."

"Perhaps they should have called it the Big Tripper," I said.

My mother laughed. "Oh Joanne, I'll have to tell that to Sadie. But I shouldn't be laughing not when poor Mrs Chisholm is on crutches and is a member of the Catholic Women's Guild. The Catholic Women's Guild members are thin on the ground as it is, so it's not good news for the funeral teas."

I told my mother she could try sending a letter to the BBC for Esther's attention. She said that was a good idea and that's what she'd do. She said to tell Josh not to be too upset about the yellow belt as she had one he could borrow until he got a proper one.

Intuition told me I'd be better off not mentioning that to Josh.

# 7

## AT LAST, THE SHIP'S CAT

The next day, armed with the flea treatment and the instruction leaflet and with the dog tied to the kitchen table, the phone rang. I nearly ignored it, and wished I had. It was my mother wondering if I'd heard of lion's poo. I tried to sound interested, but it wasn't easy.

"Lion's poo, Mam?"

"Yes, it's for keeping cats from using your bark chippings as a litter tray. Or so Percy, from two doors down tells me."

"I don't have any bark chippings."

"I know, Joanne, but I have some around my Azaleas and Percy says his son swears by lion's poo for keeping the cats off. I don't think Percy would be kidding me, he seemed perfectly serious although the second time he mentioned it, instead of poo he did say the 's' word. I didn't mind really, because poor Percy was in the Jarrow March when he was only ten years old and all he had on his feet were his brother's hob-nailed boots. He's marvellous for his age, Joanne, does his own garden, clips his own hedge and cleans his bottom windows even though they say he caught a bit of shrapnel in the Pacifics. He has a beautiful topiary cockerel in a terracotta pot which he says started out as a hedge clipping. He says he likes nothing better than sitting on the front doorstep on a sunny morning, with his cockerel between his legs giving it a once over. What's that noise, Joanne?"

"It's the dog dragging the table across the kitchen floor and the chairs clattering off the tiles."

"Oh! It's that sort of thing that makes me glad I haven't got a dog. Well I might ask at the garden centre for lion's poo. What do you think?"

I said it was possible Percy could be having her on and that she should ask for it discreetly.

"Yes dear you could be right. Sadie and I will go tomorrow and I'll let you know how I get on."

Could I stand the suspense? Now where was I? Flea treatment. I read the information on the pack, Millie would be relatively easy to treat, I was sure of that. According to the instructions, all I had to do, was find a spot between her shoulder blades and the base of her neck and squeeze the contents of the phial onto her skin. Could that be any simpler? It became a major operation.

Millie, determined to see what was going on behind her back, spun round like a skater on ice to find out. She didn't trust whatever it was that was going on behind her back. In fact, whatever it was that was going on behind her back, she was going to eat it.

I needed help. Josh couldn't help, he had got to level six on Doom and couldn't leave it. Lucy couldn't help she was just about to go to Chloe's.

Okay. They were grounded – and the weekend was included.

They stampeded into the kitchen falling over one and another. Then, following my instructions, Josh held Millie's front paws to the floor while Lucy held a piece of cheese just above the dog's nose and, hey presto, in seconds it was mission accomplished.

It became apparent though, that treating the house was

going to be a whole different ball game. Did mattresses really have piping? I was due in work at 12pm. I decided to ring in sick, take the day off and get the whole thing out of the way once and for all but, I hated having to lie to Ian. Not that it was a principle thing, it was just that he was so damned obnoxious. I was only thankful I didn't have to face him every day, three days a week was just about bearable. I decided on a kidney infection. Knowing Ian, I would just have to take a chance that he wouldn't expect a urine sample for analysing.

"Ian, it's Jo, I'm really sorry but I can't come in to work today, I've got this horrible kidney infection and I'm going to need some time off, possibly even the rest of the week." Might as well be hung for a sheep as a lamb. I held my breath.

"Oh, poor you. That's okay, Jo, you take as long as you need, I'm sure we'll cope."

Huh! He was on holiday last week. Had he had a personality transplant?

Then he said, "Just over there, Simone, that's brilliant." Then back to me, "Okay, Jo, see you when you're feeling better. Bye for now."

The creep, I'd forgotten the new merchandiser, the glamorous Simone, with legs up to her armpits and a chest that came with a foot pump was doing her stint in the office this week. Oh well, the diversion would keep him off my back.

The beds were stripped and sprayed and as mattresses really did have piping, as instructed, that piping received my full attention. I sprayed the carpet as instructed, paying particular attention to the edges. I kept the windows and doors closed for the recommended two hours, while I did the same in the other two bedrooms. Two hours later, I opened the windows, vacuumed, polished, dusted, washed and, as I slid down the wall of my bedroom into an exhausted heap, I noticed a damp patch on the carpet beside the radiator. As soon as I can move, I told myself, I'll have a better look at that.

Then Josh barged in.

"Mam, Mam, you gotta see this, Millie's doin' bright green shits!" His voice was a mixture of excitement and astonishment.

"Er, rephrase that please, Josh."

"Oops! Soz Mam, I mean she's shittin' bright green poos."

As that was probably as good as it would get and as I was too exhausted to care, I hauled myself off the floor and followed him into the garden.

"If this is a wind up, Josh..."

It wasn't.

"Apollo Veterinary Centre, Mavis Moffatt speaking, how can I help you?"

"It's Joanne Charlton, I think I've got a bit of an emergency."

"*Another* emergency, Mrs Charlton? Perhaps we need to reserve an emergency appointment for you and Millie every couple of weeks." She snorted a silly, mirthless laugh. "Just my little joke, it's the mood I'm in today, I've had everyone in stitches. Eileen says I must have been on the whacky baccy at lunchtime."

Ms Moffatt, I wanted to say, you are sad and delusional. They are laughing at you, not with you.

She went on, "And what can we tell Mr Robinson Millie has been up to *this* time?"

"She has a stomach upset."

"And have we got rid of the little visitors?"

"Yes."

"We have had a cancellation for 4pm if you'd like to bring her along then."

Lucy was having tea at Chloe's. Josh was pointing his controller and shooting and whooping and refused to come to the vet's. I told him I would be back within the hour and left him with instructions to do his homework and with strict instructions to lock the door behind me and not to open it to anyone.

The cancellation arrived at precisely 4pm with her cat. Crossed wires, apparently. This meant I had to wait until after the last appointment to be seen by Mr Robinson which turned out to be more than an hour later and which gave Millie more than enough time to deposit a green heap in the middle of the surgery floor. Normal would have been bad enough, but bright green with green steam coming off it was somehow excruciating.

I left the vet's with Millie, some white stuff in a bottle, and a receipt for £40.

It had started to rain. I turned into our street and spied Lucy sitting on the garden wall kicking her heels against the brickwork and with a scowl on her face that would scare the Grim Reaper. I pulled up. Apparently Josh had refused to let her in. He said he had strict instructions not to open the door to anyone.

"You said you wouldn't be long, Mam!" she said accusingly, her hair dripping around her face.

"I know, but the cancellation turned up with her cat. Anyway, I thought you were at Chloe's."

"For God's sake! That was an hour ago."

"Don't blaspheme, Lucy."

"Like you, you mean?" she said under her breath.

I rang the bell and Josh came grinning into the hall. I watched him through the letterbox.

"Yes, who is it?"

"You know who it is, Josh, stop playing silly beggars and open the door."

"Sorry, I haven't to open the door to anyone."

"We're getting wet, Josh. Open-the-door – NOW!"

He opened the door and got a reprimand threatening the loss of privileges from me and a condescending smirk from Lucy, which was no more than he deserved.

I put the kettle on for a much needed cuppa. While waiting for it to boil I squashed Millie's medication with some cheese and pushed it into her mouth. She wagged her tail and begged for more. She didn't get anymore, but being hand-fed cheese was obviously doggy speak for, 'Millie, the upstairs ban has been lifted', because…

"Mam, can you get here quick? I mean like NOW," Lucy called frantically from upstairs.

I sighed and switched off the kettle.

Josh burst into the kitchen.

"Mam, I've found out why Millie's been shittin' green poos. She's been eatin' the loose cloth from underneath my snooker table!"

With the flat of my hand on his chest, I moved him to one side, "Not now, Josh."

Lucy was standing on her bed struggling to hold up a four-foot poster of the Black-Eyed Peas. "Mam, Millie's pinched my Blu tack. Can you get it?"

Millie shot under the bed then peered out defiantly. I knelt down, grabbed her front paws, dragged her out and demanded that she drop the Blu tack, NOW!

She looked straight at me and with an exaggerated gulp; swallowed it.

"Like-er what happens now, mam?" Lucy demanded to know, one hand holding up the poster the other hand on her hip.

"Don't worry, Lucy, I'm sure laxatives will have the same effect on Blu tack as they do on snooker table cloth."

"I meant about my *poster*!"

I had just reached the top of the stairs and flinging myself down them seemed like the best idea I'd had all week, when:

"Mam, come back quick, urghh! Millie's bein' sick, urghh!"

I stared at the puddle of frothy green vomit with the ball of Blu tack in it and it occurred to me, and not for the first time, that perhaps I'd been multi-murderer Mary Ann Cotton in a previous lifetime and this was payback time.

Shooing the dog downstairs, I cleaned up the sick, rinsed the Blu tack under the bathroom tap and offered it to Lucy who gagged.

Josh called up the stairs, hardly able to contain his excitement, "Good and bad news, mam, that laxative's brill stuff, Millie's just shat the ship's cat out and you know how long that's been in there."

"And?" I waited.

"She didn't quite make it outside."

# 8

## COLD IN THE KIDNEYS

My mother rang to tell me she had found lion's poo. It was on the shelves in the garden centre but it was £6.95 for a tiny bit, so she had decided to put up with the cat's poo as that doesn't cost anything. She wondered why lion's poo is so expensive because after all, lion's must produce huge amounts?

There didn't seem to be any answer to that so I didn't attempt one. She went on to say that after the garden centre she and Sadie went to the precinct to wait for the new Alzheimer's charity shop to open, but although they had waited and waited, it didn't open. Sadie said they must have forgotten, so they just got the bus home. Since then, my mother said, she had been feeling a bit queasy, she'd put it down to a shop bought prawn mayonnaise sandwich.

I said I'd pop round. She said there was no need. I said I'd feel better seeing her.

"Lucy, Josh, coats on please, we're going to Gran's."

"Whaaa," said Josh, "you have to be joking! I've just got one more level then I'm finished this game and anyway it's boring at Gran's. She hasn't even got a DVD player, only VHS and ancient videos, so you can count me out."

"Me too, Mam, I mean I love Gran to bits but I'm waiting for an important message on Facebook from Emma, and she'll expect a reply, so I can't possibly go."

"Okay, you win. But please be warned that break time tomorrow will find me at the school gates waving a scarf and gloves for you, Josh, in case it turns cold, and for you, Lucy, I'll have the pink and green cardigan Gran knitted for your last birthday, which you thought you'd hidden."

That worked a treat. I honestly surprise myself.

My mother looked okay, albeit a bit pale. She was pleased to see us, but she said she didn't want kisses, in case we got her germs.

"I certainly won't have prawn mayonnaise again, Joanne, I didn't even like it much. Something was telling me I should stick with my usual cheese and tomato, but you have to move with the times. Sadie had bacon with lettuce, seemed an odd combination to me but she said it was very Moreish. She picks these things up from the telly. Anyway, while I was out, I got some new videos from Scope for the children. It'll come to me in a minute where I've put them."

Josh said, "You don't get *new* videos from charity shops, Gran."

I shot him a look and said they were new to *us*. Lucy said there was a Scope bag at the side of the settee, they might be in that. They were.

My mother spread the videos out. Danger Mouse, Pocahontas and My Girl. Josh sniggered.

"Do you want cold in the kidneys, Lucy?" my mother asked.

"I've never heard of it, Gran. Who's in it?"

"Who's in what, dear?"

"Cold in the kidneys."

"You young ones," said my mother shaking her head, "ne'er cast a clout till May be out, Lucy."

Lucy looked at me, puzzled. I smiled, I knew how she felt. I went into the kitchen to put the kettle on.

Josh followed and whispered, "Mam, Gran's puttin' My Girl on. I'm *not* watchin' it."

"Well close your eyes then, or else sit in here with me and Gran."

He passed his grandmother in the doorway on his way out.

"Joanne," said my mother, "Lucy's all bare round her middle and I'm worried about her kidneys."

"I know what you're saying, Mam, but it's the fashion."

"Fashion is as fashion does, Joanne. We may have had an occasional warm day, but one swallow doth not a summer make. Lucy will be riddled with arthritis by the time she's my age. I mean just look at my finger joints and I've never gone round with nothing round my middle."

I picked up a plastic tub from the bench. "I didn't know you were taking Ginseng, Mam."

"Oh, those, I found them at the back of the cupboard. Someone told me Ginseng works wonders for your memory. I was taking them a while ago then I put them in the cupboard when the decorators came and forgot about them."

I looked at the tub. "These are three years old!"

"Are they? How time flies," she said.

"It's probably those that have been making you feel ill. Get rid of them and I'll get you some more when I'm out tomorrow."

We sat in the kitchen with our tea and my mother said I was not to call on Friday as she and Sadie would be going to Mr Foster's funeral. They would go to the church but not the crematorium as that was all uphill.

"Poor Mr Foster, Joanne. He dropped down dead while waiting in the queue at Boots for the one hour photo service and there was only three minutes to go. Poor Mrs Foster, said every time she looked at those photos, it would remind her she need only to have paid for the next day service, as under the circumstances, that's when she got to see them. Oh! I nearly forgot, Joanne. Sadie's niece, Claire is going to try that Ivy F again to become pregnant and if nothing happens this time round, she's going to have her downstairs laminated. I'll let you know how she gets on. By the way, Joanne, did Ernest call?"

I said he hadn't but I had a couple of scares. One of which turned out to be a man collecting for the Salvation Army and other was the gas man come to read the meter.

"Oh, well, I suppose there's still time," she said.

Then she asked if I'd heard how 'poor George' was getting along. It was a mystery to me why George had become 'poor George' since we had split up, but there we are. George and my mother were fond of each other. My mother would have liked a son, but as she had been in her forties when I was born, I remained her first and last. George's mother had died when he was three and he'd been brought up by his father, Stan, so my mother had become a kind of surrogate. Five years ago, before he had retired with his new bride to Portugal, Stan had left his small and limping, building business to George. This had really impressed my mother, who was ever so proud to have a 'businessman' as a son-in-law.

As I was happy my mother seemed okay, I reached for my coat and said I'd see her over the weekend. She gave me the Scope bag, and said there was something in it for me. I went into the lounge to collect the kids. They were red-eyed and snuffling and the credits for the end of My Girl were rolling. Perhaps they were normal after all.

On the way home they nearly came to blows over who would be first to use the computer. Josh said it was his turn, he wanted to download some Slipknot, for his iPod. Lucy said she needed it first to see if Chloe was logged onto Facebook. I said I would toss a coin to decide who was to go first and they could have half an hour each before bed. I said I'd never known children like them for arguing all the time. Lucy said it was a recognizable fact that most children's behavioural problems stemmed from bad parenting and it didn't help that they were now products of a broken home. I said adversity was character building.

Back home, the arguing and conciliation over the use of the computer proved to be inconsequential as the decision had been pre-determined by the dog who sat wagging her tail in a nest of chewed up computer cables. Lucy screeched and stomped her feet and Josh swore under his breath.

I poured a glass of Australian Chardonnay then I opened the Scope bag, the contents of which I pushed into the mouth of the video machine to be grabbed, swallowed and regurgitated into that, which along with the frustration over the computer, was guaranteed to persuade my children to have an early night; The Sound of Music.

# 9

## MOVE OVER JOAN CRAWFORD

The next day was a bright and sunny start to the last day of May. The birds whistled and sang and preened and fanned their feathers; elaborating their mating dances. Butterflies fluttered and fat bees buzzed as they claimed their fragment of earth and sky. The tranquil, warm, early summer breeze silently lifted the remnants of the waxen white Magnolia blossom, floating its faded petals to the ground, like a fluttering of early summer snow. The line of washing billowed and danced to the tune of mother nature and the morning sun escaping through the leaves of a neighbouring birch, created moving mosaics on the patio paving.

Buoyed by last night's film, I pushed open the windows and trilled to the outside world that high on a hill was a lonely goat-herd. I sang Edelweiss into my coffee cup and, lifting the hem of an imaginary dirndl skirt and pinafore, I swirled about, treating my dancing partner, the washing basket, to a rendition of My Favourite Things. I put stuff into the washing machine and Millie, taking full advantage of my exuberance and before I'd gotten round to closing the washer door, pulled them out again. Josh, silhouetted in the dappled sun on the patio, picked dog dirt from the grooves in his trainers with a screwdriver while Lucy, from her bedroom, could be heard singing into her karaoke, "Don'cha you wish your girlfriend was hot like me. Don'cha?"

I was Julie Andrews, the children were the Von-Trapps and George had been killed in the war.

Then, the singing upstairs became a squeal as Lucy, bounding down the stairs with the squeal echoing behind her, charged past me and tore outside to accuse Josh of drawing lipstick and bras on her Arctic Monkeys.

Josh shrugged and said they looked better as girls. Lucy said she knew who would look better as a girl.

Tranquillity lifted her skirts and floated over hedges and fences to settle into neighbouring gardens peacefully bereft of teenagers and dogs. The cute Van Trapps set about killing each other while the dog danced around them barking her head off.

I went to the sink, filled a bowl with water, took it outside and threw it over them. They gasped. They hung their arms ape-like and dripped. The dog shimmied water from her coat then ran for cover.

I stood for a minute with the dripping bowl. I was losing the plot. I knew it would just be a matter of time. I ran, guilt-ridden, to the phone to ring George. I asked him if he remembered the children he had fathered because I'd nearly drowned them on the patio? I said I had to be the worst mother in the world, the children would be taken into care. I said I made Joan Crawford look like Mother Theresa and I demanded to know what he intended to do about it. And while I was at it I told him about the mortgage he needed to take out to pay for the dog damage and the vet's bills and to come and get the dog.

"Calm down, Jo. Take a chill pill for God's sake. The

children won't go into care, it's care in the community these days. A bowl of water would not have been enough to drown them and you're actually quite a good mother – all things considered."

*Quite* a good mother! All things considered! And when exactly had he became an authority on the subject I should like to know?

"Just trying to be helpful, Jo."

"Well keep trying and who knows, one day you might succeed!"

"I didn't ask you to ring. Although as it happens I was just about to ring you because, the thing is, Fran and I are about to leave for Florida. Her brother has an apartment out there, so I won't be able to do anything about anything for the next three weeks or so."

*He* was going to Florida while *I* was going dool-bloody-ally.

And because there was silence from my end, he added, "We thought it would give us a chance to check it out and perhaps take the children next year."

"Oh, is that right? Pull the other one, George, you'll hear bells jingle!"

"Actually, Jo, it's possible the dog might be a bit of a problem. Fran's not a dog lover, so this could be a bit tricky."

"Not a dog lover! So you haven't got that in common then."

Stuff sisterhood.

Sighing and sounding like the long suffering martyr he considered himself to be, he said, "I'll ignore that, Jo, you do seem frazzled and sarcasm is your forte after all. Look, as soon as I'm back I'll be in touch and we can talk dogging then. Er... you know what I mean."

I put the phone down.

Lucy and Josh were dripping behind me. They had linked arms comrade fashion and with the dog at their feet they were defiant, united against the enemy: me,

Lucy huffed. "When you're quite finished with the phone, Mam, we're ringing child-line!"

Handing the phone to Lucy, I thought it only fair to mention there was every possibility of Esther being otherwise occupied; after all, she had the problem of Mrs Chisholm's Big Slipper to sort out.

# 10

## STAY! NO WAY

I have decided to set myself three 'goals to achieve' in my newly single life. Although I've been putting it off, being under the illusion that eventually dogs must surely sort themselves out but which hasn't happened with Millie, number one on my list is training the dog. This needs to happen while I still have a house with some decent furniture in it as Millie is determined to decimate the lot. Goal number two is to be nicer about Fran (well in front of the children, anyway) and purely for George's sake. Last but definitely not least is to get myself a life and, after stagnating for the last eighteen years as a wife and mother, I wouldn't say no to a life infused with a bit of romance, if that's not too much to ask.

So, as there's no time like the present, I have decided to start the ball rolling and do something about training the dog. Trudy from the vet's, aware of my ignorance in all matters canine related, has given me the number of Sue, a renowned and much respected dog trainer.

Upon ringing Sue to arrange my first session, I was left in no doubt that Sue meant business. I had feebly explained that

I was a novice dog owner and as such, I wondered if I might be allowed to be cut a bit of slack. Sue was having none of that. It seemed nobody, but nobody went from Sue's classes without benefitting from her much-in-demand expertise and there was no possible reason to believe that I wouldn't also be a benefactor.

And so, with more than a smidgen of trepidation on my part, arrangements were made for me and Millie to attend the new session which was to begin that afternoon at Sue's farmyard home.

Millie knew there was something up. She sensed it. She sniffed the air as we pulled up. Countryside! Manure! Utopia! She leapt from the car dragging me with her. She was over-excited. She'd never been so near a farmyard before and the smells she was encountering were something that needed investigation and she was determined to investigate. I was dragged through a muddy field and into an even muddier farmyard while she sniffed and pawed and rolled on her back onto the remains of something dead and too horrible to contemplate.

"If you're quite ready over there, we would like to get started," called a woman's voice directed at me. It was obviously Sue. She was standing at the outside of a group of people and their dogs who were waiting for me to join them. Millie looked up at the sound of Sue's voice, noticed the other dogs, forgot the distraction of the decaying dead thing and bounded over to meet them; dragging me with her. Sue tutted and rolled her eyes, she was plainly going to have her work cut out. I could almost read her mind, 'there's always one'. She was wearing a brown, dog-tooth checked riding jacket, jodhpurs and knee-high boots. She held a riding crop in her hand which she kept hitting against her thigh. I mean she might have just dismounted from a horse for all I knew so why I should have found this get-up intimidating I'm not sure, perhaps it was the thigh thwacking that batted my morsel of confidence into the next field and beyond. Her hair was cropped no-nonsense short and her face scrubbed so clean it would be positively virgin territory to a mascara brush or a bit of lip gloss. She wasn't tall, yet if there was a wrestling match staged between her and a bull, my money would definitely not be on the bull.

There were five of us at the new training session and we were introduced to each other. There was Star, the German Shepherd with owner Gillian; Stanley, the Afghan Hound with owner Jim; Betsy, the Cockerpoo with owner Stacey; and Pip, the little black and white mongrel with owner Joan. Introductions over, we were then led by Sue into a disused barn whereupon everyone was instructed to line up against the far wall with their dog. Sue then proceeded to climb a seven-rung step ladder from where, sitting on the top platform step, she called out our instructions, well barked them really, but that just seems too much of pun.

Dogs were to be kept on the left and in a sitting position. Leads were to be held by the left hand and taken across the body with the slack taken up by the right hand. At the command of Walk we were to step forward, always with the left foot, while simultaneously leading the dog. If the dog strained on the lead, the lead was to be tugged backwards with the command Heal. If the dog responded well, praise and treats were to be given.

And so, with these instructions ringing in our ears, off we marched around the perimeter of the barn. Star was living up to his name. He stayed loyally beside owner Gillian as if he was protecting a roast beef dinner with all the trimmings. Stately Stanley pranced gracefully like a dressage pony. Betsy frolicked, eagerly doing her best to please owner Stacey. Pip yawned, he just wanted a lie down, have forty winks, this wasn't his scene, so that owner Joan had to jolly him along. Millie, being unused to orders or structure wasn't sure if she approved. Copying the other dogs yet totally bemused by the whole episode she reluctantly kept at my side allowing me to think that perhaps all was not lost. But, after the second lap, Millie had had enough. There was more to life. She had her eye on Betsy, felt sure with a nod in the right direction she could get Betsy on side for a bit of roll-about fun. She just had to get rid of me and this damned lead. And with that in mind she spun on her hind legs and pulled and tugged and circled me so that I ended up from the waist down trussed up like an Egyptian mummy. I was so tangled in the lead and as Millie was now choking to death, there seemed no alternative but to loosen it off. Until that is, Sue yelled from her observatory tower, "No. No. No. Do not even think about that, Joanne!" She disembarked from the steps by sliding frontwards down them and she strode over, thwacking her thigh as she came. Millie, sensing an impending threat pressed hard against me. Sue tucked her riding crop under her arm, unceremoniously grabbed Millie by the collar, loosened the lead and while untangling me, said, "Well that didn't go quite according to plan, now did it?" Then addressing the others, "Okay folks the show's over, as you were." She then took Millie and the lead and proceeded to show me how it *should* be done.

Millie went from being class clown to top dog. She now positively adored Sue. At last, this was someone she could look up to, respect. She would jump through hoops for Sue, should that be coming up. Betsy was history.

After a sturdy, stomp around the barn, Sue returned Millie to me, expressing her hope that I had learnt something from my observations, because in her experience – extensive experience – she might add, unruliness was very rarely down to the dog, without exception the fault lay in the hands of the owner. Suitably chastised and trying to ignore the sympathetic looks from the other owners, I meekly nodded my agreement.

Then, with a determined thwack of the thigh, Sue decided it was becoming too hot for the dogs in the barn and so the next part of the session was to be done outside, in a sectioned off corner of a nearby field.

Everyone agreed that the fresh air was exhilarating after the stuffy, smelly barn and so it was with renewed enthusiasm, that we lined up to set about the Sit and Stay exercise. The dog was to be pressed down gently on its hindquarters into a sitting position with the command Sit. This was to be accompanied by a 'forefinger in the air' hand signal. That accomplished, the owner was then to face their dog and walk one step backwards while simultaneously commanding the dog to Stay. The Stay command was to be accompanied by a 'flat of the hand' signal. If the dogs responded positively it was to be praised and given a treat. Two steps backwards and still all was going swimmingly. I couldn't believe my luck. Millie was obviously still, either in rapturous awe of Sue or else she was just enjoying the treats. But then, when we were to turn from the dogs while still giving the Stay command, Millie took off. Perhaps she had just become bored, having a miniscule boredom threshold, or perhaps she felt, as I'd turned my back on her and without the restrictions of the lead, she could do as she pleased. In any event, she ran to the privet hedge which sectioned the exercise plot and crawled through it, completely ignoring my 'flat of the hand' signals and yells of Stay. She was now in the main part of the field.

I've tried to blot this next bit from my memory, but it comes back to haunt me. I can see Millie in a corner of the field, in pounce position waiting for me to get to almost touching distance before she bolted. This went on with Millie running from corner to corner of the field and me chasing after her until I was too exhausted to try to get her back. Sue strode over while the other owners observed. She tried all of her 'extensive experience' to get Millie to come to her but Millie thought she'd just come to join the fun and so became even more excited. Sue shrugged, shook her head resignedly, said at least the field was securely fenced and with a few hard thwacks on the thigh, strode off

I tried persuasion; Mill-ie, come, Mill-ie, treat, until it became GET.HERE.NOW. It was becoming dusk. I saw the last of the owner's cars drive off. Steam was now coming from Millie who was a crouched heap in a far corner of the field.

I gave up, admitted defeat. Exhausted, I sat in the field in a foetal position and closed my eyes. All I wanted to do was to grab the stupid dog, beat a hasty retreat, go home and file the episode in the 'things never to be repeated' folder. I mean I had never, ever expressed any desire to have a dog. This dog had been George's silly idea. I mean he wasn't vindictive so what had possessed him to do it? If he'd given the kids a cat or a rabbit it would have been a lot less bother and I wouldn't now be sitting in a muddy field, a figure of fun, too exhausted to move, wishing the dog would run away and never come back.

But then I heard panting. It was coming closer. I didn't move. Then she was nudging my arm, I still didn't move. She nuzzled my neck, I didn't respond. She began to whimper, but I wasn't falling for it. I had a feeling that she would still bolt if I made a move. Probably thinking I was dead, she crawled limply under the arch of my legs where she lay, a steaming, sweaty, tongue-lolling, worn-out heap. I sensed the shadow of a figure standing over us. I opened my eyes and looked up. It was Sue. She wondered if I wanted my name down for next week's session? I silently shook my head and with a nod of agreement and a thwhack of the thigh, she walked away saying, "You know where the gate is when you're ready to leave."

"Crickey Mam! Look at the state of you! I thought you were taking Millie to be trained!" said Lucy, incredulously.

"What sort of training was that!?" Josh wanted to know. "You look as if you've been combat training with the SAS or something. And where's Millie?"

"She's in the garage, cooling off till I get round to rubbing her down. When I've been showered and changed, I'll tell you all about it?" I said, wearily.

Training the dog is still on my 'goals to be achieved' list.

# 11

## STRANGE ENCOUNTERS
## OF THE CANINE KIND

'Smile and the world smiles with you'. This is to be my motto for today, because this is the first day of the rest of my life. It's Monday morning, back to school, back to work and back to normal.

Josh was complaining because he couldn't find one of his school shoes and that was before he'd even looked in the dog basket. Lucy was screeching blue murder in her bedroom because most of the cover of her Spanish exercise book had disappeared. The bit that was left was blue with the texture of blotting paper.

"If the book had been put onto a shelf or zipped into your schoolbag, Lucy, the dog would not have been able to get at it, so if it's in shreds it's your own fault for leaving it where the dog *could* get at it," I said, all calm and smiley.

"That's like so not fair," she said, "Mr Bosanka will kill me."

"I very much doubt that, Lucy." I smiled benignly.

"I'm not scared of old Bosanka," said, Josh, "me and my mates call him Bosanka the Wa…"

"Do *not* go there, Josh," I threatened, smilingly. "Now, if the two of you don't get a move on, the bus will go without you."

"Why are you smiling like that, Mam? It's freaking me out," said Lucy. I tweaked her nose playfully while ushering them out of the door still munching toast and shoving stuff into their bags. Then, humming a merry tune, I followed behind them to the car, to start my day in the office.

As I opened the gates to the drive, a petite, Posh Becks look-a-like, looking as though a puff of steam could knock her out, came round the corner on the opposite side of the road, walking her dog. Walking actually being a euphemism for Posh gripping the lead with both hands in a frantic attempt to stop the dog from breaking into the run which would be guaranteed to pull her off her feet. The dog, a huge brute of a thing, was later identified to me as a Rottweiler.

I gave Posh a good morning smile, although with sunglasses the size of bin lids covering most of her face and concentrating on trying to keep her feet on the ground, I couldn't tell if she saw me. However, it soon became apparent that the dog had.

Having opened the gates I turned to walk back to the car when my legs were suddenly buckled by something like the force of a cannonball. It dragged with it, the stumbling, screeching and totally ineffectual Posh as it proceeded to grip my waist with its huge paws, pinning me to the car bonnet, whereupon seven stones of heaving, drooling and panting dog began thrusting at me from behind. It was probably this that wiped the smile from my face.

Posh continued to screech and, with her sunglasses and baseball cap flying off in different directions, she tried, but without any success whatsoever, to pull the dog off me. I struggled to breathe under its weight, but managed to push its enormous paws away from me as a man passer-by, grabbed the lead from Posh and tugged until the dog lost its grip and gave up.

Posh apologised profusely. She just didn't know what had

come over Jeremy. Of course there was no doubting what had come over me – bloody Jeremy.

By this time, an audience out collecting their morning newspapers and mother's with pushchairs had gathered around my gate. I heard a man's voice sniggering and saying to whoever was listening, "That lends a whole new meaning to that dogging carry-on that does."

And how they all laughed.

Straightening myself up and wriggling my skirt down to where it had started out and with as much dignity as I could manage, I walked back to my front door, fumbled with the key in the lock, opened it and went in. Once inside I fell back against the closed door, took some deep breaths then wobbled my way into the kitchen. Flopping into a chair, then toppling out of it again, because Millie had been at one of the legs, I wondered what on earth had made that dog do that. I mean I wouldn't mind being pounced on by, say, Daniel Craig or Ewan McGregor or even Ade from the hairdressers would do at a push, but a dog! That's really sad, even by my standards.

I needed some time to pull myself together, to get changed, wash the dog drool out of my hair. I was already late for work. I had to ring Ian. It was beyond the realms of possibility to expect him to believe that I had been sexually assaulted by a Rottweiler, so I'd tell him the car wouldn't start.

"Ian, I'm sorry but I have to wait for the AA, I can't get the car to start."

"For Christ's bloody sake, Jo, we have a disciplinary at ten o clock."

"I know, Ian, sor-ree."

"Have you heard of buses, Jo? Big red things on wheels. You get on, pay your fare to some miserable sod with a shite attitude, take a seat then get off. Comprehendo, Jo?

I wanted to say, "Red! That's soh yesterday," instead I said, "Yes, Ian, I'll get there ASAP."

"Friggin' great. I'll have to tell Shaun friggin' Elliott we can't do his lateness disciplinary, cos the human resources assistant is friggin' late. Well done, Jo."

I put the phone down. I might report him, he shouldn't speak to me like that. Smiling! I just wanted to cry.

I was still feeling sorry for myself when the door opened and my children walked in. Lucy was floppy and red-eyed and Josh had his arm stretched up and over her shoulder, protectively, but he was too short and Lucy was too tall and the gesture just didn't work.

Self pity disappeared quicker than Gary Glitter from Top of the Pops. I jumped up and along with Josh, helped the collapsing Lucy into one of the non-collapsing chairs. What on earth was going on? Why was Lucy in this state? Why weren't they on the bus and on their way to school?

Call it a mother's intuition, but a quick glance at Josh was all it took for me to realise that Josh's brotherly concern was thinly disguising a smidgen of repressed glee which also meant that whatever had happened to Lucy, it probably wasn't exactly life threatening.

Trying desperately to keep the excitement from his voice, Josh did the explaining. He said while they were waiting for the school bus, a little brown dog, out on its own, had grabbed Lucy's leg with its paws and sexed it. Josh said while the dog was sexing Lucy's leg it had got its willie out and he had actually seen it. He said he'd never seen a dog's willie before; it was a little pink thing.

Lucy moaned. She gripped my arm. She was hyperventilating. I told her to take deep breaths.

Josh said the other kids in the queue had gathered around Lucy and the dog. They were cheering the dog and egging it on. Then the bus came but Lucy couldn't get on it because the dog wouldn't get off her leg. He said Vicki Pearson sniggered and said, 'Everyone knows you're desperate for a boyfriend, Lucy, but that's ridiculous,' and all Vicki's chav mates laughed and chanted, 'Who let the dogs out'.

Mrs Murphy, who drives the school bus had got out of her cab and tried hitting the dog with her bag saying, 'Get off that poor, innocent child, you rollocking little eejit'. Josh said Mrs Murphy, who was Irish, called everyone a rollocking little eejit. He said Mrs Murphy had called Craig Bolton a rollocking little eejit when he had thrown a water bomb and it landed in her cab and she'd had to pull over. I told Josh I'd got the message and I did NOT want to hear that again.

He said as Lucy was so upset, Mrs Murphy said it might be better if Josh were to take her home and return to school a bit later when everything had calmed down. Mrs Murphy asked Josh if he had a dog in heat. Josh wasn't sure, so he just said no. Josh said the bus went off with everyone cheering and shouting through the windows and then the dog got fed-up, got off Lucy's leg, sniffed about for a bit then ran off.

Josh said, "Just think, Luce, some of the kids had their phones out so chances are you could end up on YouTube and get loads of hits and become really famous."

I steeled myself against the anticipated wrath which I was sure would follow that remark but it didn't come. Instead she calmly processed that thought. Was a dog sexually assaulting your leg at a bus stop with loads of kids watching and cheering worth the price of fame? She'd have to think about that. In the meantime we had a cuddle and some hot chocolate.

I wondered if Mrs Murphy was right about Millie being in heat. Perhaps I should go to the library and get a book on dogs. Or google it. Or perhaps I should just get rid of the damned dog. I rang the vet's and, with somebody else's luck, Trudy answered.

"Trudy," I said, "this might sound a bit silly, but is it possible Millie could be in heat? She's only about ten months old but my daughter and I have had some strange encounters of the canine kind and it has made me wonder."

Trudy said at ten months it was more than possible. She asked if I'd noticed Millie's vulva becoming soft, swollen and pliable.

I said, "Eh!"

She said I should look for tell-tale signs: droplets and stained bedding. She said unless I wanted to breed from Millie I should consider having her spayed.

Josh tapped my arm and mischievously asked if heat was a dog's period and if it was, would Millie need a tampon up her bum.

He was pushing his luck, I ignored him.

The consideration to have Millie spayed was decided upon in about three seconds and arrangements were made to have the spaying done. I was to wait until Millie's heat was over and in the meantime I was to collect an 'Anti-Mate' spray to use on Millie, to help, in Trudy's words, to deter unwanted attentions from other dogs. 'Fastening the stable door after the horse had bolted' came into my mind and that shocked me. I'm only thirty -nine and I'm already thinking in adages. I'm turning into my mother!

I thanked Trudy and before I hung up I decided it might be an idea to mention the bowl of mandarin and pomegranate pot-pouri Millie had eaten that morning, in case of repercussions.

Trudy said most dogs preferred Frolic.

I put the phone down just as the doorbell rang.

The man looked normal enough: cardigan with saggy pockets and football buttons, corduroy trousers, sandals over socks, a long bit of hair combed over his bald head, newspaper under his arm.

"I would like you to treat this as an enquiry," he said, officiously. "Are you familiar with The Son of Aurora Whirlwind?" I looked at him. This was not the sort of thing I expected to be asked from a stranger on my doorstep. I expected to be asked if I was happy with my gas supplier or did I want my drive resurfaced, because the person asking just happened to have a truck load of tarmac round the corner. He waited for an answer.

"I haven't lived here long," I lied.

He ignored me. "The reason I ask, is that The Son of Aurora Whirlwind is the kennel club name of my dog, Sultan. A name which any responsible dog owner would be familiar with."

Again he waited. I wondered if perhaps he'd missed his medication. I looked around. He didn't seem to have a carer with him, so I was glad I'd kept the chain on the door.

He went on to say that his occupation over the last few days had revolved around trying to find the source of discontent of The Son of Aurora Whirlwind, aka Sultan. He said his endeavours had proved fruitless, until, that is, while out collecting his newspaper that morning, he had witnessed the unfortunate incident between myself and a particularly aroused Rottweiler. Putting two and two together, he had no alternative but to conclude that the offender must reside in this property. He said The Son of Aurora Whirlwind was well known in the dog world, was impeccably bred, a best of breed champion and much in demand as a perpetuator of the breed. It was inconceivable therefore, that this magnificent animal should be displaying the behavioural instincts of a common-or-garden mongrel, i.e. howling and baying like a wolf at the moon and, uncharacteristically attempting to mount his wife.

I said I was sorry for his wife, as, from my experience that morning, I knew how she must be feeling.

"Those sugar-coated sentiments cut no ice with me," he said, dismissively. "Am I right in assuming you are the owner of a, er, lady dog? And, am I right in assuming that that lady dog is in season?"

I shrugged, non-committedly.

"And do you intend to breed from your lady dog? Because if the answer to that is no then in my opinion irresponsible dog owners such as yourself, who allow unspayed ladies to contaminate the atmosphere, should be served with an Anti Social Behaviour Order as you pose as great a nuisance to ordinary law abiding citizens as do Hoodies. "

I had a madman on my doorstep.

It was still only 10am yet up until now, one way or another, this had been the longest morning of my life. Being ravaged in public by a rampant, sexually charged canine was not my idea of a spectator sport because I had not, as far as I was aware, suddenly morphed into Lassie. Add to this the implication that I was somehow responsible for the sexual urges of the entire dog population and, with premenstrual, hormonal activity pounding through my veins, the contemptuously, supercilious person on my doorstep should consider himself extremely lucky if he were to walk away unscathed, because at that moment, reaching for the spider plant from the hall table and smashing it off his pompous head while telling him to go away in something four lettered and Anglo Saxon, was what I wanted to do more than anything else in the world. But instead I smiled, and with the utmost restraint I said, "Mr Aurora Whirlwind, why not go the whole hog, take out a court injunction against me then do us all a favour, bugger off and get yourself a life." Then I closed the door.

"Who was at the door, Mam?" asked, Josh.

"Oh, just somebody wanting to tarmac the drive."

I came down from my shower to find Lucy back to normal and eager to get to school as Chloe had texted her with some amazing news! Josh said all the stuff he'd had to deal with that morning had taken its toll and it was doubtful if he'd be able to manage going back to school.

I ruffled his hair and said he'd survive.

I dropped them off at the school gates, before dropping my clothes off at the dry cleaners. Then I went to work.

Ian was sulking and ignored me for most of the day. Shaun Elliot had rung in sick which meant the disciplinary had had to be rearranged and that had rendered my lateness neither here nor there and that had peed Ian off.

In the afternoon I got a text from Alison to say she would call next Friday night after she'd been to Weight Watchers, if I was going to be in. If I was going to be in! Was she kidding? My mother had more of a social life, than I had. This was good news, I needed some like-minded company and Alison fitted that bill nicely.

I rang my mother and told her about the visit I'd had from the horrible man and the ASBO threat. My mother said, "That's all very well but you need to be careful about Aspro, Joanne, it's been proven to play havoc with the lining of your stomach."

# 12

## THE WEAPON OF MASS DESTRUCTION

It was the day of Millie's operation. I dropped her off at the vet's in the morning with arrangements made to collect her when I'd finished work that night. I'd had a horrible day at work. Although I didn't think it possible, Ian had been even more obnoxious than usual. He was in trouble with both the union rep and the store manager for allegedly sacking someone without following the proper procedures and, in an effort to vindicate himself, which was never going to happen, he'd had me chasing around looking for pretend files and correspondence, which we both knew didn't exist. It all terminated in the guy being reinstated and Ian being given a warning.

I just wanted to collect the dog, go home, have something to eat, do the obligatory half hour of nagging the kids to do their homework then sit in front of Crimewatch with a glass of chilled Chardonnay. But until then, while waiting for Millie to come round from the anaesthetic in the recovery room, I would settle for a few minutes quietly flicking through the magazine I'd picked up from the table in front of me, an enthralling read entitled, 'Your Pet-Your guide to Pests and Diseases'.

Of course, it goes without saying that a few quiet moments was never going to happen because, although there were plenty of vacant seats in the waiting room, a man chose to sit beside me and not only to sit beside me but also to tell me about the operation his dog, Susan was having done to flush out her ears. *Why* do people do this? Did I have 'bore me to tears with stories about your dog' tattooed across my forehead?

The man said his dog was an Irish Wolfhound and this one, Susan, was his twelfth (it seems he had always kept two at a time). Apparently he'd had an obsession for the breed since he was eight years old when one had licked him on the cheek. I stifled a yawn, like I said it had been a long day. He then proceeded to fish about in the inside pocket of his jacket before producing a wallet which was stuffed full of photos of the damn things and which, one by one he pushed in front of my face. This is Shirley, this is Wendy, this is Becky, this is Ruby... on and bloody on... this is Emma, this is Lottie, oh, and this is my wife. I didn't get a look at the one of his wife because he looked at it for a minute, then, as if he'd been enlightened by some sort of divine intervention he seemed to check the picture of his wife against the one of Lottie. Was he comparing them? Surely not. I looked at him a bit more closely and Mr Aurora Whirlwind came to my mind. Were they related? The mad-as-hatters. Yet again he looked normal enough: Farmer Giles type; pink cheeks, sandy coloured wiry hair, tweedy jacket with leather elbows covered in dog hairs.

Then, as a moth-eaten, gangly thing with soulful eyes and about the size of a donkey wobbled its way out of the recovery room, he gathered up the pictures, stuffed them back into the wallet and with the wallet inside his jacket, he hurried over to the dog. He hugged and kissed it. He produced a stuffed toy rabbit from his jacket pocket which he held to the dog's cheek while he made comforting there, there, noises.

Surely his wife couldn't look like that! If she did no wonder she wasn't with him. She was probably holed up in a kennel somewhere, or in Ireland chasing wolves.

As Susan and the man wobbled their way outside and into the man's mud-caked, Land Rover, a floppy, rolling eyed, get-me-outa-here, Millie, was led from the recovery room by Trudy, who produced a massive plastic cone thing which she euphemistically, it seemed to me, called a collar and which she tied around Millie's neck. This, I was told was designed to stop Millie attacking her stitches.

Getting droopy Millie *and* the collar into the car proved to be no mean feat. In her drug induced state it seemed she no longer recognized the concept of a car, preferring instead to flop about in the car park.

Treats were no inducement and as I had to be careful of her stitches, by the time I'd managed to lift her in, the collar, which had the cutting edge of a machete, had sliced into my finger, torn my tights and ripped a hole in the seat cover.

She tried circling the back seat before eventually giving up and flopping onto it. I watched her through the rear view mirror as I started the engine. She looked back at me through drooping eyelids, as if she would rather be dead and I felt a twinge of guilt. But then I bucked up, told her and myself it had been done for the best. Neither of us would any longer have to put up with unwanted sexual advances from rampant members of the opposite sex and that just had to be good news. Hadn't it? She exhaled a long, mournful sigh that sounded like, yeah, yeah, just 'cos you're not getting any. This was true. Well not from my own species anyway.

# 13

## GREASE IS THE WORD

Josh said, "Mam, why's Millie's head in a lampshade?" and both him and Lucy laughed their heads off at Millie in her collar. The laughter didn't last long though. In fact it ended abruptly the next day when the anaesthetic had worn off and Millie was bounding around back to her normal self, except misjudging distances and objects and banging the collar into everything and anyone foolish enough to get in her way. Lucy, not for the first time that day, stood on a chair begging me to get Millie out of the way so she could get down without risking her tights being ripped to shreds or worst, her legs.

I was still on a bit of a guilt trip about putting a dumb animal through the ordeal of an operation and Millie, being that dumb animal, not only knew this but took full advantage. She decided she couldn't quite reach into her feeding bowl because of the overlap of the collar and she looked so sorry for herself that Josh, losing the toss of a coin, was assigned the job of hand feeding her and holding her water bowl to her mouth so she could lap from it, a process which meant that everything within splashing distance got soaked which included Josh. It was obvious Millie thought hand feeding was no more than her due after what she had been through, but Josh said it made him want to puke. Lucy said watching Millie trying to lick her stitches made her want to puke. (And this from the girl who has aspirations of becoming Michaela Strachan's sidekick in a wildlife conservation.)

Millie took to standing square in front of the television, just to be annoying, but knowing, for the time being anyway, she'd get away with it. I wondered she wasn't brazen enough to take charge of the remote control. I went round repairing torn wallpaper and touching up paintwork and quietly cursing the dog and the damn collar and trying to remember if I'd ever had a decent life.

But then, Friday night brought with it, Alison, who brought with her, a bottle of wine and a big bag of Kettle crisps. She was fresh from Weight Watchers and was celebrating a two pound weight loss. Alison, plump and pretty as always and looking glamorous in her wide-legged white pants and floaty orange kaftan, was now sporting a swishy new hairstyle, which I was really jealous of as it's all I can do to stop my unruly mop from imitating Violet Elizabeth's damned ringlets.

Millie, full of her usual exuberance but with the destruction capability of an Exocet missile, charged down the hall to greet her.

"Aargh! What the hell is that!?" yelled Alison, who, as she turned to face the wall in a gesture of self preservation, dropped the crisps. Millie, who up to that point had been luxuriating in the guilt-driven indulgence of being hand fed, without any hesitation, forgot about the restraints of the collar, grabbed the crisps and ran with them to her basket where she proceeded to tear open the packet and devour the lot and no-one, fearful of the risk to life and limb, was brave enough to stop her. Thereafter, Josh was relieved to be relieved of his hand feeding duties.

Lucy and Josh had their respective friends, Chloe and Jack staying for supper and they had asked for, and were being allowed, the treat of a pizza delivery while I was cooking something special for Alison and me. The pizzas were delivered and paid for and the kids took them upstairs.

I opened the wine. Alison bemoaned the loss of the crisps. She said while some people wanted to smoke cigarettes with alcohol, she wanted to eat crisps. I told her to think positively; little pickers wear bigger knickers, and she said she couldn't get knickers any bigger. She said the next step would be to go commando.

"Jo," she said, "you know when I go for a bikini and leg wax and to put up with the pain, I have to think of it being done in a good cause, because that night I'll be going to bed with David Beckham? Well, lately, when I think of David Beckham, he morphs in my mind into Richard Madeley. What do you think that means?"

"Hmmm, it probably means you have a secret yearning to be Judy Finnigan."

She wrinkled her nose and said damn, that's what she had been thinking. We laughed, wine induced laughter.

We calmed down and she showed me a tattoo she'd had done on her stomach, just above her belly button, a tiny rose. I said she'd need to be careful she didn't get pregnant or she might end up with a bloody big hydrangea. She said, hell! She hadn't thought of that.

We were off again. We laughed our way into the kitchen, propped ourselves onto kitchen stools and opened another bottle. I asked how her romance with Nigel was going?

She said, "Don't ask." She said, most things she could turn a blind eye to, his dancing for instance, was exceptionally cringe worthy, but she usually got round that by pretending he was somebody she'd just picked up and who she didn't know from Adam. Then there was his insisting on using Nature's Way toiletries because they're not tested on animals. She said she agrees with the sentiment, she just wishes he wasn't so damned sanctimonious about it. But, she said, it's the little things, like the other day when he came in with a packet of seeds to grow his own herbs and a book on the power of herbs for healing. Then the other night, she'd asked him to call at the garage on his way home because she was desperate for a bar of fruit and nut, but – and it wasn't as if she wasn't grateful for the thought and all that – he had gone miles out of his way to Holland and Barratt and bought organic cocoa stuff instead. He had said it was the principle of the thing. She said try talking principles to your hormones when they're screaming out for fruit and nut... they just did NOT want to know.

The thing that was really peeing her off though, was that Nigel was a Lib Dem and getting more Lib Dem every day. He was putting himself forward as a party candidate and he was doing three laps round the park every morning before breakfast, to get fit to fight the Council elections. She said she wouldn't mind so much if he looked anywhere near decent in Lycra shorts and a bum-bag, but he didn't. And as Alison had no desire to see the park at dawn, she had told him that her allegiance lay in being apolitical and he said it that was just the sort of attitude that had the country on its knees. Which, she had told him, was how she would be after three laps round the park before breakfast. He was going to knock on doors canvassing as a Lib Dem candidate and he would like to think he could count on her support. Was he kidding? she said, wearing a yellow rosette and knocking on doors around their area! They'd get knocked out. She said it was eco this, eco that and eco the other. Talk about an Eco Worrier! He said she should be more concerned about the planet, but she said she was doing her bit she really was.

She was becoming as eco-friendly as anything. She had stopped using hairspray, mainly because her new hairstyle didn't warrant it, and she separated her rubbish into the various recycling bins, although she knew it all got chucked in together when the men collected it. She was all for people using public transport which was no more than she'd had to do since the clutch went on her car, but somehow, gaining and retaining knowledge on carbon footprints, was prohibited by a distinct lack of enthusiasm. She had tried watching Question Time to improve her mind and to impress Nigel, and to be honest, what else was there to do on a Thursday night before the weekend got going. But, try as she might, she either fell asleep or she found her finger clicking onto the shopping channel.

I sympathised… men… I poured some more wine.

"What's that sack thing hanging on that hook?" Alison said, pointing to the back of the kitchen door.

I reached it down. "Sack thing!" I said, in mock astonishment. "I'll have you know this is a natural, top-notch, made-in-India, hessian peg apron."

"What the hell's a peg apron for?"

"To hold pegs of course."

"As in?"

"Clothes pegs. For pegging out washing."

"Bloody hell, Jo."

I told her she wasn't the only one saving the planet, because not only had I been saving the planet for my children's future but I'd also been saving money on my electric bills by pegging the washing outside instead of using the tumble dryer. And, my mother, to show how impressed she was by my economy, had bought me this peg apron.

"And the upshot is?" Alison asked.

"Not good. You see, being the simpleton that I am, I'd always thought you just stuck pegs in the clothes and the wind blew them dry. But, oh, no. My mother came round and re-hung everything it had taken me ages to hang out. She wasn't altogether sure the line had been wiped down properly. Then the clothes should have been hung inside out so that the sun wouldn't bleach them and with the openings hung in the direction of the wind. The pegs should always be put in the thickest part of the garment, i.e. the waistband, and sheets should be hung from their four corners. And to top it all, as I was bending over to get the clothes out of the washing basket, the bloody pegs fell out of the pouch of my apron all over the garden and I thought, bugger this for a game of soldiers so I gathered up the pegs and the washing basket and made for the tumble dryer. So, if you'd like to be the proud owner of a peg apron, be my guest."

Alison said, she'd pass on that.

I lit the oven and turned the gas on under the pans. We were having salmon in a dill and rocket dressing, with new potatoes and green beans and for dessert, pears poached in red wine with scrunched up meringue and clotted cream. I said I hoped I wasn't dishing up too many calories. Alison said not to worry as she'd never known a calorie she didn't like. She said it sounded lovely, it was ages since she'd had salmon.

I said, "Ah yes, but this isn't *any* old salmon. This is Marks and Spencer salmon. Prime salmon caught in the clear cold waters around the Scottish coast by fourth generation conservation minded fishermen from the small fishing town of Peterhead in the North of Scotland." (And in case there was any doubt of that, I had the label to prove it.)

Alison said of course it was, and the dill and rocket for the dressing had been grown in soil of fairy stardust before being teased from the earth by the wave of a magic wand, to be then picked by the soft, gloved hand of Alan Titchmarch. Then, and only then, was it sprinkled with Lourdes water for cleansing before being gently floated into extra, extra, extra virgin olive oil. Oil produced from rendering down ripe, eighteen year old virgins from the remotest corners of Sardinia, where the excesses of man were virtually unknown and where were to be found the only eighteen-year-old virgins inhabiting the earth.

Then we ate it.

We cleared the table, stashed the dishwasher then went into

the lounge with our glasses and the bottle. A Grease CD was playing on repeat. This was nostalgia. This was school disco time. We put down our glasses and sang Grease is the Word into each other's faces.

We flopped onto the sofa and giggled.

We sang along with John Travolta and with breast stroke arm movements to Greased Lightning, but the strains of Sandra Dee was our cue to pump up the volume, kick off our shoes and jump onto the sofa. I was Olivia Newton John and Alison was Stockard Channing.

Alison had just finished the 'Elvis! Elvis!' bit, when struggling to focus through blurred eyes, I became aware of the figure of Lucy, standing in the doorway, arms folded, watching us. I nudged Alison and we wobbled to a halt.

"Are you two drunk?" Lucy demanded to know.

"Drunk?" I slurred.

"Drunk?" Alison slurred.

"Course not," We slurred together, indignantly.

"Well that's what it looks like from where *I'm* standing."

I nearly slurred, 'Well stand somewhere else then.' But I didn't.

We tried our best to straighten up, look sensible, sober, adult, but it wasn't easy, bleary-eyed and wobbling about shoeless on a sofa.

Lucy went to the stereo and turned it down. "For goodness sake, Chloe and I can't hear ourselves think!" And with that she flounced out muttering something about some people never grow up.

Never grow up! We pulled faces and stuck out our tongues at the closing door, then fell into hysterics.

It was the most I'd laughed since George was chased around the bird sanctuary by Percy the Pelican. Although then I'd actually wet myself.

Alison said it was the most she'd laughed since we'd met

Gemma Graham, who had her baby in its pram. Being baby-phobic, Alison had held back, while I'd gone straight for it, peered into the pram to say what a cutesy little thing it was, but was struck dumb by how un-cutesy it actually was. Alison said the expression on my face was the funniest thing she had ever seen and we missed the next two buses while she calmed down.

It's amazing how the thought of un-inebriated parents coming to collect their off-spring can transform tipsy, overgrown, overblown disco queens into something resembling normal.

Strong coffee, a fresh slick of lipstick, a comb through our hair and Chloe and Jack were called down to be dispatched to their sensible, sober parents and then Nigel came to collect Alison.

He had with him, by virtue of killing two birds with one stone, a wad of Lib Dem fliers which he had decided he might as well push through neighbouring doors while he was in the area. He also had a carrier bag filled with lager bottles and cans which he had collected from the streets on his way over and which he was going to take home to 'dispose of properly'.

Alison looked at me, rolled her eyes and said she'd be in touch.

# 16

## HEN PECKED

"Mam", said Josh, looking up from his homework, "you know how you're sort of soft and squidgy?"

"Hmmm," I said, wondering what was coming next.

"Well Fran isn't like that. She's like a cardboard cut-out and when she kisses you on the cheek it's like being pecked by a hen."

"OMG," said Lucy, "as if you'd know what it's like being pecked by a hen! You are such a nerd, Josh."

"I can imagine it, can't I, Mam?" he said.

I didn't say anything, I wasn't sure where this was leading.

"Well, I like Fran," said Lucy haughtily, "she gave me a really nice nail polish the last time we visited."

"I didn't say I didn't like her! I just said she's like a cardboard cut-out and she kisses like a bloody hen," said Josh, indignantly.

"All right, Josh, that's enough of that and don't let dad hear you saying things about Fran because he won't like it." I said.

"For God's sake! I didn't say she goes around killing people!"

And with that he picked up his books to finish his homework upstairs.

O-kay, I shall consider that little episode as number two on my 'goals to achieve' list, ticked off. No need to overdo it.

# 17

## HI GUY

The most gorgeous man I have ever set eyes on has unexpectedly jumped into my life. He is an artist and for this week only, he is a guest speaker at my interior design course.

His name is Guy.

Oooo. Hi Guy.

Naturally of course, there has to be a downside and it is this. I have come straight to the class from work. I am wearing a plain white blouse, which somewhere along the line has acquired a coffee splash on the front, a naff length, well-worn pencil skirt which has the beginnings of knee indents and a shiny bottom, yukky flesh coloured tights and low heels. This boring ensemble constitutes my business-like work wear and is not a good look. Add to this my make-up, which hasn't been touched since it was put on in about three seconds flat at seven thirty this morning and my hair (which has a mind of its own) is pulled back tidily but boringly into an elastic scrunchy and you get the picture. This is not the look I would have decided upon to meet the man of my dreams, but hey, Sod and his law and all that.

Guy came into the room and introduced himself. He

unhooked a haversack and a guitar from his back and stood them in a corner before perching himself crossed legged in a sort of Hari Krishna chanting pose on the front desk. He shuffled about on his backside, making himself comfortable while at the same time flicking back both sides of his slightly wavy, ash blond, shoulder length hair, which then fell back into exactly the same position. His Daniel Day Lewis cheek bones accentuate the most amazingly beautiful sea green eyes, and a vaguely discernible bit of stubble gives him a sort of Jesus Christ Superstar look. Of course the guy from Jesus Christ Superstar, didn't wear a wide necked tie-dyed tee shirt, a plaited leather thong necklace and Jade beaded bracelets, but otherwise...

He has come to teach us about colour; the language of colour, colour and light, colour and proportion and colour combination.

He looked around the room, bringing colour to the cheeks of the assembled females, well mine anyway, with the most stunning smile, then said:

"Colour is a basic human need... like fire and water, it's raw, it's indispensable to life..."

*–I'm drooling, I just know he's using colour as a euphemism for sex.*

"... It's a universal language, it stimulates emotions, it evokes nature and personality traits and has a human dimension which is irresistible. It affects perception and mood..."

*–Told you.*

"... Seeing colour, using it and surrounding yourself with a personal palette that works for you, produces a calming backdrop for daily life..."

*–I'm mesmerised, the only colour I'm interested in being the turquoise of those spectacularly beautiful eyes.*

"... The colour wheel works by linking the primary colours of red, blue and yellow with the secondary colours of violet, orange and green and with the tertiary colours..."

*–I'm using the power of consciousness to get him to notice me.*

He untangled his legs, pushed himself off the desk and produced from his haversack a colour wheel which he proceeded to stick onto the blackboard. He's wearing loose fitting jeans; low slung, turned up at the bottom, bohemian looking. I could do bohemian. I could live with gorgeous Guy in a commune at Stonehenge singing 'Kumbaya'; in fact, I'm there now...

*Meandering waist deep through fields of golden barley in my gypsy top and beads and my long tiered skirt and Doc Martens. My untamed hair is hanging loose and wild about my shoulders with the occasional burdock burr in its tangles. The barley ebbs and flows, waving about me like tinsel. The wicker basket looped over my arm is filled with the fruits of my labour. In the near distance I see the rising smoke of camp fires, joss-sticks and Marijuana. Plaintive notes coaxed from the mouthpiece of a harmonica, waft on the breeze.*

*My mother, dressed in a hessian sack tied round the middle with a hemp rope belt, is in a corner knitting fingerless gloves. Her hair is standing on end giving her a vaguely mad look, like Ken Dodd but without the teeth. She is waiting for me to return with my spoils, the nettles for soup and the dandelions for tea. She has picked over a drum of elderberries for winemaking and she has some milk thistle pods brewing to extract a medicine for a healthy liver. She is saying things like, 'What doth it profit a man to gain the whole world yet suffer the loss of his own soul'. Sadie, with a beanie hat pulled low on her head and wrapped in a bit of old carpet is whistling something non-descript while giving the milk thistle pods a good stir round with a hawthorn twig. Lucy, with a circlet of bluebells and ivy in her hair, blows the seeds from a dandelion clock then blows into her panpipes and prances and frolics a barefooted little wood nymph dance while Josh, a dirty little urchin, kicks an inflated pig's bladder into a makeshift goal.*

Chairs scrape the floor. Coffee break time! Hell! I'd drifted off. I hope he's not going to ask questions, although it's possible I could hazard a guess as to his jeans size.

I was about to join Christine and the others to goz about gorgeous Guy, when he called my name and asked if I had a minute.

He waited until everyone had gone then he asked if I'd be interested in sitting for him in his studio. Sit! I'd run up the walls and hang off the chandelier. He said I have an unusual profile which he would like to get onto canvas. Sort of Barbra Streisand-ish. He wondered if I might be Jewish. Bloody hell! Perhaps he *is* Jesus.

The power of consciousness had worked. He had singled me out. He wanted me to sit for him. I wasn't used to attention from gorgeous men, I had to grab the moment, hold onto it. I said, "Actually, I'm not Jewish, but my maternal grandfather worked for Isaac Cohen in his raincoat factory before the war." I felt lightheaded. Perhaps I should have eaten more at lunchtime. I babbled on. I told him about the tatty old envelope my grandmother had kept in her cutlery drawer with the yellowing paper flyers in it. The ones I used to take and out look at when I was small and having tea there. I even recited a couple of the versus:

*If it's raining, don't be blue,*
*Step inside for something new,*
*You'll stay dry and you'll look posh,*
*In your Isaac Cohen mackintosh.*
And:
*Why drip,*
*When you can drop,*
*Into Isaac Cohen's*
*Mackintosh shop.*

Then I stopped. Here was the Artist Adonis who wanted to draw me and I was gabbling on about the stuff in my Granny's drawers! What was wrong with me? Thankfully, he didn't seem to have been listening. He was studying me but I was wishing I had gone with the others. Then he surprised me by saying how much he liked the definitive cupid's bow of my lips and the hazel-green colour of my eyes with their gold flecks which seemed to reflect the freckles on my nose and the burnished copper of my hair.

Bloody hell!

My classmates trooped back from their coffee break wondering where I'd got to. I shrugged and smiled enigmatically; who needs Gold Blend when you've got gold flecks…

When the lesson was over, Guy picked up his haversack and guitar, said he was hurrying to meet a friend for a jam session and handed me a scribbled note of his address and phone number and the time of Saturday morning at 10am.

Saturday at 10am would be perfect. Lucy will be in Starbucks with Chloe eyeing up the new waiter who had, and I quote, eyelashes to die for and Josh will be at five a-side.

I vaguely remembered saying goodbye to my classmates as I levitated into the car park. I somehow found the car, got into it and turned the ignition key. The car engine hummed as I sang the 'My Guy' song from the sixties.

Perhaps I'd driven home or perhaps a passing cloud had towed me. In any event the car found its way into its space on the drive and I floated to the front door.

My mother had given the children their tea. "Joanne," she said, "I'm worried about the children's health. Lucy has told me computers can have viruses and I heard on the radio recently that penicillin is in short supply so I don't think it's a good idea for the children to be around viruses."

Lucy smiled sweetly.

"Mam," said Josh, indignantly, "they want to experiment on us at school. They want us to take fish oils, innit. I'm not taking them, it's not like I'm a bleedin' seal, is it?"

My mother squinted her eyes, peered at me then asked accusingly, "Have you been drinking, Joanne?"

Lucy said, "You definitely look a bit spaced out, Mam."

I just smiled as I turned to check out my interesting profile in the mantelpiece mirror.

# 18

## THE HERO FROM ZERO

I was in the kitchen draining pasta and singing the 'My Guy' song when the front door was flung open and Josh's school bag, with the aid of a kick, came flying through it. Josh followed, punching the bag affectionately as it fell to the floor. The light fitting swung precariously and the phone was knocked off its hook. School was out!

There was something about the way that bag came into the house that spoke volumes. Sometimes, quite often actually, it was kicked along the floor in the manner of a petulant footballer taking his frustration out on the ball after scoring an own goal. This meant Josh had been in trouble and was about to protest his innocence, a protestation which was liable to continue for much of the night or until either me or Lucy said, OKAY-ENOUGH! But more often than not the bag was dragged along behind him, like a dead body, and that meant he was fed-up, he'd had a horrible day, he hated school, school was the pits, he had loads of homework, nobody's life was worse than his and if there was something for tea with Broccoli in it he would just kill himself – NOW. But today, the bag came flying through the air like a chicken to its roosting coop.

"Mam, school was mint today! Police were trawling the place with sniffer dogs searching for deadly weapons and stolen goods while a copper-chopper was circling the grounds looking for the robber. Honestly Mam, you had to be there, it was SICK!"

Huh! I turned from the sink. This was Willow Grove Comp not down town L.A.

Lucy, following behind him, rolled her eyes and said, "O.M.G! Get-me-out-of-here! I have just about had enough of small boys with small minds making out Craig Bolton is the next hero from zero, when in actual fact he is just the same little nerd he has always been." Then she snapped a banana from the bunch, went into the living room, flopped into a chair and switched on Home and Away.

Josh, too excited to give in to the urge to wrestle Lucy to ground, she having had the temerity to call Craig Bolton a nerd, pulled out the only kitchen chair which still had four legs, straddled the back of it, grabbed an apple and between mouthfuls said the whole thing had kicked off because Craig Bolton had decided to bunk-off from doing PE.

"There are two things Craig always bunks off from, Mam," said Josh, as if it's Craig's prerogative to do exactly as he pleases, "one is Citizenship, because Craig says that's just for the gays, and the other is PE."

"Sorry. Josh, but I won't have you using the word gay in that derogatory fashion."

"Huh! It's Julian and Adrian, Mam! They are 'the gays'. They call themselves 'the gays'."

"Oh," I said, not sure what my response should be.

"Anyway, Craig, right, says PE is for tossers and if the teachers think they can get him to prance around like a fairy doing PE, then they have another think coming, innit. So, he

91

hid in the toilet block until the coast was clear enough for him to sneak out to have a fag behind the science pre-fab."

"I hope you don't think that is acceptable behaviour, Josh, because it isn't."

"Yeah, yeah, anyway, as Craig peaked out of the door to check the corridor for teachers he clocked the new school secretary, Miss Smith coming out of her office with her arms piled high with papers. She locked the office door behind her but she didn't bother to take the key out of the lock. So when Miss Smith was out of sight, Craig decided he wouldn't bother having a fag after all and instead he would let himself into Miss Smith's office and photocopy his bare arse, which was something he had always wanted to do, innit."

"Re-phrase that please, Josh."

"Yeah, yeah, wha'ever, anyway, Craig, right, had just got sat on the photocopier, with his pants down, when some bloke with tights over his head and a gun from the Pound Shop, burst in and demanded Craig tell him where the dinner money was kept. Craig recognised the gun straight away because his kid brother had one exactly like it. Craig pointed to Miss Smith's desk and while the robber was rifling the drawers, Craig jumped off the photocopier and stumbled out into the corridor, locking the door behind him and locking the robber in.

Just then old Humphreys, the geography teacher, came round the corner and demanded to know what Bolton was doing outside the secretary's office with his pants round his ankles. Before Craig could tell him what had happened, old Humphreys grabbed him by the back of the collar and dragged him along the corridor saying Mr Clayton would know how to deal with the likes of him. Craig was trying to pull his pants up and trying to tell old Humphreys about the robber in Miss Smith's office, but old Humphreys wasn't having any of it. He said the school had its reputation to think of and it could do without perverted little bastards hiding in corridors waiting to expose themselves. And he went on and on about the effect taking drugs and sniffing glue had on developing brains, although he didn't think that applied to Craig Bolton as he doubted Craig had any brains to develop."

"Er, stop right there, Josh." I said, "There is no way Mr Humphreys would have used language like that!"

"Honest, Mam, it's the truth. You can ask Craig if you don't believe me, innit!" Josh protested, secure in the knowledge that that scenario would never happen.

"Anyway, Mam, if you will stop interrupting! Old Humphreys right, told Mr Clayton that not only had Craig been hallucinating about robbers, probably as a result of sniffing glue, but he had also been found in the corridor with his pants down, waiting to expose himself to poor Miss Smith.

"Mr Clayton was shocked. He said it didn't bear thinking about that a pupil in his school would be capable of such behaviour, although nothing would surprise him when it came to Craig Bolton. He said Bolton was, and always had been, a menace and a troublemaker and a disgrace to the good name of the school and drug taking and glue sniffing and exposing himself in a school corridor, would not be tolerated under any circumstances.

"Craig was still trying to tell them about the robber, but they told him to zip up both his trousers and his mouth. They said he would gain nothing by inventing ridiculous stories and the sooner he was off school premises the better. Then Clayton rang Craig's mother and asked her to collect Craig as he was to be suspended indefinitely. He told her that not only had her son been using hallucinogenic drugs and as a result had been making up silly stories, but by intending to expose himself to a vulnerable young woman, he also had the makings of a pervert.

Craig said his mother, who was as hard as anything and had AC/DC tattoos up her arms and across her back and could deck a bloke with one punch when she'd had a skin-full, went ballistic at the mention of drugs and pervs and he heard her screeching down the phone. 'HE'S WHAT!!! WAIT TILL I GET MY HANDS ON HIM, I'LL SWING FOR THE LITTLE BUGGER.'"

I tutted, and Josh said, "I'm just telling you what Craig's mam said, innit. Anyway, Craig, right, told Mr Clayton that his mother would kill him if she thought he was taking drugs and had become a perv and Mr Clayton said better that than he should die from taking drugs while on school premises. After all, the school had its reputation to think of.

"Then was an almighty scream from the other end of the corridor. Mr Clayton and old Humphreys looked at each other before rushing out of Clayton's office. They were followed by Craig, who, on his way out, had grabbed some chocolate hobnobs off a plate on Clayton's desk and was stuffing them into his pockets.

"The scream was from Miss Smith who had unlocked her office door and had been knocked for six by the robber running out of it. A couple of teachers were running down the corridor to get to Miss Smith who was yelling that the man had threatened her with a sawn off shotgun. Then the teachers started yelling for someone to get first-aiders and to ring the police.

"Just as they were about to leg it down the corridor, Clayton and old Humphreys were stopped dead in their tracks by Craig's mother, who had come bursting in through the side doors. Craig said his mother had her blue hairy jumper thing on and she looked like Sully out of Monsters Inc, only scarier. And he heard Clayton say through his teeth, 'Christ Almighty, Richard! The proverbial brick shithouse or what?'

"And old Humphreys said through his teeth, 'You're not wrong there, Keith.'

"Then, because they now knew Craig had been telling the truth and there had been a robber locked in Miss Smith's office, they both started grinning like Cheshire Cats, and as his mother got closer, Craig said he could hear a sort of humming noise coming from the back of Mr Clayton's throat.

"Mr Clayton shook Craig's mother's hand and thanked her for coming so quickly but he was really looking down the corridor watching everything kicking off. Craig said he nearly puked because Clayton put his arm around his shoulders and said it was obvious there had been some misunderstanding and Craig deserved a pat on the back for his bravery. He said Craig was a credit to the school and he wished all the boys had Craig's bravery and integrity. Craig said Clayton was licking up to him like mad, because he knew if they had listened to him in the first place, the robber could have been caught and Craig said he would tell that to the police, if they asked him.

"Mr Clayton, who was still grinning like an idiot, said, 'Now, now, Craig, let's not be too hasty about what we should or should not be telling the police.'

"He told Craig's mother that he would leave them in the capable hands of Mr Humphreys, as armed police, newspaper reporters and medics for Miss Smith were now invading the school. Before he went he said Craig and his mother were to avail themselves of the coffee machine and the plate of chocolate Hobnobs which they would find in his office. Then Craig heard Clayton whisper to old Humphreys, 'Keep a close eye on those two while they're in my office, would you, Richard?' And old Humphreys said, 'You can rely on me, Keith.'

"Craig's mother told old Humphreys that it would take more than a gob full of Hobnobs to keep her quiet. She said she intended to sue the person in charge of education as soon as she finds out who it is and she will stick out for every penny she can get her hands on because nobody calls her Craig a druggie and a perv and gets away with it. And she hopes their Barry doesn't find out, because God knows what he'd do about it. He was banged up for bare-knuckle boxing but was due out shortly. Well at least their Barry had said it was bare-knuckle boxing and she didn't fancy anybody's chances who said it wasn't.

"Craig said old Humphreys was brickin' it and he said, 'Now, Mrs Bolton. The only reference to drugs had been to find out if Craig had been taking any medication which might cause an allergic reaction to any medication he may need as a result of his ordeal.'

"Craig's mother said, 'BOLLOCKS!'

"So what do you think about that then, Mam? Awesome innit?"

"Hmmmm," was all I could manage.

"Anyway Mam, I think I'll nip round to Jack's to tell him about Craig, he wasn't in school today, he was having grommets put in his ears."

"Well ask his mam's permission first, he might not be up to the excitement; think of his ears and keep your voice down."

While I was digesting Josh's story, music signalling the end of Home and Away wafted into the kitchen bringing Lucy with it.

"Please tell me the Craig Bolton saga has finished," she said, "I couldn't stand that for another minute! Honest Mam, talk about pathetic. The boys were carrying Craig Bolton around on their shoulders chanting, Ree-spect! Ree-spect! I mean, how juvenile! Anyway, Symphony Evans was back at school today because her mother said it would cost too much to take the case of Symphony refusing to wear school uniform to the European Court of Human Rights. And Symphony's dad said if she came back to school without any fuss, he would fork out the thirty pounds it would cost for her to have acrylics done. And because the girls were soh not interested in the carry-on over stupid Craig Bolton they all gathered around Symphony to say how edgy and fabulous the acrylics were and how dead jealous they were. Well everyone except me and Chloe that is. Symphony said it had taken her ages to choose the colours because she couldn't decide if she wanted each finger different or what. But eventually she decided to have alternating baby pink and frosted silver with crystal swirls embedded in them. Well everybody *thought* they were swirls, but Symphony said they were actually S's, as that's her initial. Honest Mam, me and Chloe nearly gagged, they were soh pretentious! I said if I had thirty pounds I'd adopt a gorilla online. Chloe said she'd go for a snow leopard."

The Craig Bolton story made Headlines in the following day's Northern News:

## SCHOOBOY COMMENDED FOR BRAVERY

Fourteen-year-old Craig Bolton, of Willow Grove Comprehensive, was declared a hero yesterday after attempting to foil a masked raider who had broken into the school. Craig had been in the secretary's office photocopying his anatomy project when a masked man broke into the office demanding money. Craig said the man was brandishing a weapon which he recognised as a gun. Craig diverted the robber's attention before running out of the room and locking him in. Mr Clayton, Headmaster of Willow Grove Comprehensive, said it was an act of unparalleled bravery and Craig Bolton was to be applauded, not only as a credit to the school, but as a shining example to other pupils.

When asked to comment on her son's bravery, Mrs Bolton said it was no more than she would have expected of her Craig. But, Mrs Bolton said, Craig's brothers, five of them including Barry who was doing a stretch for bare knuckle boxing, weren't too happy about Craig being called a druggie and a pervert, just because he had been caught with his pants down after checking himself out, thinking the shock he had suffered had caused him to have an 'accident'. She expressed her hope that her son, Barry, didn't find out who was responsible for blackening Craig's good name because Barry had gotten used to prison–quite liked it–so it would be no skin off his nose to do another stretch. Even a long one.

Mr Clayton, when asked about accusations made of Craig using hallucinogenic drugs, said the suggestion was scurrilous and unfounded. The mention of drugs had been made merely to ascertain if Craig was taking anything which might give rise to contra-indications, such as hallucinations, if any medication was required following his ordeal.

When asked how she was feeling after her ordeal, Miss Smith, in a temporary position as school secretary, said she would find it impossible to regain her confidence after finding herself looking down the barrel of a gun in the hands of a violent robber. Miss Smith considered it most unlikely that she would be able to secure further suitable employment given the extreme, recurring dizzy spells, chest pains and headaches she was suffering. As well as the loss of her confidence, Miss Smith said she had also lost a number of valuable possessions in the raid.

When Craig was asked if he had any comment to make, he said, nah, he couldn't be a***d.

The following week, Josh brought home a letter from school, signed by Mr Clayton asking for donations to help Miss Smith replace some of the items she had lost in the raid. The items, which were not covered by the school insurers were, a high spec camcorder, an Apple laptop, an iPad, an iPhone and a substantial quantity of valuable jewellery, which she had kept in a drawer in her desk in the event of being invited out, unexpectedly, straight from work.

Mr Clayton's letter concluded by wishing Mrs Brody, who was on maternity leave, a speedy return to her position of school secretary.

# 19

## BYE GUY

It was Saturday, the day I had been waiting for all week. From the car window I checked the address against the note Guy had given me. It matched the tall, red bricked, terraced town house, three or four storied, grand and probably Victorian.

I looked at my watch, it wouldn't do to be too early, or too eager. My watch said 9.55am. I had been up and dressed since 7.30, which, on a Saturday morning had never been known, could that be considered eager? Of course it could.

Well here goes, I told myself, in for a penny and all that. Butterflies were having a field day in the pit of my stomach.

I got out of the car, locked the door and walked the narrow, shrub-lined path, side-stepping the straddling branches of a small, brownish shrub, a shrub which I know from past experience has thorns powerful enough to rip the flesh from your legs, while smiling sweetly through tendrils of little white flowers. I gave it a knowing look and a wide berth as I continued up the path which led to a short flight of concrete steps and the front door. Plaster Acanthus leaves, like open hands, circled the tops of two bulbous plaster pillars standing like guards at each side of the door. Victorian ostentation at its best, I thought. I nearly grabbed an enormous brass knocker but somehow its size put me off, so I pressed the bell instead. Then as Guy, gorgeous Guy, pulled the door open, the butterflies did a final flutter before flying off and leaving me to it.

"Oh, you've come," he said, smiling dazzlingly while tossing back his hair.

Try keeping me away, I thought, smiling back, as he led me into the hall and towards a very impressive staircase.

The top buttons of his white cheesecloth granddad shirt were opened and folded back showing off his plaited thong necklaces. His sleeves were rolled up and turquoise beaded bracelets hung loosely from both wrists. His white linen trousers were rolled up at the bottom to skim his ankles. He didn't have anything on his feet. I suddenly felt overdressed. I didn't think it was possible but he was actually even more gorgeous than I remembered.

"We're right at the top," he said, "it's a bit of a hike."

He led me across the black and white tiled hall to the staircase which rose to the right of a heavily embossed wall, the colours of red and cream separated by a wide, carved dado rail, the colour of fudge. Gilt framed pictures lined the walls. All old. Some portraits and some eighteenth century hunting scenes and one strangely enough, of a dog looking a bit like Millie, being cuddled by a child on a velvet chair.

The stair treads splayed wider at the bottom with a mahogany banister sweeping down and into a large flat circle which reminded me of an oversized counter from a draughts set. My hand just about covered the width of the banister as we ascended the stairs and I wondered how many bottoms had been unable to resist sliding down it over the years, making it as smooth and shiny as glass. Guy's bare feet slapped the stripped wooden treads while my heels tapped them, and both sounds echoed.

"Did you have any trouble finding the address?" he asked.

I hesitated. Had I had any trouble? It had all been such a blur of butterflies.

He waited. I mean it wasn't as though he'd asked me when Toulouse Lautrec decided he would paint prostitutes for a living, now had he?

I tried to think of something interesting to say; something witty, but I couldn't think of anything, so I just said, "No."

"Oh," he said flatly, "just most of these terraces look alike."

We reached the top of the stairs. The sun shining through an elaborately stained glass window had sprinkled the walls, floor and ceiling with the colours of melted fruit gums. I felt foolish. The little confidence I possessed was suddenly in danger of bursting like a balloon. He had asked me a perfectly ordinary question and I had answered in a word of one syllable! And, after thinking about it forever. No doubt he's now thinking, it's just as well her profile is interesting because her mind is moronic. I told myself I must do better, be humorous, confident. Hey Guy, is that ya paintbrush in ya trouser pocket...

We turned on a landing and climbed another staircase which was equally grand and colourful then up a narrower, shallower flight which led into Guy's loft studio, and into a different world.

Walking in, I immediately turned my head and squinted against the momentary dazzle. Everything was white. Walls, ceilings, paintwork, everything, pure white. For someone espousing the virtues of colour this was certainly some contradiction. As my eyes adjusted, I expected to smell bleach but instead I smelled heat. Something like singed paper.

The room seemed huge, although long and narrow. The outside wall was probably about ten feet high. The opposite wall was twice as high and the ceiling sloping between the two included three huge velux windows. I had to admit, I found the starkness slightly disorienting. Guy closed the door behind me and being white it sort of disappeared.

Some of Guy's canvases were hung on the tall wall. Varying sizes, yet somehow hung perfectly symmetrically. Abstract landscapes and seascapes; illusions of scenes and objects in water colours. Underneath the hung canvases and propped up against the wall were dozens of charcoal drawings. Single profiles; some facing left, some facing right. Double profiles; some facing each other, some turned away from each other. A pair of hands clasping. A pair of hands with fingers barely touching. A fingerless hand. A head with no body. A body with no head.

I wondered that the paintings didn't melt or at least fade in the sunlight. Guy said they're not there long enough. He said they're either commissioned or they go into exhibitions and are sold from there.

He indicated a stool for me to sit on. I had to look hard, it was draped in a white sheet, so it wasn't that easy to see. In fact Guy's head, hands and feet seemed to float independently, dressed as he was, all in white.

I put my bag down on the floor and stepped up and onto the stool. My profile, my 'interesting' profile was about to join the others lining the walls, drawn by gorgeous Guy in this awe-inspiring room. Romance? This was it. Fully fledged. No holds barred. This is what dreams are made of, well mine anyway and I just knew this moment would stay with me forever.

Then someone walked through the wall. It was still hard to see where the door was. He asked me if I would like a coffee and I said yes. He disappeared before returning with the coffee and a guitar. Guy introduced him as Gareth. There was something about Gareth I couldn't quite put my finger on. He was wearing bib-n-brace dungarees over a bare chest. He was handsome, although not as handsome as Guy of course, but he was toned and tanned (although a bit orangey for my liking) and he obviously worked out. His hair was shorn and he had earrings in both ears. As he put my coffee cup down, the bib of his dungarees flopped forward and I noticed he had nipple rings in both nipples. Oooh, bet that hurt, I thought.

The sun shone through the glass, the room was warm, the smell of singed paper was fast becoming my favourite smell and I was comfortable perched on my stool. My shirt buttons were loosened just enough to bare my shoulders and my 'burnished copper' locks spiralled warm against my skin. I was about to be charcoaled by this dazzling man who looked into my face as though he were looking into my soul.

He gently lifted my chin and turned my neck into position with his fingertips. My nerve endings tingled.

The soft strumming of a guitar emanated from somewhere across the room. I was beginning to feel orgasmic.

A soft voice accompanied the strumming. He was singing the song Mary Magdalene sang to Jesus in Jesus Christ Superstar.

'... And I've had so many men before...'

I watched Guy. A secret smile played on his lips as he listened. I glanced sideways at Gareth, he was smiling coyly at Guy. They caught each other's look, but not before I did. I had dissected it, bisected it and turned it inside out.

It was theatre. It *could* have been Mary Magdalene singing to Jesus; albeit with ambiguous connotations. It was pantomime. 'Look out, he's behind you'. Well, he certainly would be if I wasn't there.

It was romance, their romance. I hadn't left the starting block. I was an interloper, a voyeur. I suddenly did not want to be there. The room was impressive but claustrophobic. I wanted to be outside to see the green of the grass, the blue of the sky, my little red Peugeot. I wanted to feel the breeze in my hair, see branches swaying, leaves falling. I wanted to kick a can, hug a tree, join the Moonies. The brightness was blinding. Okay, so I wouldn't be waking up with gorgeous Guy but I didn't want to wake up with conjunctivitis.

I told him I was sorry but I couldn't stay. I said I'd remembered something I'd forgotten. He looked confused, as well he might. I buttoned my shirt, slid off the stool, grabbed my bag and tripped over the empty coffee cup. I didn't see it, it was white, and where the hell was that damned door!

# 20

## PLAY IT AGAIN SAM

I'm in shock!

My mother, my eighty-three-year-old mother, has just rung, excitedly, to inform me she has a boyfriend and is going on a date!

This is not something I would normally expect to hear from my mother on a Monday. Monday is pension day and what I expect to hear, is how long she waited in the queue at the Post Office, and, who was before and who was after her in that queue.

I expect to hear that poor Mr Arthurs, bless him, waited a full half hour and all he wanted was an airmail envelope to write to his daughter in America. This is the daughter who insists Mr Arthurs should be using email as that was the reason she sent him the money to buy a computer. But Mr Arthurs says it was airmail that had got him through the war, it wasn't email. I expect to hear that Vera Clegg who has an ASBO said, 'Sod this for a game of soldiers' and stormed out, which meant Mr Pringle was able to move up a place. I expect to hear that poor Mrs Gaffney, can't get her feet into a decent pair of shoes because of her chilblains and that there is now only £60 between Mrs Stewart and her Stannah

Stair Lift. I expect to hear that Mrs Mason from Number 11, knows for a certain fact that *her* from Number 10 has been at it again with the co-op delivery man.

What I do NOT expect to hear, is that my mother has a boyfriend and is going on a date.

Nevertheless, she continued to inform me that the *boy*friend is one Sam Pickles, who, my mother says, had been her first love and who she had never quite forgotten.

Oh yes! And where, I wondered, did my father feature in all of this?

My mother said she had not set eyes on Sam Pickles for more than sixty years. He had left prison and moved away and the last she had heard he was on the merchant ships. Then, to her amazement, and I might add, transparently undisguised joy, he had turned up at the Old Thyme Formation Dancing a couple of days ago.

"There I was, Joanne, with my back to the door, chatting to Dorothy from the corner shop about her sister's operation while we waited for Geoff to set the music up, when I heard a man's voice asking Sadie if this was where the Movers and the Shakers hung out? Sadie said, 'Well Movers is stretching it a bit but there's plenty of Shakers', which had made the man laugh. Well, I remembered that laugh as if I'd heard it only yesterday and when I turned, there he was, large as life, Sam Pickles. And he recognised me straight away. 'Gwendoline Griffiths!' he said, 'as I live and breathe.' Of course he only knew me by my maiden name. And that was that. We only had eyes for each other for the rest of the afternoon."

I said, "Er, sorry to interrupt mam, just for a minute back there I thought you mentioned prison?"

She said, a bit too dismissively I thought, "Oh Joanne, it was something or nothing. These days he would just have to clean graffiti off the walls of the underpass."

Then her tone softened as she said, "He was just a naughty boy really."

Bloody hell! My life is going from bad to worse. My mother is consorting with a criminal, she could have been a gangster's moll in a previous life and I have been lulled into a false sense of security with treacle tarts and rhubarb crumbles. When I put this to her, she said, "Oh for goodness sake Joanne, lighten up. Sam is not a gangster and never has been, he's a sailor and anyway, it's better than going out with pond life."

Lighten up! pond life!

She said I sounded just like my grandmother, who wouldn't hear of my mother having anything more to do with Sam Pickles when he went to prison, said he was a bad lot. Then Gerard, my father came along in his Trilby hat and his made-to-measure suits and his Fair Isle cardigans in autumnal colours, with pockets for his carefully folded hankies, which of course had to be initialled with a G, and his nail file and his Fisherman's Friends – God rest his soul, she added, more, I suspect, for my benefit.

Then she said brightly, "Anyway, Joanne, I'm going on a date with Sam but I'd like you to meet him first. He's coming for tea on Saturday and I'd like you to come too."

I asked her what they intended to do on this date, don masks and striped pyjamas and take a trip around Wormword Scrubs for old time's sake perhaps?

She ignored me and said they were going ten pin bowling and I wasn't to worry about her bad back as Sam said there were contraptions which, after you pointed the bowl in the direction you wanted it go, did the hard work for you. Afterwards, Sam said they could either stay in the centre for a couple of beers and a game of pool, or else go into town for a pizza.

And what, might I ask, was wrong with an old person's toddle round the park and tea and toasted teacake in the café? I mean it wasn't as if I minded my mother having a boyfriend per se, her neighbour Harold was nice enough, gentlemanly, and he had taken a shine to my mother, asked her round for tea a couple of times but he had never drummed up the excitement that this Sam Pickles has. I mean who was he? Some ex-con dredged up from the sea bed!

That night I woke up in a cold sweat. I dreamt my mother was a patient of Harold Shipman.

I didn't tell Lucy and Josh their grandmother had a boyfriend. It was too bizarre. I needed to get used to the idea myself first. Just as well I was to meet him on Saturday as Josh would be at the fun-fair with Jack and his parents as part of Jack's birthday treat and Lucy would be in Starbucks with Chloe, making eyes at the new waiter, the one with the eyelashes.

Well, Saturday came round and I'd no sooner hung my coat in my mother's hall when the doorbell rang. My mother hurried past me to answer it and in bowled Sam Pickles.

He had a box of chocolates, a miniature rose in a plant pot and a kiss on the cheek for my mother. He impressed me as not so much a sailor, more a pirate. Not so much Captain Birdseye, more Popeye. Not so much a gangster, more a bookie's runner.

My mother introduced us. Sam took my hand into both of his and shook it vigorously. He said although I was pretty enough I was not a patch on my mother for looks. My mother coquettishly fluffed at her apron and said, "Sam Pickles, what *are* you like?" Then off she went into the kitchen to make tea and to put scones and currant buns onto plates with doilies, while I was left to entertain Sam.

What on earth did my mother see in him? He was wearing a collarless shirt rolled up at the cuffs, a red and white spotted bandana knotted around his neck, white Adidas trainers and combat pants with braces. The body parts I could see, his hands, knuckles and lower arms, were heavily tattooed with anchors and crossbones and what looked like a version of noughts and crosses. He was on the short side. My father had been tall. He had a round face, a ruddy complexion which I put down to sea spray and piercing blue eyes which twinkled impishly for an old man, I thought. He had bushy white side-whiskers which stood out against the red of his cheeks. His white hair was thin and combed straight back, and, it needed a double take, but I spied a wispy little ponytail tied with a red stretchy band at the nape of his neck! He wasn't wearing earrings, although I checked for piercings and both his legs were intact, but otherwise, a parrot on his shoulder wouldn't have looked too out of place.

My mother had said men were in short supply at the Old Thyme dancing, but it seemed to me there was short supply and desperation. My father, who had been a department manager in a large department store, had been an excellent ballroom dancer. And indeed his father, an articled clerk before his early demise, had medals for it. No bushy side-whiskers, no tattoos, and definitely NO ponytails there, thank you.

I asked Sam if he had any family. He said he had never married, couldn't keep his land legs long enough, said he would still be on the ships if he hadn't gotten too old. He had been living in Portsmouth with his sister after he retired, but she had died and so he'd come back up North. He had a strange, sea-faring sort of accent. I asked him if he thought things had changed up here. He said, changed! He would never have recognised the place, motorways and shopping malls everywhere. He had gone in search of the motorbike shop which used to be on the High Street, but found it was now a Kwik Fit garage. He said he quite fancied another motorbike, had one when he was young. He said my mother could ride pillion and they could 'burn up' the countryside. His eyes glazed over. My blood ran cold. My mother riding pillion! Had he had his kicks on Route 66 or, after a pint and a pizza and a good old revving of his Harley Davidson, did hope spring eternal?

*Between the arch of his legs, his lean mean pullin' machine vibrates expectantly, then splutters and dies. He strokes it, he coaxes it. He revs, it shudders. He revs again, it pulsates. He revs again and it throbs, ready for action. He punches the air triumphantly yelling, 'Born to be Wild' at the top of his voice. His unzipped leather jacket shows the printing on his tee shirt, 'A Friend with Weed – is a Friend Indeed'.*

*My mother, with hair by Kawasaki, is waving to me with one hand while clinging onto his waist with the other. She has 'Bat Outta Hell' printed on the back of her leather jacket, the fringe of which flies back in the sudden gust of takeoff. She's calling, "We're hittin' the highway Joanne, then we're hittin' the sack. Don't wait up..."*

I glanced sideways at Sam. He looked miles away, a smile tickling the corner of his lips. Was he reminiscing or was he planning?

I asked him if, apart from my mother, there was anyone else he recognised from the old days. He looked startled for a minute, as if I'd poked him in the ribs with a stick. Then, clearing his throat, he said he had noticed one or two familiar faces but he had trouble putting a name to them. He said there was one bloke in particular who he had seen recently at the formation dancing and who he remembered from the dances at the Palaise, after the war, "Thought he was Fred Astaire with knobs on. Still does if you ask me, can't think of his name though."

Then he called to my mother in the kitchen, "Gwen, who's that bloke goes to the formation dancing, thinks he's the dog's bollocks?"

My mother called back saying she couldn't think who he meant.

Er. *My mother*, trying to think of someone who thinks he's the dog's bollocks!!

"You know who I mean, Gwen. Smarmy bugger, smells like a whore's handbag. Looks like that lecherous git off the carry-on films. Whatsisname?"

"Sid James," my mother offered from the kitchen.

"Sid James!" said Sam, astonished, as if my mother had suddenly lost her marbles.

"No Gwen, he plays that slimy bugger, says ding-dong when he sees a bird he fancies."

My mother didn't respond. Sam looked at me. I shrugged. Then he clicked his fingers. "Leslie Phillips! That's him."

"Leslie Phillips, Gwen," he called to my mother, "I knew it would come to me sooner or later."

My mother came in with the tea tray,. "Leslie Phillips, Sam? I don't recall anyone by that name goes to the formation dancing."

Sam looked slightly bewildered.

I smiled, drank my tea, made my excuses and left them to it.

Two days later my mother rang to tell me it was all off between her and Sam Pickles. She had asked him if he would mind if best friend Sadie joined them on their date as she and Sadie went everywhere together.

Sam had said, "Hell's Bells, Gwen, I didn't have you down as a lesbian."

I'm not sure if this is why my mother has finished with Sam or if she has decided a walk on the wild side is more than she can handle. Perhaps it's a bit of both.

# 21

## PARTY ANIMAL (ORANGUTAN) STYLE

I looked from my face in the mirror to my hands and feet. I loosened the belt of my dressing gown and looked down at the rest of me then quickly tied it again. "OH-MY-GOD!!" I heard myself screech. How in God's name had this happened and how was I supposed to go to work looking like this? I fell backwards onto the bed.

Then through the haze, it dawned. Work! I was supposed to be there! I sat up quickly, too quickly, my head exploded. I took some deep breaths and waited in dire agony for the fall-out from the explosion to settle.

I had to be dying. This couldn't possibly be just a hangover. Could it?

There was no way I could go to work looking and feeling like this. I would have to ring Ian.

I picked up the phone, pressed the buttons and swayed. I was going to be sick. He answered, somehow I held onto it.

"Ian, Iss, Jo." I was slurring my words, "I'm really shorry, but I can't come to work today. I've got - er, terrible shystitis."

I realised too late that I should have given that some thought.

"For fuck's sake, Jo, you're ringing now? You should have been here an hour ago. Oh-kay – let's – seeee." He was going to make a meal of it. I could tell. Was it possible he'd heard me making party arrangements with Alison?

"Cystitis this week, kidney infection last week. I might be wrong but shouldn't that be the other way round? You're not taking the piss are you, Jo?' Cos, if you are, I suggest you take a sample of it to the doc's, have it checked out, then let me know the results. Pronto. Comprehendo. Got that in one, Jo? Good-o."

Just how obnoxious was he? He was supposed to be the Human Resources Manager, for God's sake. Job description: humane, approachable, sympathetic should the situation demand it. Talk about a square peg in a round hole, or is it a round peg in a square hole? Oh, who cares. I'll ask my mother, she'll know. If only I'd said I had a migraine or something. Too late now.

"I'll give it a couple of daysh' Ian, and if I'm no better, then that'sh what I'll do. I'll be in touch. Bye."

I threw down the phone, hung onto my mouth and got to the bathroom just in time. URGHHH!!

I wiped my eyes and mouth with toilet paper and hung there, my chin resting against the cold ceramic of the toilet bowl while chinks of clarity began opening up.

Something was making me cringe and I wasn't convinced it was entirely down to the vomited alcohol. An image was circling somewhere in my brain, something I couldn't quite get to grips with, something coming and going, waving at me, tantalizing.

Then suddenly there it was. I was tumbling out of a taxi, punching the air and singing at the top of my voice, 'Hey, He-y baby, oo-ah', before waving manically at Siobhan and Sophie who were still in it and who I hadn't known from a chip in a tea cup three hours previous to that. There I was blowing them kisses and telling them tearfully how much I loved them. Oh-my-god! Please let this have been a dream, ple-eese. I mean I might come across them again sometime.

Then I was stumbling up the drive, singing 'I Will Survive' very loudly and Kev from next door was calling down from his bedroom window, "You and Gloria bloody Gaynor might survive, Jo, but I might not. I have to be up at five for my shift."

I'll have to apologise to Kev – albeit by post, considering the state I'm in.

I hadn't wanted to go to Selina's fortieth anyway. It didn't seem right having a party on a Sunday night with the kids having to go to school from my mother's and me with work the next day. I only went to keep Alison company. Nigel had some Lib Dem thing or the other to go to and although Alison had said she could quite easily have persuaded him to go to the party instead of the Lib Dem thing, there was every possibility he might have felt the urge to dance, and she couldn't risk that, not if that malicious cow Stella was going to there. So, with his overnight bag in his hand and Alison's pretend regrets in his ears, he was chivvied off and I was recruited instead. And anyway, I reckoned if I was to 'get a life' I had to start somewhere.

I had only intended to show my face for an hour or so then come home, take advantage of the peace and quiet with the kids staying at my mother's and read some Jane Austen. I'd felt the need coming on all week for a fix of good society and pleasant aspects.

Alison had said she wasn't going to be late either, she had an early morning train to catch to get to Glasgow for a training meeting.

The last thing I remember before falling out of the taxi, was head-banging and playing air guitar to Meat Loaf in the middle of the dance floor and Alison pointing to her watch saying she had to go and telling me to be careful with that stuff as it was pretty potent. I remember poo-pooing that advice and saying it was just like pop; then nothing.

But, at some point after coming home, I'd obviously done this! It must have been after seeing how tanned and glamorous party girl Selina looked after her holiday in Greece, and how untanned and pasty I looked by comparison.

My knees were hurting. I really had get off this floor, lift my head out of the toilet bowl, yet I couldn't move.

I mean, how the hell was I supposed to get on with my life looking like this? Okay, it was more of a PG than an X rated sort of life, but as far as lives go it was mine, and it had to be lived. I needed a miracle. I had to beg, do a deal, do what I always do at times like this: grovel.

I clasped my hands together across the toilet bowl, closed my eyes and promised God faithfully that I would never miss Mass again and I'd go to confession at least once a month. Although once a month is the norm, in reality it's far too often and I would just end up inventing sins, but so be it. I might even put my name on the church cleaning rota. But then again, I might not. If I know that sanctimonious old Tilly Magee, with her rubber gloves and can of Mr Sheen, she'd probably push me out of the way and say she's perfectly capable of doing the cleaning and the flowers herself, thank you. And off she'd go, polishing the pews as if the devil himself were prodding her up the backside. Something I will do though, is buy loads of poppies this year to compensate for raking out and dusting off last year's one. I was on a guilt trip for ages over that. Oh, and St Anthony definitely isn't camp. Just my little joke. St Anthony camp! Chances are he's as butch as anything. As butch, if not butcher than say – Vinnie Jones or Tom Jones or Danny Dyer. I'll send money for the missionaries in Africa, if they're still in Africa and I'll try to like the dog. I'll be so nice, I'll be unrecognisable. Please God. Pleeese – I swear I'll do anything. I'll try to persuade Josh to join the priesthood and Lucy to be a nun, and if things don't get any better than this, I'll join them. Although it's possible I might not be up to the kneeling.

I pulled myself up by the toilet cistern, heard a creaking noise as it came away from the wall, swayed my way to the bathroom cabinet, forced down an Alka Seltzer then crawled back to bed.

Lucy tapped me awake asking if I was okay. She had never before known me to be in bed when she'd come from school and she was worried. I turned to face her, forcing my eyes open and stretching my mouth into a groggy, but hopefully, reassuring smile.

She stepped back in horror and said, "Urgh! Mam. What's happened? Urgh!! Should I call the doctor or something? Should I ring for Gran?"

A sleepy, alcoholic reality dawned. I shook my head, and it felt as though it would fall to the floor. With a pathetic stab at feigned cheerfulness, I told her I was fine, she wasn't to worry, it was only spray tan, it would wear off – eventually.

Before she flounced out she reminded me in no uncertain terms, that it was Parent's evening at school tomorrow and if it hadn't worn off by then, there was no way I would be allowed to meet her teachers looking like *that*! "And," she said, as she turned from the door on her way out, "you'll never get a boyfriend if you go on like that!"

I leaned over to reach a hand mirror from the dressing table and for a second the earth tilted off its axis. When things stabilised I looked into the mirror. It seemed the more I was sobering up the worse I looked. My face was streaked in varying shades of very dark brown and sludgy orange. The exception was a blurred, whitish ring around my mouth and blurred whitish streaks down my chin which had, I assumed, been caused by being sick before the damn stuff had dried. There was also a track of streaks from each eye where I must have shed tears while being sick.

I got shakily out of bed and groped my way downstairs.

Josh pointed and laughed fit to burst. He kept jumping out at me from behind things, saying, "Have you ever been tangoed, missus?" until I felt the need to throttle him.

The dog barked. She thought I was a stranger. Then she ran under the table and wouldn't come out.

I heated up some beans for the children, threw some Winalot in the direction of the dog's bowl, then went back to bed.

Then as day two dawned, with it came a miracle! While cursing the dog for pulling out the contents of the bathroom bin there it was, one of the cans I'd used, and there, akin to the miracle of Lazarus risen from the dead, rising up at me from the back of the said spray can, was a helpline number. A helpline number! Oh Glory Be! My prayers had been answered. THANK-YOU-GOD. You won't regret this. When I'm fit to be seen, I'll be out there buying dozens of Big Issues. OH YES!!

I grabbed the dog and kissed her before she ran for cover back under the table. Then I stood on the front doorstep and waved the children off to school with joy in my heart. Lucy begged me to go back into the house. I tweaked her hair playfully. I was not to be fazed.

I stashed the breakfast dishes in the sink, they could wait. Prioritising was the name of the game today and I had a helpline number to ring.

I rang and it answered.

*–This is the helpline number for Take-a-Tick-and-Tan. Your call may be recorded for training purposes. Please continue to hold and you will be connected to your personal advisor as soon as one becomes available. –*

I held the phone at arm's length. Paul McCartney and Stevie Wonder warbling their way through Ebony and Ivory was more than a person with the remains of a hangover could be expected to endure. Even a person without the remains of a hangover, come to think of it.

But then, after what seemed like an eternity, my personal advisor became available, sounding as chirpy as the proverbial budgie on speed.

"Hello there, how can I help you today?"

"Oh, hello. Erm… well, I used your product and the result isn't quite what I was expecting. I wonder if you could suggest something I could use to like… tone things down a bit… quite a bit actually… get back to normal really?"

"To whom am I speaking?"

"It's Joanne Charlton."

"Hi Joanne, I'm Sonia, but please feel free to call me Sonn. Now what seems to be the problem?"

"Well, like I said, er, Sonn, I wonder if there is something I can use to… you know… tone things down a bit… a lot?"

"Okay, Joanne, let's start from the beginning, shall we. Did you read and follow the instructions included in the pack? Did you depilate? Did you exfoliate and moisturise?"

"Erm."

"Erm doesn't sound very convincing, Joanne. We know a lot of people take the easy route and cut out the important bits. Oh, can't be bothered with all of that, they say. Then when the product hasn't worked satisfactorily, of course it's never their fault. Yet it always is. As my nan Molly, would say, why spoil the ship for two penneth of tar because if a job's worth doing, it's worth doing well. Can I ask you, Joanne, what number is on the container you used?"

Number? I twiddled the can. "Er – number six."

"Number six is for Afro Caribbean complexions. Are you Afro Caribbean Joanne?"

"N-No."

"What then?"

"Well, just ordinary really. A bit pale, a few freckles."

"And you used number SIX. WHY?"

"I don't know. I didn't check. I just picked it up in Beautiful

Bargains. They had it on offer – two for one – they must have wanted rid of it – there can't be much demand for spray tan for dark skinned people, can there?"

"Admittedly, it's not one of our best sellers, but some dark skinned people can, unfortunately, be susceptible to disorders of skin pigmentation and find our products helpful. Just out of curiosity, did you use both of the containers you purchased?

"Yes."

"Oh, poor you. Now, let's think positively. Where do we go from here? You didn't follow any of the preliminary procedures, you used the strongest colourant and you used both containers…"

"The thing is, Sonn, I've still got a splitting headache from a really bad hangover, so if you wouldn't mind…"

"A hangover, Joanne! Please don't tell me you used the product while under the influence of alcohol."

"Ermmm…"

"As my Nan Molly always says, Joanne, when drink is in, wit is out. So, to re-iterate again. Preliminary procedures were not followed, two containers of the strongest colourant were used and it was applied under the influence of alcohol. As this is a free phone number, Joanne, perhaps you wouldn't mind holding while I have a word with a colleague to see if we can come up with any suggestions for you. Fingers crossed then."

"Er, Sonn…"

Too late, Sonn had gone. I didn't want suggestions, I wanted another damned miracle. Bet they're having a right laugh – She WHAT? Used number SIX! Two containers! A bit pale, a few freckles. Oh-my-God, What an Idiot!

Yes, yes, ha bloody ha. Sometimes I think I'm living a parallel life to Forrest Gump. My head was pounding. I nearly hung up, but curiosity, the sort born of sheer desperation, kept me hanging on.

"Are you still there, Joanne? Thank you for holding, your call is important to us. Well, I've spoken to my colleague and we think a good alternative would be camouflage. The Army and Navy stores have an excellent range of all-in-one camouflage suits and worn with a wide metallic belt and plenty of gold-coloured chunky jewellery, the look can be very cutting edge. I've seen pictures of both Katie Price and Sienna Miller carrying this look off to perfection when worn with Ugg Boots. And let's face it, Joanne, with the war in the Middle East, it could also be considered patriotic, a tribute to the troops, that sort of thing."

I said, "Ugg boots, Sonn? It's the beginning of June!"

"Joanne," she chirped, "high fashion is seasonless. And what better time to have used a high colourant spray tan than now, when big, and when I say big, I mean humungous, shades are in. Look no further than the 'Oliver Pope' range and you will see, Joanne, that, with a bit of ingenuity, all is not lost."

Well why did I feel like a burst balloon then? Limp and deflated with nowhere to go but the bin. We had something in common Sonn and me, we were both clutching at straws. Crumbling ones. But because I had the feeling Sonn was genuinely programmed to try to help, I said – and I wasn't trying to be sarcastic or anything, I just somehow took on her chirpy voice - "Thank you, Sonn, you've been an inspiration. I'll find the nearest Army and Navy Store, and as I don't want to frighten passing children or dogs, because after all, Halloween is a long way off yet, I'll pull a balaclava over my head, the sort with eye holes as favoured by the SAS and bank robbers, and who knows, I might even set a whole new fashion trend. Bye Sonn, thanks again, you have a nice day now." And I put the phone down. So much for bloody miracles.

For two days I've rubbed and scrubbed and just about managed to keep a layer of skin on, but it's still streaky and sludgy and I'm still a mess. But, there's nothing else for it, I have to go to work and face the music or else Ian will demand a hospital report.

I had to cover up, cover my legs. I searched through my wardrobe. Trousers were allowed in the office, as long as they were smart but I was a jeans girl and the only smart trousers I had were black, part of a suit, and it was a beautiful sunny day, but they'd have to do. Something with long sleeves and a high neck was next. I could only come up with a black polo neck. I tried to cover my face with tan coloured make-up, but it didn't work, so I rubbed it off and used a very pale powder instead. It was debatable as to whether that was an improvement, but as miracles were no longer an option, I decided to go with it. I normally tied my hair back for the office, but today, needing all the help I could get, I used the straighteners and pulled it down at the sides, like curtains, it would be something to hide behind. Then out came the new, humungous sun glasses which I had ordered on next day delivery from the NEXT catalogue, and which I knew I would be pushing my luck wearing in the office, but that applied to people who had a choice.

Helen, the receptionist, was busy on the phone, so I sneaked past, keeping my head well down and letting my hair fall over my face. A bit pointless really, as I was pretty much unrecognizable anyway. I tip-toed into the office. Ian was on the phone. The conversation went something like:

"He's done what? A full consignment? One friggin hundred? Why do we employ these morons? What a shower of shit! Did he not realise that if glass was falling out of the packaging it was a knockin' bet the table tops, being glass, would be smashed? Yet he still signed for them!? Well, that's it. No more chances. He's had a verbal and a written now it's out the friggin' door. Send him up. Oh, and if he gives you any crap like, 'what gives him the right to sack me?' Tell him, why does a dog lick its balls? BECAUSE IT CAN."

I cowered into my chair, switched on my computer screen and felt for the mouse. I couldn't see much, you can't when you're wearing sunglasses indoors.

Then, from the other side of the room and it being only a matter of time, Ian clocked me.

"Well if it isn't Yoko friggin' Ono. And have we just flown in on Air Cystitis or what?"

I couldn't see him but I could sense his self-congratulatory smile at his wit. I half turned in my chair and while peeling off the sunglasses, I flicked back a curtain of hair and gave him a sad little look that said, 'Ian, you can't make me feel any worse than I already do.' I was just about to come clean about the whole sorry episode, when he stepped back, in fact it was only the wall behind him that kept him in the room.

"Hell's bloody bells, Jo. What's happened to you? My God you look terrible." Then pushing himself further against the wall, he attempted a grovelling, camaraderie sort of smile. He tried to sound light hearted but ended up sounding like the gangster boss in the Supranos.

"Hey Jo-Jo, you know me, bit over the top, bit of gobshite, eh! Ha ha."

Then he turned serious. He was worried. Not on my account obviously, but because he thought if I were to expire and he hadn't taken my sick calls seriously, there could be consequences and he was mentally weighing up what they might be. After all he was still on a warning.

"But bloody hell, Jo, kidneys and stuff can be a bit er, worrying. I know cos when I was a kid I had Yellow Jaundice… sick all the time I was… yellow stuff… horrible… I looked like a miniature Chairman friggin' Mao… but Christ Almighty, if you don't mind me saying so, Jo, you look a helluva lot worse than I did. You look a bit like," he squinted his eyes, "a bit like… an Orangutan or something, it's the colours. Orangey, browny. Okay, that's a bit of an exaggeration, but you get the picture… and muffled up like that, this weather, it's not normal. Tell you what, Jo…"

His feet walked nearer although he kept his head well back,

he obviously didn't want to breathe the same air. He picked up my bag and all but threw it into my lap. He held the back of my chair at arm's length and swivelled me round to face the door. It was clear he wasn't going to risk getting in too close, which was probably just as well really.

As he propelled me on the castors towards the door he said, and I think it's possible I might have detected a teensy bit of concern in his voice… "You go home, take some time out… rest up… book some dialysis or something. Don't worry about this place… I'll get a temp in… might even be able to get into Simone… er, I mean get Simone in, yes get Simone in… Okay, Jo, you take care now."

He all but tipped me out of the chair and into the corridor. My conscience was telling me I should confess, come clean, I wasn't entitled to take time off, I wasn't ill. You couldn't take time off for being stupid. But it had gone too far.

I straightened up and walked towards the reception desk and Helen. My conscience twanged as I passed Helen, she being the most saintly person you would find this side of heaven and me being a fraud. When she wasn't on reception, Helen helped to run a kitchen for the homeless. I tried telling myself that was the sort of thing you could do if you were childless, but deep down, I knew childlessness and charity didn't necessarily live side by side. Helen was just a good person.

She looked up as I passed and I gave her the sort of shaky little smile you would use if you weren't long for this world. I tried to shamefacedly scurry away but she called me back.

"Jo," she said, "I'm sorry to see you looking so poorly. If you wait a minute, I've something for you." She fished about in her bag before producing a phial of Lourdes water.

"Honestly, Helen, there's no need, really. I just need a few days off that's all. Keep that for somebody who really needs it."

"Nonsense, Jo, you take it." She pressed it into my hand while saying she would remember me in her prayers. I thanked her piously, like the fraud I was and I scurried towards the outside doors.

This pretence was taking on a life of its own and it seemed that in my case, it was suggestion that was the mother of invention, because once outside, an ache started in my back, just about where my kidneys were. I felt a bit sick and dizzy. Perhaps I needed to lie down, take Ian's advice and book some dialysis. I walked to the car park and got into my car.

I should have relished some time off, but I didn't. I was a cheat and a liar and it was probably the guilt that was making me feel ill.

I decided I'd call and see my mother.

I drove into the street, along the row of neat, semi-detached bungalows, differentiated from one another only by the window dressings and the various hanging flower baskets. Elderly people in two's and three's stood chatting at their gates no doubt marvelling at the sunshine. Normally I would have given a passing cheery wave and remarked to them myself about the weather through a wound down window, but not today. Today I kept a low profile, skulking behind my curtains of hair and my sunglasses, as though I was Katie Price and they were the paparazzi.

I pulled up at my mother's gate and with my head down I walked the short path and rang the bell. My mother opened the door slightly, peered out, and before closing it again said, "Not today thank you." I rang again. She opened the door as far as the chain would allow blinking her eyes against the sun. She was just about to say another, not today thank you, when recognition dawned. She loosened the chain.

"Oh, Joanne, it's you! What on earth is wrong. Come in. Sit down. I'll put the kettle on. I thought you were that Gypsy woman who sells the heather. She has a swarthy complexion, although having said that you couldn't call her streaky."

"It's okay, Mam, I'm fine, really I am."

"You certainly are not fine. Put that cushion behind you. I'll make us some tea. I won't be a minute. Say a decade of the rosary, while you're waiting. If it doesn't do you any good, it'll do you no harm."

"Honest, Mam, I don't need a cushion or tea, or rosary beads or anything else. I know I look weird, but it's only spray tan."

"Spray tan, Joanne! I'm not senile. People wouldn't make stuff that makes you look like that! Nobody would buy it. You can't fool me. It's that mobile phone."

"Eh!"

"It's the radiation. I've read about it."

"Honestly Mam, trust me, it isn't the mobile phone. I used a spray tan meant for black people. I bought it in Beautiful Bargains by mistake."

"Spray tan for black people! Beautiful Bargains must have seen you coming Joanne."

Day four and normality is rearing its pasty head, although I'm not quite out of the woods yet. I've cleaned the house from top to bottom in an effort to expend some of the guilt of not being at work. I've dragged the dog out from under the table and wearing my humungous sunglasses, I've taken her for long walks. I needed the fresh air and you're not so conspicuous if you have a dog. She's still cowering around with her tail between her legs, sneaking to her food bowl when she thinks no one is looking then scurrying back under the table, as if she's in the presence of something evil. Stupid dog. She knows it's just me. Talk about attention seeking.

I rang Ian and told him I was much better and I'd be back to work on Monday. He said that that had reminded him to check his first aid certificate as he thinks it might have run out.

My mother has written to David Dimbleby to find out his take on mobile phones.

Day five and I'm pretty much back to normal. I actually seem to look even more doughgirl-ish than I did originally.

These have been five days in which:

I have had alcoholic poisoning and the mother of all hangovers.

Used two cans of a black person's spray tan and somehow unintentionally managed to achieve a fairly good facial impersonation of a broken-hearted Smokey Robinson, with the track of tears etc.

Pledged myself and my children into the services of the church, then decided not to bother.

Had a lengthy, yet ultimately pointless telephone conversation with a helpline canary.

Needed to push a written apology through my neighbour's door – couldn't knock in case they thought Halloween had come early.

Cringingly, drunkenly and worryingly declared my love for people who three hours previously, I didn't know from a hole in the wall.

Scared the dog, who still needs to be dragged out from under the table. Beginning to think she must get a buzz from having her front legs almost pulled from their sockets.

Missed Lucy's parent's evening.

Nearly throttled Josh.

Imagined myself at death's door.

Worried my mother half to death.

Had Helen on reception have a Mass said for my intention.

Received unjustified sympathy from Ian.

And vowed to double check all small print on every product purchased and never, ever again, drink copious amounts of Archer's and lemonade.

# 22

## IN AT THE DEEP END

Why, when all I wanted was to sit with my feet up in front Prime Suspect, did Josh decide to tell me, when he'd had all night, in fact all week, to do so, that he needed pyjamas for his swimming lesson the following morning? He was being taught life saving; on a brick. I sent him upstairs to look for some pyjamas. He said he had looked but couldn't find any.

I grudgingly trudged upstairs to turn out his drawers while suspecting it was probably a futile exercise, as Josh had grown so much lately I kind of knew the only pyjamas not being worn or in the wash, would be half way up his back. And I was right. However, there were some with a picture of Donny Osmond on the front that had been passed from Sadie's family to us, via my mother, who said they had hardly been worn.

When I suggested those to Josh he said, "You have to be kidding! I'd rather drown myself than wear those poncy things!" Lucy patronisingly said she had been going to suggest he could borrow her outgrown Care Bear ones, but drowning himself was a much better idea. After he'd pulled her arm into a Half Nelson and she'd deposited a backwards kick on his shin so that he hopped around on one leg, he said I'd have to write him a note to excuse him from swimming. I said he should have told me earlier and I would have sorted some pyjamas out. He said he did, he had told me last week but I took no notice. He said I was too busy looking at my profile in the mirror.

There was no arguing with that but I was in a dilemma. I thought it important that Josh should learn life-saving techniques, albeit on a brick, but could I be bothered to stay up till midnight washing and drying pyjamas which would just be dunked in water anyway?

Who was I kidding? I pulled some from the washing basket, rolled them in a towel and made my way downstairs, hoping to catch the end of Prime Suspect.

As I passed the phone in the hall, it rang. It was Alison.

"Jo-ooo," she said, ominously.

"Ye-es," I said, equally ominously.

"How – do – you – fancy… ablinddate?"

"A blind date!"

"Yes. You see Nigel has this friend Michael, and Michael has this friend Colin who Michael says could do with a bit of cheering up – bringing out of himself – you know the sort of thing, and he thinks some female company might just do the trick."

"And?"

"And – Nigel thought of you."

"No, I mean, AND what's the back story?"

"There isn't one really. Just it seems Colin's wife ran off with his sister to live in a Norwegian wood where they whittle wildlife out of sticks."

"That's story enough. I don't think so somehow."

"Oh go on, be a devil. You know you want to."

"Are you kidding? He could turn out to be Hannibal Lector, for God's sake."

"No he couldn't, that was Anthony Hopkins. Anyway, Colin's a policeman."

"So?"

"Sooooo. Play your cards right and you might cop off."

"Ha, ha. Have you seen him – this Colin? What does he look like?"

"I haven't seen him, but I think Nigel might have. He's in the kitchen, hang on, I'll ask."

"Mam," called Josh, from the living room, "Millie's on the coffee table, lapping at your wine, innit. Should I get her down?"

Oh, for goodness sake! "Well what do *you* think, Josh?" That's all I need, a drunken dog to have to sober up.

"You still there, Jo? Nigel says he has seen Colin but only from a distance. Big bloke, broad, smartly dressed, didn't get a look at his face though and he doesn't know much about him apart from what I've said."

"Hmmm… Okay, I *might* think about it. The emphasis being very much on the might. When do you need to know by?"

"Just whenever."

"As long as he doesn't want me in handcuffs. Been there, done that. Don't suppose you know any Donny Osmond fans in need of pyjamas… hardly worn?"

She said if she did, she wouldn't admit it.

I put the phone down while telling myself that if I wanted to 'get a life' then this was the sort of thing I would need to do. Prime Suspect was forgotten as I continued to sit on the chair in the hall. A blind date! I'd never been on a blind date before. Come to think of it, excluding George and that Kevin Scott from the school disco, I'd never been on any date before. A blind date! If I did decide to do it, I wouldn't tell anyone – it smacks of desperation. Of course Alison and Nigel would know but I'd swear them to secrecy. Anyway, if nothing else it would give me a chance to dress up. I had that really nice skirt and top which had yet to see the light of day and I'd been waiting for ages for an excuse to have some red highlights put in my hair. I'd get those done.

I realised I was talking myself into it. Oh, why not? Life's too short. In for a penny and all that. I smiled indulgently at my impending decadence. Then I shuddered. What would I do if this Colin turns out to look like Robbie from the loading bay? G-o-d! Run a mile that's what!! But then again, he might turn out to look like Leon from the Trading Office. I wouldn't run then, no sir-ree.

I couldn't decide if I felt excited or scared. He might turn out to be the man I've been waiting for all my life, yet knowing my luck, he's more likely to be a homicidal maniac who should be doing life.

Oh, what the hell! I knew, although Alison's 'just whenever' had been said ever so nonchalantly, she would be bursting at the seams to find out what I'd decided. I would ring her tomorrow and tell her I'd do it.

I'd need to brush up on my cheering up techniques, that's for sure. Actually, I'd need to acquire some first. I practised in the mirror, "Is that ya truncheon in ya pocket…?"

# 23

## TAMPON TROUBLE

Josh was eating his Weetabix while planning his revenge on Bobby Peterson. Bobby Peterson had told Josh it was fun to chew silver paper on a filling. Josh had only recently acquired a filling. Josh said he would jump out at Bobby Peterson as he walked past the science lab, get him in a Half Nelson, push soil into his mouth and if the soil had a worm in it then so much the better.

"That is *enough,* Josh," I said, "I don't want to hear any more of that nonsense. If Bobby Peterson had told you to jump off a bridge, would you have done that? Of course you wouldn't, now go upstairs, get your bag ready for school and if I get reports from school about any bad behaviour, boy will you be in trouble!"

On his way out he said, "Do you think I should just turn the other cheek, Mam?"

I was surprised, moreover, impressed. I said, "Yes, Josh, that's exactly what you should do. Well done. Was that something Gran told you to do?"

He said, "Nah. Miss Nightingale was twittering on about

turning the other cheek during Spiritual Studies and Craig Bolton stood up and dropped his pants and said, which one Miss?"

I groaned, "Upstairs NOW and don't forget to clean your teeth."

"Please Mam, ple-eese."

"No, Lucy, I've told you before, I've got all the responsibility I can handle at the moment, without taking on a gorilla."

"But Mam, the poor thing's an orphan. Its parents have been murdered..."

"That's as maybe Lucy, but the thought of my foster child gorilla, stomping about in a huff and bashing its thirty-stone chest in a strop because he would rather have Signorney Weaver as his foster mother, is not something that appeals to me somehow. Perhaps if it was on only child, but I've got you and Josh to contend with as well."

"But Mam, this is just a tiny, cute baby."

"It won't stay tiny and cute forever, Lucy. Trust me."

"But all you have to do, is pledge some money every month and Michaela Strachan will actually look after it."

"Lucy! How could I possibly hand over the care of my poor little gorilla to a complete stranger. It doesn't bear thinking about."

"Mam! It's Michaela Stra-chan, it's not a stran-ger," she sing-songed.

"Sorry Lucy, the answer is no. As I told you last week when you wanted a horse, anything to do with money is not an option at the moment I'm afraid."

"Huh! It wasn't that when Josh got a new football *and* new footie boots."

"Hmmm. A new football and boots compared to a horse. Could there be something of a fiscal discrepancy there? Something in the region of say four thousand pounds perhaps? Then of course there's the after care costs, stabling and livery, versus a tin of Dubbin. Oh and have we forgotten the trip to Miss Selfridge last week and your new jeans and top?"

"Yes Mam, but I'm not talking about clothes or a horse now, I'm talking about a poor little gorilla whose parents…"

"I know, Lucy, have been murdered."

I said she should try her dad when he comes back from Florida. She huffed and said that was ages away and anyway, Benjy would probably have been snapped up by somebody else by then.

I said there would be other gorillas.

She said not like Benjy there wouldn't, and anyway her father would probably say no.

I thought, Oh I don't know. They say charity begins at home. George shouldn't have any problem sponsoring a gorilla; fellow swingers and all that.

Then Lucy said, "Mam, what's Millie eating?"

Millie had been rifling in my bag. She'd obviously eaten the other half of the chocolate flake I'd left, because the wrapper was on the floor and she had lip pencil on her nose and teeth, so that had gone the journey as well. In a stern voice, because someone said it's all in the tone of voice, I reminded her that my bag was out of bounds. I also reminded her about the cage in the local cat and dog shelter with her name on it. She exhaled one of her sighs, the one that sounded like, 'God that old chestnut'. I said, "Make no mistake about it pooch, you will not be hitting the high life when you go there. Oh, no. You're not guaranteed Pedigree Chum and Winalot mixer, it'll be supermarket brands or whatever kind animal lovers have donated into the drums at the exit doors of the supermarket." I expected her to sigh a, yeah, yeah, as she usually did when I mentioned the cat and dog shelter, but she didn't, instead she started to choke. She began clawing at her mouth while rolling back and forth on her back.

Lucy had gone upstairs to get dressed and I called her down. It was obvious the dog had something stuck in her throat.

I really had to shout for Lucy as she was sulking over Benjy and ignoring me. Eventually, realising I meant business, she stomped downstairs. I had Millie on her back and I told Lucy to hold her down securely so she wouldn't be able to turn away from me until I could see what she had in her mouth. Forcing her mouth open and although she was struggling to get away, I could see the string of a tampon hanging out of her throat. My God, this was serious. If the pad of the tampon started to swell Millie would choke. I pushed my fingers into her mouth and tugged at the string but it wouldn't budge. She was retching and clawing at her mouth and struggling to get away from me. Lucy was begging me to do something. I shouted for Josh. I tried the string again. It was no use the tampon wouldn't budge and if I pulled the string too hard it would just come away.

Josh came downstairs.

I pushed Millie down and onto her stomach while the children put pressure on her back to keep her still. I forced her head to one side and jammed my knee into her mouth to keep her jaws open while I pushed my hand down and into her throat. I managed to grab the tampon between my forefinger and thumb and was able to ease it out. Just in time. It was really quite swollen.

Panic over, I sat on the floor with Millie's head between my legs stroking and shushing her until she stopped retching and became calm. Lucy was tearful. She had thought the dog would die. Josh was putting on a brave face. Millie seemed okay and we were all relieved.

Then I had a scary thought. It actually dawned on me that had the dog needed the kiss of life, I probably would have done it. What was my life coming to?

It was my day off from work, the sun was shining, the kids had missed the school bus, the dog had nearly choked to death on a tampon so, to the astonishment and delight of all concerned I took the unprecedented, executive decision to ring school and say we'd all come down with a bug; a twenty-four hour thing, then I packed a picnic and we all, including the dog, piled into the car and went to the beach for the day, all the while keeping a low profile in case the education people were on the lookout for truants.

Later that night I rang my mother and told her about the morning's drama with the dog. She said, "I told you those tampon things were dangerous, Joanne. If God wanted you to have cotton wool up there, he'd have made you like that!"

# 24

## IT'S A COP-OUT

Lucy and Josh were to stay with my mother, both complaining bitterly that they were old enough to be left at home on their own. As if! Lucy said Chloe's parents trusted *her* to be left on her own.

I said, "Chloe doesn't have a brother."

Lucy said, "That doesn't make any difference."

"Oh," I said, "it does."

Josh said Jack is sometimes left on his own. I said, Jack doesn't have a sister, and so it went on. I told them I was going out with the girls from work, just for a meal and I wouldn't be late. Lucy said red and copper highlights seemed a bit of an extravagance just to go out with the girls from work, and if I could afford those, which must have cost a fortune, I could afford to adopt a gorilla. Josh said if Gran puts Jason and the Argonauts on again, he wouldn't humour her this time, he'd keep his eyes shut till it was finished. I dropped them off still grumbling and complaining, then I returned home to get ready for my blind date with Colin.

Arrangements had been made, via Nigel, for me to meet

Colin in Marco's, the little Italian place on the High Street. I liked Marco's. I liked the red and white checked tablecloths and the dark wood furniture and I liked the dripping red candles in the utilitarian empty wine bottles in the centre of the tables. I liked the attentiveness of the uniformed waiters with their affected accents and Al Pacino noses and I liked the way the smell of garlic hits you as you walk through the doors. Marco's isn't a place you'd go with the girls, it's a place for romance, for holding hands across the table, so here's hoping...

The taxi got there before my mind did. It pulled up while I was still rehearsing my walk on scene. I wasn't ready. I hadn't decided what my adopted persona should be. Should I go in smiling, confident. Blind date! Bring it on! Or should I be shy, reticent, coy... be gentle with me? One thing was certain, I couldn't go in looking the way I felt, as if I was about to meet an untimely end at the hands of someone who, for all I knew, could be the next Fred West, albeit with a police uniform and a truncheon at home. Perhaps I should go around the block a few more times, like they did in the films when the bride had arrived at the church before the groom. Or perhaps I should just go home.

The driver asked for the fare and I fiddled in my purse then lost concentration and looked out of the window. The door to Marco's was inviting with its gleaming brassware and rich mahogany wood, and I knew inside it would be cosy with couples; intimate, or hoping to be. Yet I was about to be coupled with a complete stranger. He could be anyone. Peter Sutcliffe, anyone. Why was I putting myself through this? Cheering up some saddo! Come off it, Joanne. Who are you trying to kid? Dawn French meets the Samaritans you are sooo not. You're here because in your own stagnant little pond the prospect of a bit of excitement, whatever the packaging, floats your boat. So who's the saddo now, eh! And don't think Colin won't have realised that. He probably thinks he's doing *you* the favour.

How many women would agree to a blind date unless they were desperate?

The driver looked at me through the rear view mirror.

"Have you got the fare then, or what?"

"Oh yes, sorry. I was miles away."

"Which is where I should be, so if you don't mind…"

I paid the fare and stepped out and onto the pavement. I stood in the street like one of the concrete bollards, staring at the door to Marco's, unable to move while the taxi sped off.

My mother thought I was out with the girls, so if I ended up dead in a ditch, she would be no help.

Nigel and Alison knew where I was and who I was with so if I *was* to come to a sticky end, they'd be able to point the finger. But what good would that do me if I was dead in a ditch and my children motherless?

With a bit of luck, Colin would have had second thoughts and not turned up anyway. Or without the luck he would be sitting inside, checking his watch, drumming the table with his fingernails and wondering where the hell I was. And with my luck, I knew which one it would be.

So, I straightened up, took some deep breaths told myself to get a grip, because if Colin was inside he was probably feeling just as nervous as I was and just think how much worse he would feel if instead of cheering him up, I stood him up?

A few more deep breaths, a smiley face and I dragged my feet in their concrete boots to the door, and walked through it.

I looked around as a man jumped to attention. That must be him, I thought. I followed a uniformed waiter who showed me to the table where Colin was standing, straight as a lamp post and as if he was about to march on parade. The waiter pulled out a chair for me, then Colin and I sat down, in unison. I couldn't help thinking it would have broken the ice a bit if he had been really naff, stood behind my chair, bent his knees as I sat down and said, "Let's be havin' yer."

He wasn't a Robbie from the Loading Bay look-a-like, thank the Lord, but neither was he Leon from the Trading Office. He was broad and muscular with a jaw-line as square as a kitchen tile and if it was a cross between Arnold Swarzenegger and a Welsh rugby player that got your juices flowing, then Colin was your man. He was clean-shaven, soberly but immaculately dressed in a checked shirt, striped tie and knife-pressed chinos and he smelled nice. He was probably the most scrubbed-up man on the planet. What did it for me though was animation, twinkly eyes and a bit of stubble, but as I mentally crossed those off my wish list, I decided I'd settle for a smile and hopefully a bit of humour. But, it soon became apparent that Colin didn't do smiling. Or humour. I kind of felt I might have my work cut out cheering him up; first impressions and all that.

A smile was still stuck to my face, vacant, with not much behind it other than a touch of panic. When we were seated, and speaking as solemnly as if he was giving a statement in court about a murder, Colin knitted his brows together and said it was the first time he had been on a blind date and he didn't mind admitting, he had been brickin' it all week. Although, he added, he was pleased to see I didn't have a face like a burglar's dog.

My smiley face jammed. I looked surreptitiously around hoping nobody had heard that. Even in my limited, very limited experience of chat-up lines, that one slid to the bottom of the pile. He said he'd never seen so many ugly, sloppy women around and, although Nigel had said I wasn't one of them, he had still been worried, because after all, one man's meat is another man's poison.

Bloody hell!

We chose from the menu and ordered wine. A white wine spritzer for me, nothing too potent, in case of a quick getaway and a bottle of red for Colin. The conversation was, as expected, a bit stilted until I asked what had attracted him into the force; then I wished I hadn't. He said, solemnly, that he had wanted to be a policeman from being a child. He said it was always the policemen in comics and on the telly that had caught his imagination. PC Plod in Noddy, the policeman in Punch and Judy, Starksy and Hutch, Elliot Ness, Ironside, Columbo, Dick Tracy, anything with cops in it... Kojak, Officer Dibble, Chief Wigham, Officer Barberry...

I think it was around here I lost consciousness.

Then I came to... Inspector Linley, Frost, Morse, Bergerac... Then the food came and to change the subject, I quickly told him about my interior design course. Now, if what had gone before was odd, what followed next had the element of the surreal about it, possibly to do with the fact that I had been married for years to someone who thought a shell suit under an anorak was as high fashion as it got. Colin, although still solemn but now with a discernible touch of animation, said he could tell I had good taste as soon as he saw my matching bag and shoes which picked out the tan colour in the pattern of my skirt. He said he liked the green diamante hair clip I was wearing which he thought was exactly right with the red and copper tones of my hair. He said he always noticed things like that, which I thought for a burly policeman with bulging biceps and an encyclopaedic knowledge of fictional policemen, seemed kinda cute. Odd, but cute-ish.

He seemed to be getting into his stride. This was obviously what turned him on. He said my bag was exactly the right size for a shoulder bag, anything bigger would just look clumsy. He said his favourite bags of the season had to be the ones in the new pastels from Marc Jacobs. He asked where I'd bought the clothes I was wearing and before I could answer, he said, "Let me guess. I'm pretty sure I've seen that skirt and top in Zara. Am I right?"

I really wanted to think he had clocked the stock in Zara while grappling with a shoplifter. I really wanted to think that... I mean, I'd heard of the fashion police, but...

I said he was right, the outfit was from Zara. He said he knew it, and he was pleased to see frilled-edged cardigans back for another season as he thought they were really feminine. He also thought the clothes in Pur Una had upped the profile of Marks and Spencer, and he had written to them to congratulate the buyers, although he did think the horizontal striped, high-necked cardigans with the different coloured buttons had had their day.

This was sooo no longer cute, so I asked him how he found his Seafood Linguine. He said it was fine. He asked me about my Carbonara, I said it was very nice. He ordered another bottle of red, although I put my hand over my glass. Being entirely sure this was not my kind of date, I thought it best to keep that clear head for that quick get-away. I was going to ask him about his favourite holiday destination, but I had the feeling an afternoon checking the rails in Principles would have been as good for him as week in Alicante, and as he hadn't asked me, I didn't bother.

Yet, I suppose in his own way, he was making an effort and as usual, I was being a nit-picking cynic. Okay, I decided I would put some effort in. He was interested in fashion, so what could I contribute to that. Who did I know on the designer front? There was Stella McCartney. Actually, me and Stell did have something in common. Both of us, along with the rest of the world, having intuitively marked Heather Mills' card as a manipulative man-eater. This was long before it had dawned on poor old Sir Paul, hidden away as he was somewhere in the Mull of Kintyre with his sheep and his mega millions and his freezer full of Quorn and polluting the air with his wacky baccy. And even though lurid tales of Heather were being dredged up in every newspaper worldwide and Channel 4 had dedicated a whole programme to her wicked ways and even the dogs in the streets were barking their heads off about her; it seemed poor old Sir Paul, was the only person on the planet who hadn't an inkling. Perhaps it's just me, but I considered that divorce to be a blessing, because somehow, I just could never have brought myself to think of Heather as 'Lady' McCartney, it just would *not* come naturally. Anyway, I digress. What about the square shouldered jackets Stella was reinventing this season to wear with short skirts? Surely they'd be worth a mention. On the other hand, they're nothing to get excited about. I'll leave those jackets for her mate, Sylvester Stallone, they'd be right up his street, bulk him up a bit.

Or there's Vivienne Westwood, but I didn't know enough about her to make a conversation with, except she's that weird old bird who made safety pins fashionable and at some point married that geek from the Sex Pistols, Malcolm somebody or the other.

Then for some reason I became silly. I asked him if he thought Donny Osmond pyjamas might make a come-back. He kind of glared at me over his glass. So I took that as a no. Cheering up a humourless policeman was proving to be no mean feat. There was a joke somewhere in the back of my mind about policeman's balls, but it wouldn't come to me. There was a distinct possibility it would have bounced off him anyway. I smiled secretly at my wit, admitted defeat, thought bugger this for a lark and concentrated instead on the desert menu and a very good-looking waiter at the bar.

I was enjoying a silent moment of decadence over the prospect of tiramisu when Colin asked me what cream I preferred. If I'd downed another glass or two of wine, there's every possibility I would have tapped the ash off an imaginary cigar and said in my Groucho Marx voice (which I do very passably, actually) are we talkin' haemorrhoid or vaginal thrush, Colin? Instead, I said, demurely, "Well I think I prefer full cream, I can't be doing with that squirty stuff that disappears as soon as you put your spoon into it."

He rolled his eyes, he was obviously finding me extremely hard work. He said he meant face cream, the sort with proretinols and pentapeptides. I spluttered a mouthful of wine across the table then apologised profusely, saying I'd swallowed the wrong way.

As the tasty looking waiter collected the desert order, he gave me a flirty look, or perhaps it was wishful thinking or perhaps it was the other way round.

Ho-hum, I tapped the table with my fingernails and checked the date box on my watch. No – it wasn't April 1st.

The desserts came. Colin was hitting the wine a bit – a lot. He seemed to be getting slightly maudlin. He slumped onto the table swirling his Malibu ice cream with his spoon but not eating it, whereas I was positively devouring my tiramisu while keeping an eye on the good looking waiter.

Colin was slurring. Not surprising really, after two bottles of red. He asked me what I couldn't live without. I had the feeling he was thinking along the lines of Max Factor or Chanel. Still, I thought it only fair to give the question some credence, think about it for awhile, hum and ha, what could I not live without? It seemed like a sensible question so I stroked my chin, I cupped my forehead in my hand like the bust of 'the thinker', then, I counted on my fingers, "A pulse, my children, lipstick, peanut M&M's, Kitchen Roll…"

He interrupted and lunacy prevailing he said what he couldn't live without was 'Elle' magazine.

I said, "Elle magazine, Colin?"

He said after his wife had left him he had cancelled her subscriptions to 'Woodworking for Beginners' and 'How to get your claws into Hawking', but he had kept the subscription to 'Elle' going. He said there were some hard bastards in the force and to qualify this he punched his right fist hard against the open palm of his left hand. I had to grab my coffee cup as the table shook. He said he didn't want to end up like those fuckers and that's why he read 'Elle' because it kept him in touch with his feminine side.

Now, although I consider myself to have a fairly high 'oddball' threshold, given the practise I've had, tonight the walls were closing in. Nice bare plaster walls with stencilled pillars and falling ivy and sketched maps of Italy and hangings of Venice and Gondola's and Michelangelo's David, they may have been; but they were still closing in. And okay, I knew it would soon be over and I'd soon be home and one day I might even be able to smile about all of this, it just didn't seem like that. I'd had enough. I wanted to shake hands, say it had been a pleasant evening and that perhaps we could meet up again sometime, all the while being certain that by virtue of Colin being a fully paid-up card-carrying oddball and me being not, that scenario would never happen. I was on the verge of making my excuses to leave, when he asked if I thought it would be possible to live without the principles of Feng-Shui.

I knew I should have gone ten minutes ago. My reservoir of Zen, never brimming at the best of times, was bone dry. Feng-shui! Colin, luv, I have enough angst without the addition of Feng-Shui angst. I have enough trouble finding time to *make* the damned beds without wondering if their position is compatible with the door.

I looked at my watch and gasped theatrically, was that really the time? I stood up, said it had been a lovely evening, but I really must be going; children and child-minders and all that.

I think by now his state of wine-induced Zen was impenetrable. He didn't hear me. I left half the money for the bill and fled.

The next day Alison rang, excitedly asking how things had gone with me and Colin.

Now, my mother has this saying: if your ears are burning, it's left for love and right for spite.

I asked Alison if Nigel was there. She said he was in the bedroom. I asked her to ask Nigel if his right ear had been burning between about, say, 8.30 and ten o clock last night.

She asked him. He said no more than usual. I said perhaps he should find that a bit worrying because around that time, I really wanted to put Nigel into thumbscrews while giving him a Chinese burn and a chest wax.

Alison said, "Oh, so not great then?"

# 25

## YOU'RE KNICKERED

My mother said the trouble had started when Vera Clegg, who has the ASBO, stood up demanding that *she* should have won the full house as May Simmons had made a late call.

But Ned Lewins, the floor walker, although in Ned's case, hobbler, because of his war wound, said May's call was fair and square and as far as he was concerned, May had won the full house.

Vera Clegg said Ned Lewins would say that, as he had always fancied May Simmons and there was no point in Ned trying to deny it, because Vera said she remembered one night, just after the war, seeing the pair of them behind the Palaise ballroom, and you didn't Trip the Light Fantastic with your trousers round your ankles.

Everyone in the hall gasped at that except May Simmons, who squealed.

Then Hattie Smith, who takes the tea round at half-time, said that was a terrible thing for Vera Clegg to have said about poor May Simmons who was a well respected member of the community and who had taught lots of the local children to play piano. Vera Clegg laughed sarcastically and said, "Well, she certainly had Ned's crotchets quavering that night behind the Palaise."

Somebody from the back called out that that remark was typical of Vera Clegg, whose sister Mildred had gotten more than Nylon stockings and a jar of beetroot off the Yanks.

Then everyone began shouting and taking sides then bingo cards, counters, and markers started to be thrown about.

Ned Lewins waved his stick in the air in an attempt to restore order but his good leg gave way and as he toppled over, he knocked Mrs Mossop's hat off her head. Mrs Mossop had worn that hat for her daughter's wedding in 1960 and her daughter had married a farmer, so Mrs Mossop considered that her lucky hat and she had worn it for bingo ever since. Mrs Mossop tried to retrieve her hat but she leaned over too far, fell forward and out of her wheelchair and landed on top of Ned.

Someone called for the caretaker and the caretaker called the Neighbourhood Watch.

My mother said it had all seemed a bit over the top considering the prize for the full house was an Asda sponge pudding and a tin of custard. So she and Sadie had got the early bus home.

My mother and I were in the fruit and veg aisle in the Supermarket and she had just finished telling me about Monday night's shenanigans at the 'Autumn Leaves' bingo, when Rita, who does my mother's shampoo and set on a pensioner's Thursday, loomed out at us from behind the organic bananas.

"Hello, Mrs Morrison. Hello, Joanne. It's turned out nice after all, hasn't it? Don't you just get sick of all that rain? Still we'd be the first to complain if there was a water shortage, now wouldn't we, especially if the shampoo and sets had to be cancelled because of it." She gave a little chuckle, then she got down to brass tacks.

147

"Ee, Mrs Morrison, Joanne. Did you hear about that Vera Clegg? She's just gone and got a warning from the police yesterday. Been causing trouble again she has, this time for cutting down Marion Marshall's washing line while her washing was still on it, because she said the trollop always hangs her flimsy underwear on the bit of line which faces her kitchen window and her Alfie can never get onto his pudding for concentrating on his meat and two veg. I mean, Mrs Morrison. Alfie Clegg! As if…"

My mother said, "Whatever next?" She didn't know what the world was coming to when people couldn't be trusted not to cut down other folks' washing lines.

"Well," continued Rita, "Marion Marshall said that was the last straw, she was fed up to the teeth with Vera Clegg and so she rang for the police. When the policeman came, he told Marion Marshall not to rush out to replace her underwear as there was a new shop opening shortly in the precinct, part of a well known chain which sold fantastic underwear, on a par with Agent Provocateur but without the price tag. He said he'd read about it in a magazine. Marion Marshall thought he was having her on. She thought Agent Provocateur sounded like a French Spy, but she had her son check it out on Google and it was right enough; a knicker shop. Fancy a policeman knowing something like that!"

I smiled. Because the evidence would suggest…

# 26

## TOO MUCH REFLECTION

My mother rang. "Joanne, I've got some news for you. But first of all; a warning. Sadie and I were in the library yesterday because Sadie's granddaughter Ruby has a little part-time job in there and we called in to see how she was getting on, and guess what? They had a vagrant in. Poor soul might have just wandered in for somewhere to sit and keep warm but nevertheless he was handling the books with dirty fingernails, so, if you get a book from the library, remember to sponge it down when you get it home as you don't know who has been there before you. Anyway, do you remember me telling you about Sadie's niece Claire, who said if she didn't get pregnant with the Ivy F this time round, she'd have her downstairs laminated? Well, guess what?"

"She's pregnant!"

"No, she's had her downstairs laminated. Sadie says it's beautiful, just like a ballroom. But there's a problem. Claire has this dog, a big dog, lanky, I can't think of the name of it. Oh, yes, Hector. Well anyway, the poor thing can't keep its feet on the floor, ends up face down and sprawled out in all directions, so much so that now it won't even come into the house, just stays outside whimpering. It has started sleeping rough under a tree at the bottom of the garden, but Claire says she's terrified in case there's a storm and the tree is hit by lightning and the poor thing ends up dead, so although she loves it and it will break her heart, she has decided to get rid of it."

I perked up, "She's getting rid of the dog? How? Where?"

"Not the dog, Joanne, the laminate flooring. Oh, and something else. Remember Florence who won the raffle for the spare seat on the bus to go to the walled garden? Well Florence has just found out that a great uncle of hers was once hanged. What you think about that?"

"I should think once was probably all it would take."

When the penny dropped, my mother laughed. "Oh Joanne, that's really funny." And I mouthed it while she said, "I'll have to tell that to Sadie. Anyway, Florence says she wants to find out more about this hanging carry-on and so she's going to do one of those family tree things that everyone's doing these days. But as I said to Sadie, that won't be a five-minute job and as Florence must be eighty-five if she's a day she's going to have to get a move on. Anyway, Sadie and I have been trying to work out where the spare seat on the bus will be and the only conclusion we can come to, is that it must be beside Mr Arthurs, because poor Mr Pringle who would have been in that seat, wasn't sure if he would be able to travel, what with his prostate trouble, God-love-him, so we're beginning to think he must have pulled out. As soon as I find out I'll let you know. Anyway, Joanne, I'm off to read the riot act to my California Poppies while the sun's out."

I put the phone down thinking I really needed to get out more – no – REALLY needed to get out more, when Alison rang. She was bored. She had arranged a day's holiday to catch up with some jobs around the flat, turning out cupboards, that sort of thing, but couldn't get motivated. She said she was swirling a finger of Kit-Kat in a cup of hot chocolate and although she felt as guilty as sin because her Weight Watchers weigh-in was tomorrow night, she couldn't wait for the chocolate to melt so she could lick it off.

"So Nigel's not back from that conference thing yet then?" I said, "because, if he was you, wouldn't be eating Kit-Kats you would be eating fairtrade biscuits from the Co-op." I told her that last night I'd put some Minstrels into a bowl and put them into the microwave for thirty seconds then sucked the chocolate through the still crispie coating. She said she would definitely have to give that a go. She asked if I fancied a pub lunch, I said I had a plumber coming.

"Oh! Well why didn't you say something?" she said.

"Not literally," I said, and I told her about the leaking radiator, well the radiator that had started leaking but was now... she interrupted.

"Sorry, Jo, no offence, but talk of a plumber coming had me well interested but a leaking radiator! No matter how well intentioned, that will bore me rigid."

So instead I told her about the win I'd had on the school raffle. How Josh had come bursting in with news that I was on the list of winners. And how I'd hunted high and low for two days for the ticket as Josh said there were some awesome prizes. TV's, Ipod's, stuff like that.

"Go on then," Alison said, "what did you win?"

"Guess."

"The school hamster, cos they can't be arsed with it anymore."

"No."

"A dusty old box of Christmas deccys that had fallen behind the art cupboard and forgotten about – till now"

"No."

"Okay, give up, what did you win?"

"I won... da da... a launderette voucher for the washing of a large item."

She laughed her head off.

151

"You might mock," I said, "but at least I didn't win the set of spanners. Scott Johnson's mam won those."

"Well at least she could sell those on Ebay, but a launderette voucher! Bloody hell, Jo, it could only happen to you."

"URGHH! Wait till I tell you this," she said, changing the subject. "Do you remember Charlotte Greener who was a couple of years below us in school? Well I saw her the other day, pushing a pram. I tried to pretend I hadn't seen her and was just about to cross the road because you know how baby phobic I am, but she saw me and called me over. So, I looked obligingly into the buggy, as you do, and it was actually quite a nice-looking baby, so that was okay, but you'll never guess what she told me? She had this rubber ring thing hooked onto the buggy handle and I asked her if she was going swimming. She said, no, she wasn't going swimming, but that ring went with her everywhere because when she was giving birth, she'd pushed so hard, she'd pushed out a great big pile. I said, in all innocence, a great big pile of what, Charlotte? And she said, as if I was some sort of moron, 'A haemorrhoid, Alison!' And now she needs that rubber ring because when she sits down it's like sitting on broken glass. Surely that cannot be right, Jo?"

So I told her about the woman I met in hospital when I was having Lucy. She was onto her tenth and she said her muscles were now so slack she had to push the head back if she coughed, yet when she was having her first, she'd pushed so hard giving birth that her eyeball had come out and was resting on her cheek and had to be put back in. I didn't believe her of course, not, that is, until I actually gave birth and realised it wasn't so far-fetched after all.

Alison said, "Right that's it, that's my non-existent maternal instincts well and truly extinct. Joooo," she said, again changing the subject, "how do you fancy a spot of Bungee jumping? Tell you why. I was driving over the bridge the other Sunday when I noticed these girls having their nether regions strapped up by some v-e-r-y tasty looking Soldier boys in uniform and I thought I could fancy a bit of that, would fill in a Sunday morning very nicely that would. What do you say? Would you be up for it?"

"Oh, I don't know," I said, "knowing my luck they won't be kosher Soldier boys, they'll be pervs in fancy dress, hoping for a groping, and chances are I'd do my jump and instead of dangling there or whatever it is you do, I'd ricochet back, knock some poor pensioner off his bike and under the wheels of a skip wagon and I'd be had up for man-slaughter."

"I take it that's a no, then," Alison said.

Then the doorbell went.

"That'll be the plumber," I said.

Lennie introduced himself as he stood in the doorway. He was armed with a mastic tube, a torque wrench, an oily rag, and a cheeky grin. He reminded me of someone, but I couldn't think who it was. He said he was sorry he couldn't have come earlier as he was lagging pipes.

I took him upstairs, showed him into the bedroom and indicated the radiator. The indication being somewhat unnecessary as the towel wrapped around it, the bed sheet rolled into a sausage and wedged underneath it and the fact that it was hissing like a snake while squirting water kind of gave it away.

Lennie tutted about corrosion and enquired as to the history of the leak and the age of the radiator. I told him we'd been in the house for nine years and the radiator was already installed so it was probably getting on a bit. He said he'd be able to fix it this time but it wouldn't be long before it would need to be completely renewed.

He knelt down, took a spanner from his top pocket and began to unscrew the valve and as he looked up at me he also looked into his reflection on the ceiling. His grin widened, it became less cheeky and more lecherous. In a nod-nod-wink-wink, well what have we here fashion, he suddenly seemed to find me a much more interesting proposition than the ordinary looking housewife who had let him in and, a good deal more provocative than a hissing and imminently exploding radiator.

Hell!! How could I have forgotten about that stupid mirror. I wanted to shrug it off, joke about it, tell him we hadn't lived here long, that we'd inherited it from the kinky couple who lived here previously, but I'd already said we'd been here for nine years. I wanted to say something witty but I was struck dumb. I wanted to be on the other side of the door and squeal with embarrassment. But most of all I wanted to kill George. This was all *his* fault!

Perhaps it was my imagination but it seemed Lennie's mastic tube was being held rather more suggestively than I would have liked and after he'd serviced my return 'n' flow valve, and charged me £50 for the privilege, I was pleased to see the back of him. Then it dawned. He was a Tyrone from Corrie look-a-like.

That mirror had to go. I searched through Yellow Pages where Lennie the Lecher had been listed auspiciously under plumbers, but, perhaps not surprisingly, there were no listings for ceiling mirror removers. Anyway could I stand anymore embarrassment? No, I could NOT.

The mirror had been my twelfth wedding anniversary present from George. I had wanted a microwave with an integral grill. My mother had thought the mirror was a lovely idea, and wasn't George clever to have thought of it? It would reflect light into the room beautifully, as north facing rooms were notoriously dingy. I didn't know lucky I was to have such a thoughtful husband as George, I should appreciate him more.

I flopped onto the bed and looked up and into the mirror. Before George had it installed I could switch off with the light bulb. In the dark I could wonder if those curtains were such a good buy after all, I could wonder if, by juggling Saturday mornings I'd be able to fit Josh's football practice in. I could wonder if there would be enough room to sleep all the girls Lucy had invited for a sleepover. It could be somebody else in that room; in that bed.

But the mirror reflected reality. I saw a face, my face wincing at carpet burns or trying not to giggle or just being too tired to care.

Okay, that's it. I got up from the bed. Enough reflection... pathetic pun... that mirror had to go. Now, how difficult could it be to prise a mirror from a ceiling? I was a woman for goodness sake. W-O-M-A-N. I felt like Peggy Lee and almost burst into song. I was free, liberated, emancipated. Men! Who needs them? Did Germaine Greer burn her bra all those years ago for me to baulk at the idea of removing a mirror from a ceiling? No, she did not.

I would need to get over the first hurdle, which was going into the shed for the tools. That shed was Spider World and spiders and me just didn't get on. I was terrified of them and they knew it. They deliberately built their webs across the doorway to keep me out. The sensation of the gossamer threads fingering my face and clinging onto my hair was usually enough for me to require smelling salts, and on a bad day, say if the spider was still in the web; heart resuscitation.

My last venture into the shed was with an Asda bag over my head with the handle loops pushed under the collar of my polo neck. The bag had eyes, nose and mouth cut-outs. I had needed a dibble and some weed killer and I was taking no chances. I had pulled the eye holes tighter onto my face and more in line with my eyes to better see the stuff on the shelves, when George sneaked in, grabbed me from behind saying, "How's this for a dibble," while Mr Jones, only the width of a hedge away, sang 'Hey Jude' while dead heading his petunias. It never ceased to amaze me how, even George, could find someone with an Asda bag with eye and mouth cut-outs over her head, a turn-on.

Okay, down to business. I pulled a plastic bag over my

head, as previously described, checked to make sure no one was watching who might have thought the Klu Klux Klan had come to town, made my way down the garden path and ventured into the shed. I was armed for protection with the handle that used to have a cricket bat on the end of it, pre-dog. I pulled the eyeholes tighter and looked around stealthily. No sign of anything untoward, i.e. spiders, so I got together the things I would need. A hammer, a chisel and step ladders.

I had devised a plan. I would start by loosening each corner of the mirror by wedging the chisel between the ceiling and the mirror and then hitting the chisel with the hammer. Then, I would work my way to the centre from each of the loosened corners. I protected the bed and the furniture with some muslin sheets then I set to work.

The corners of the mirror were loosening very nicely and just as planned. I now had to inch my way to the centre. I started at the first loosened corner and tapped at the chisel. There was slightly more dust falling than I would have liked but so far so good. I then went to the opposite corner and tapped again at the chisel. I was on a roll. Knock, knock, tap, tap. Then, without any warning and with an almighty crash, the mirror plus half the ceiling somehow missed me completely and fell onto the bed.

The dust was unbelievable. I couldn't see a thing. I slid down the ladder and felt my way to the door. I was on the landing, bent over, coughing and spluttering when the phone rang.

I ran downstairs. "Hu – Hullo," I spluttered.

"Hello there," the voice sounded cheery, "do you own a brown and white friendly, excitable dog. The name tag's a bit scratched but it looks like her name could be Millie?"

I hesitated. Lennie must have left the gate open.

"Hello, are you there? Like I say the tag's a bit scratched, but it looks like this is the number."

"Em, who is this?" I coughed.

"It's Dale. I'm working at the special needs school on Sycamore Street and the dog was running around the yard with the kids. It's just they've gone into their classes and nobody knew what to do about the dog. One little fella was crying his eyes out, he wanted to take it home with him."

I perked up. "Did he? What did his mam say?"

"His mam isn't here. It's just I've got the dog with me in the van, she's eating my crisps. Hey you, that's my dinner when you've quite finished, you little rascal. The thing is, I need to get back to work, I've another job to go to after this one. Is it your dog then?"

"Yes, sounds like it," I said flatly.

"Well, are you coming to get her then?"

"Yes," I coughed, "I'll be there shortly."

The dog lead wasn't in the usual place, but then it would be a miracle if it was. Sycamore Street school was only a few streets away, I would carry Millie back. I knew I must look a mess but I pulled on a cardigan and hoped for the best.

As I got nearer the school, I spied the van parked at the gates. A tanned arm was hanging out of the window and Millie's sleeping head was being cushioned by it. As I got closer, I saw Dale with his head on the headrest and with his eyes closed. They were both sleeping. He was quite nice looking in a boy band sort of way. They looked companionable, it seemed a pity to disturb them. It seemed to me Millie would be really happy riding around in a van all day eating crisps and sleeping on Dale's arm instead of being cooped up in a kitchen, relying on the throw of a coin as to who lost and had to take her for a walk. Perhaps I could just sneak away.

Too late. Millie heard my footsteps and whimpered.

Dale opened his eyes and blinked. "Hi, have you come for the dog?"

I said I had. He was actually *very* nice looking with his brown eyes open and his muscles rippling in his uncommonly (for a builder) white vest, as he pulled himself up in the seat.

"Bloody hell luv, you collided with a cement wagon or what?"

Oh here we go. I meet the village's Ronan Keating and I look like the plaster cast of clay woman. I told him I'd had a bit of bother with a ceiling.

He said I should ring his company. He said the bosses were on holiday at the moment, but someone would be there to take the call. He fished about in the dashboard then handed me his company's card:

George Charlton and Francine McGovern
Building Services and Man Power Recruitment Associates.
For all your Building and Manpower Requirements.
Let us give you a free estimate for professional service and advice.
Guaranteed to beat any like-for-like quote.

I thanked Dale for the card and took the dog who, it has to be said, was more than a little reluctant to come. Perhaps she found it too confusing trying to keep up with my colour changes; a streaky orangutan one week, clay woman the next.

So, George and Fran had amalgamated. He'd kept that quiet.

# 27

## GOING FORWARD BY GOING BACK

Three streets later and Millie weighed a ton. I'd tried putting her down and dragging her by the collar but she wasn't having any of it. So we compromised. I lifted her front legs while she walked on her hind legs and somehow we made progress. The plaster dust got up her nose and made her sneeze and she continued to sneeze all the way home which made the journey even more arduous. Eventually I staggered to the front door, opened it and all but dropped her in the hall just as the phone rang.

"Hello, Joanne it's Norah," Norah is my mother's next door neighbour, "I called round to see if your mother fancied a cuppa, but she's not well, Joanne. I think she's had some sort of seizure, perhaps even a bit of a stroke. I've called the doctor and there's an ambulance on its way."

A BIT OF A STROKE. The phrase resounded, leaving echoes in my brain. My heart pounded into my throat. I told Norah I was on my way. I grabbed my keys from the hall table, slammed the door behind me and ran.

A BIT OF A STROKE. What did that mean?

I got there as my mother, wrapped in a blanket and with breathing apparatus over her mouth, was being wheeled into the ambulance. She looked ashen. I climbed, panting, into the ambulance with her.

"I'm Joanne and this is my mother," I said breathlessly to the ambulance man who gave me a strange look.

"We'll soon have her in hospital, don't worry, she'll be in good hands," he said, while checking the equipment and giving me sly little looks out of the corner of his eye. Perhaps he thought I was a health hazard. I probably was.

I wanted to hold my mother's hands, but they were covered by the blanket which was up to her chin so I stroked her hair instead. I had forgotten how it felt, my mother's hair, how fine and soft it was. I twiddled the curls between my fingers the way I had as a child, when I couldn't sleep and she lay with me telling me stories. Was it possible that someone so significant to my life was going to disappear from it? Yet I knew it was more than possible. My father had passed away one day when I was at school. They called me out of class to tell me. His heart, dodgy for years had given up on him, on us, my mother and me. That was a terrible time but at least then I still had my mother.

Tears were welling but I held onto them. Her head was lolling to one side and her eyes were barely open but she was conscious.

"I'm here, Mam, everything's going to be okay, you'll see." Then I sniffed the air and looked around. Had Millie followed me and jumped into the ambulance? I sniffed my cardigan. Damn.

My mother was taken in as an emergency and wheeled into a side ward where her condition was assessed. I was asked to wait in an ante room. People were coming and going and giving me strange looks. After what seemed an eternity, the doctor came in and told me they didn't think my mother had suffered a stroke, but further tests were needed. He said she would be kept in a high dependency unit and her condition monitored. He said she had been given a sedative and was sleeping but I could sit with her for a while. I went in. She was wired up to monitors, one of which bleeped and a nurse came in and adjusted something which stopped the bleeping. The nurse looked at me strangely the way everyone else did.

I checked my watch. The children would be home from school soon. I should get back. The nurse said there was nothing I could do for my mother, she would continue to sleep, but if there were concerns I would be contacted immediately.

I followed the painted, oversized footprints around the twisting and turning hospital corridors until I came out of the rear doors and onto the car park. I wandered about for a while looking for my car. Then I remembered, I didn't have it. I was vaguely conscious of people looking at me. I realised I would need to ring for a taxi because I hadn't a clue about the buses, except they were now gaudy colours. I went back into the hospital to look for a call box. The taxi was a free phone number, which was just as well because I had no money; I would have to pay the driver when I got home. Everything seemed to be going in slow motion.

The taxi driver said, "You're as white as a sheet, luv, you had a shock?"

I just said, "Yes." He sounded genuine, but perhaps he was being sarcastic, I couldn't tell and I didn't care. He didn't say anything else. He pulled up outside my door and waited until I got my purse. I paid him then went back into the house.

I stood in the doorway of the living room. Lucy was in an armchair with her knees up to her chin, tormenting Josh.

"Josh and Leonora up a tree, k-i-s-s-i-n-g."

Josh was punching her knees and protesting that he didn't fancy Leonora Smithson. He said Leonora Smithson was minging and he'd only been chatting her up for Jack.

Then they caught sight of me in the doorway.

"Mam, what's happened to you?" Lucy asked. "We came from school and the door was locked, so we went to Gran's but she wasn't in, so we had to get the spare key off Janice. Mam why are you covered in that white stuff?"

I suddenly felt exhausted. "Give me a few minutes then I'll tell you all about it."

I caught sight of myself in the hall mirror. What a mess! No wonder I'd been getting all those strange looks.

I went into the kitchen and filled the kettle then I leaned onto my elbows on the kitchen bench and great big plaster tears splashed onto it. I didn't want my mother to die. I loved her, she was my mother, she had had a boyfriend last week and she had a seat on a coach to visit a walled garden. She couldn't die. I wasn't ready to lose her. I wasn't ready to be an orphan. I threw a tea bag into a cup then pulled some kitchen paper from its roll and wiped the bench, before the plaster tears set and I'd need to scrape them off.

My feet dragged me up the stairs. I ran a bath, poured in some bubbles, threw in a fizz bomb and listened while it crackled and fizzed.

The bath was warm and scented. I held my breath and submerged, my hair swirling and covering my face, until I needed to resurface to breathe. Then, as I hauled myself into a sitting position I realised I was sitting in an inch of sludge. The bubbles had disappeared and made way for a film of horrible grey stuff. I stood up and dripped gung. I reached for a towel to rub myself down and it turned into sandpaper. I stood looking down at the gung realising that if I pulled the plug the pipes would get blocked. I pulled the shower head from the taps and swilled myself down leaving the plug in.

Wrapped in a towel, I sat on the edge of the bath swirling the gung around with my fingers. My mother was in a hospital high dependency unit. My bed was covered in half a ceiling and a shattered mirror, my children were waiting for their tea and

162

some sort of explanation, the dog needed to go out and there was an inch of sludge in the bottom of the bath to be somehow gotten rid of.

I came downstairs, Lucy and Josh were subdued, they knew something was wrong. Lucy had put a pizza in the oven and was shredding lettuce for a salad. Josh had fed the dog and was about to take her for a walk. They gave me shaky, questioning smiles.

I sat them down and told them their gran was very poorly and all we could do was to hope and say prayers for her to get well. Tears immediately welled in Lucy's eyes and Josh bent to put the lead on the dog, in case I saw them in his.

We ate quietly then the children, without prompting, cleared a space on the table and proceeded to take from their bags, books for their homework. The dog, sensing something was wrong, sat under the table between their feet.

I went upstairs. Forcing the door to my bedroom open because the stepladders were jamming it, I peered in and surveyed the damage. Had this happened today? There was stuff on the bed amongst the dust. A Girl's World head, some Star Wars figures, books, a bag of vinyl records and a box of Christmas decorations. I looked up at the void that had been the ceiling and realised this stuff had been in the loft. I closed the bedroom door; it would have to wait.

I slept on the sofa in a sleeping bag and as I woke my stomach knotted. I looked at the clock, it was 6am. The hospital hadn't called, so I rang them. I was told there was no change in my mother's condition. She was being kept sedated until her blood pressure and her heartbeat were stabilised. I was told she was still very poorly; that she would undergo some tests, which would include neurology tests later that morning and I would be able to see her and have a chat with the doctor after about eleven.

It was still too early for the children to get up. As I couldn't get near the clothes in my bedroom, I pulled on some jeans and a top, which had been in the ironing basket. I hooked the dog to her lead, put my keys in my pocket and went quietly out of the front door. I ran until I came to St Augustine's church. In the porch I blessed myself with holy water before opening the door and peering in; in case a Mass was being said.

It was deathly quiet. I picked the dog up and tiptoed to near the front where rows of candles were burning; candles lit by the faithful for thanksgiving or hope. In the stillness I could hear the flickering of their flames and the dripping of the hot wax as it melted and fell onto the holders. I could smell the lingering, familiar and somehow comforting smell of the incense and candle wax which hung about in the air and which had pervaded the old oak pews and ceiling beams for a century or more.

There was another smell. I looked around. Under the eaves at the back was a bag lady swigging gin from a bottle. It was the gin I could smell. Two nuns were in the pews opposite counting prayers from big brown rosary beads which hung like rusted chains around their waists. They alternated the prayers with a kiss on their rosary crucifix. I knelt in the nearest pew and with the dog sitting beside me I looked up, behind the pulpit, to where the statue of Jesus on the Cross stood on its oak plinth. I told Jesus that I would be so grateful if he could find it in his heart to give me some more time with my mother, I wasn't ready to lose her and she wasn't ready to die, she had so much life in her still. But, if he had other plans, then I prayed he would take her quietly, while she was sleeping. I thanked him for my mother's life, for my lovely children and for everything else he had blessed me with.

The shambling figure of Father McCaffrey came out of the vestry to prepare for the early mass. As he walked across to the chancery, he was stopped in his tracks by the sight of me and the dog. I gave him a watery smile. He came and sat with me and he stroked the dog. I told him about my mother. He was surprised and saddened. He said how much he had always liked my mother, that she was a good-hearted soul who he'd never heard say a wrong word about anyone. He smiled and said he could remember as plain as day the time he called to bless my mother's new bungalow. It was the day Simon's Lad romped home at Haydock Park. He and my mother had watched it on telly then they'd had tea and homemade date and walnut cake before he went to collect his winnings. He said my mother's date and walnut cake was the best he'd ever tasted. He was doing his best to cheer me up. He said he would offer up the seven o clock mass for my mother's intention and he would have prayers said for her in the evening mass. He said he would visit my mother and that I was to remember God was good. Then he blessed both me and the dog.

The doctor said my mother's condition was still causing concern and she would continue in the high dependency unit for the time being. Her blood pressure was very low and her heartbeat was irregular and she would continue to require round the clock monitoring. She was still wired up to contraptions which lit up and bleeped and which drew haphazard lines on screens. I watched her as she slept. Her skin was as rosy and as smooth as a young girl's. I held her hand and told her what Father McCaffrey had said.

The day passed, with no significant changes. I stayed with my mother until it was time to go home for the children coming from school.

The night passed as it had before; we had tea, I cleared the dishes, the children did their homework and I continued to ignore the catastrophe that was my bedroom and the sludgy swamp in the bottom of the bath.

The next morning I again woke at 6am and struggled my way out of the sleeping bag. I was again relieved not to have had a call about my mother so I rang the hospital. I was told her condition had improved slightly and that the doctor was happy that she appeared to be stabilising. I hooked the dog to her lead, sneaked quietly out of the door and once again ran to St Augustine's. The nuns were there as before but the bag lady wasn't. I thanked the statue of Jesus on the Cross for sparing my mother's life for another day. Father McCaffrey came out as before to prepare for seven o clock mass and he saw us and came over. He stroked the dog and said prayers were still being offered up for my mother. I told him about the doctor's latest report and he was pleased to hear it. He said he hoped to visit my mother later that morning.

It was peaceful in church; calm. I decided I had time to stay to hear Mass and still be home in time to get the children up for school. A few people came in, six or seven: stalwarts, a puny congregation, tried and tested believers. They looked non-plussed at me and the dog. Perhaps if she had been a St Bernard... The responses were thin, feeble and the Mass was over in about twenty minutes. He didn't hang about Father McCaffrey. Perhaps the bookies opened earlier on a Wednesday. I walked home and as I did so I felt different. It was a feeling I couldn't put my finger on.

I was due at work, I couldn't go. I had to take some time off. I rang Ian and he was, strangely enough, sympathy itself. He said I wasn't to worry about work I had to think about my mother and I was to take as much time off as I needed. He said he would get a temp in. He was being so uncharacteristically nice and I was feeling so fragile, I felt like crying.

I saw the children off to school and tidied the house before making my way to the hospital. Father McCaffrey was already with my mother. He had his back to the door and I waited in the doorway. He was reading something to her which I assumed was probably either a comforting passage from the new testament or else the news from the church bulletin, but which turned out to be the racing form from that morning's newspaper. He was telling my mother he fancied Catherine the Great in the 3 o clock at Aintree.

"Ah, Joanne," he said cheerily, as I walked in. "Your mother and me were just discussing Catherine the Great and hoping she is as great at Aintree as she was on her last time out at York. Isn't that right Gwen? Well, I really must he going," he said, as he hauled his heavy frame out of the low, easy chair, "the poor sick won't visit themselves and Mass won't say itself. Now you take care, Gwen, d'ya hear? I'll call again. Bye now, Joanne, and don't forget you and the dog are welcome at Mass anytime."

I sat with my mother until lunchtime when I went to the café for something to eat. Afterwards, it being a lovely day, I walked out of the rear doors and onto a grassed area which was prettily dotted about with flowerbeds and wooden bench seats. I'd picked up a magazine from the shop in the foyer and I sat on one of the benches flicking through it. The sun was warm, butterflies and bees flittered noiselessly about their business, background voices were carried into the distance by the slight breeze which tickled the pages of the magazine on my lap.

The next thing I knew, a hand was gently tapping my shoulder and someone was asking if I was okay. I'd nodded off. I squinted against the glare of the sun and into a man's face. He seemed both concerned and amused and while he wasn't the most handsome man I'd ever seen, nevertheless, it was a nice face looking down at me. But I didn't dwell on that. I looked away. I blushed and mumbled and cringed at the thought of how ridiculous I must have looked.

"It's just your purse was on the bench beside you and you never know who's knocking about," he said, affably.

That had never happened to me before. I mean you prepare to go to sleep, you don't just sit down on a park bench and nod off. Old people do that. When he'd woken me my head was back and my mouth open so obviously not a pretty sight. I stood up quickly, said I had to be somewhere, grabbed my purse and the magazine, hurried inside and mentally filed the episode under 'another moment best forgotten in the Life of Joanne.'

That night I took the children to see a film and we went for a pizza. I thought it might cheer them up and they pretended it had.

I told them while Gran was in hospital it was possible I might not always be home when they came from school so I needed to know they were being sensible and mature and not fighting and squabbling all the time. I needed to know I could trust them to behave. Josh was allocated the job of taking Millie for her walk on the green behind the house and to clean up after her and Lucy was to start the tea, "Don't worry about us, Mam," they said, "we can take care of ourselves. You just concentrate on looking out for Gran."

And that's how it was during the next few days. There wasn't a cross word between them and even the dog seemed calmer.

It transpired that, while taking the dog for her walk Josh had made a new friend, Leo.

Leo was nearly fifteen, tall for his age and with a quiet confidence. Leo also walked his dog, Tigger, on the field behind the houses and Leo and Tigger were now quite often to be found in our kitchen when I got home. Apparently Tigger was called Tigger because he could jump up and down on all fours. Tigger could do all sorts of tricks and Leo was teaching Josh to do the same with Millie. She could now sit up and beg and was in the process of learning to roll over. She loved it and I was more than impressed. Perhaps she had a brain after all.

Lucy had taken quite a fancy to Leo, she asked me if I thought he was nice. I said I thought he was very nice and she grinned happily.

As well as training Millie, Leo and Josh had been busy making up raps. "Listen to this, Mam, you'll be amazed," said Josh, as I got back from the hospital one afternoon. And Lucy, who would normally have viewed any effort of Josh's with scornful disinterest was in the throes of it, accompanying Leo with the backing beat as Josh, his baseball cap on backwards and wearing his baggy jeans and T shirt – in the style of his hero, Eminem – sang – or rapped, or just yelled really:

*Spinning round the yard in a shopping trolley,*
*didn't know that school could be such fun,*
*they sent me out of class cos I didn't have a pencil,*
*are they mad, or is it me, or is EVERYONE?*

*Sitting on the toilet hoping they won't miss me,*
*got a big red ring around my arse,*
*I've been here for hours, so they haven't missed me.*
*School, what-a-bore, what-a-drag, WHAT-A-FARCE.*

*Saw a girl standing in the corner of the school yard*
*not exactly pretty, in fact she looked a bit queer*
*thought I'd do her a favour and ask her to a movie,*
*she looked me up and down and then she said, NO FEAR.*

*I want to get out*
*I just want to shout*
*I want to be free*
*Free to be ME*
*I just want to sing*
*Do my own thing*
*I want to be free*
*Free to be ME.*

"Well mother, cool or wha'?" Josh asked. For some reason, when Leo was around, Josh had started calling me mother.

"I'll say. It was great," I managed, with forced enthusiasm. Oh well, it keeps them off the streets, I thought.

# 28

## RECOVERY AND DISCOVERY

We were still going to early morning Mass, me and the dog, after I'd rang the hospital to check on my mother, who thankfully continued stable. I needed to do something and praying seemed as good as anything, anyway, I liked being there. My mother had tried for years to get me to like going to church, but it had been a losing battle, yet now I couldn't stay away. I liked the tranquillity and the dog couldn't believe her luck what with early morning runs and the attention which she was now getting from the meagre congregation.

I was still answering the phone to well-wishers and visiting my mother after the doctor's had finished their rounds.

The bedroom was still uninhabitable, but I couldn't seem to muster enough energy to care let alone do something about it.

Then one afternoon when I was at the kitchen sink, I noticed Leo sitting on our garden wall with his head down. He didn't have Tigger with him which was unusual. I went out.

"Shouldn't you be in school, Leo?"

"We finished our mocks this afternoon, so we were allowed home early," he said, still with his head down.

"Oh, wait till Josh finds out, he'll be sooo jealous, he'd love an early finish. How do you think you've done… in your mocks?"

He shrugged.

"Is something wrong, Leo?"

"Tigger has gone. My mother told my dad he had to get rid of him, or else she'll leave him. She never liked Tigger, said she could smell him all over the house. But that's not true. Tigger doesn't smell, he's a clean dog. I keep him clean."

"Where's Tigger now?"

He shrugged, "At my grandma's, till they decide what to do with him."

"Well you'll still be able to see him."

"But it's not the same."

"You can come round here whenever you like to see Millie, but I suppose you already know that."

"But it's not the same," he said, as he pushed himself from the wall and walked off, his hands in his pockets and his shoulders hunched.

The next morning I had a call from the hospital. My mother had come round and was asking for me! Oh-My-God. This was the best possible news. I scribbled a note for the kids, grabbed my car keys and took off.

Not only did my mother not die but when I got to the hospital, apart from a tube still attached to a vein in her hand and one up her nose which they said would be out by the end of the day, the bleeping machines were gone and she was sipping tea through a straw. She looked wonderful; alive. I kissed her and held her hand and stroked her hair. We didn't say anything for ages; didn't need to.

I couldn't wait to get home to tell the kids the good news and, although I kept it to myself, I couldn't wait to go to church to say a prayer of thanks. I'd been feeling all along there was help coming from that direction.

The next few days were euphoria tinged with a bit of sadness, euphoria over my mother's recovery and sadness over poor Leo missing his dog. He looked so hunched and miserable and although he still came round with Josh, he wasn't the same. His gloom had rubbed off onto Lucy and Josh and their enthusiasm for making up songs just wasn't there anymore. They just sat around in the kitchen; deflated. I felt myself being angry with his mother yet I knew I was being a hypocrite. It wasn't so long ago that anybody could have had Millie.

A couple of days later while Leo was upstairs with Josh and Lucy, Arnie, Leo's dad came round and introduced himself. I wondered how a father and son could be so different but I liked Arnie immediately. He had a kind face, open and friendly. I thought if I'd had a brother I'd have liked him to be exactly like Arnie. He asked about my mother and we chatted for a while.

Then Arnie said, "Can you call Leo down, Jo, I've got some news for him."

"I hope it's news about Tigger, poor Leo is really missing him."

"Him and me both, Jo. But not for much longer because, I was so fed up with listening to Mandy's rantings, trying to justify getting rid of the dog, that when she said I should choose between her and getting the dog back, okay, I hesitated. Not for long mind, only a couple of minutes or so, but Mandy said as far as she was concerned it was 1 minute and 59 seconds too long and if I had to think about it, even for that one second then she was out of there. And so she's packed her bags and gone to her mother's. Ironically though, that's where the dog is, so we have to get him back."

Leo heard his dad's voice and came downstairs.

"Well, kidda," said Arnie, ruffling Leo's hair, "there's good news and bad news. Your mam's packed her bags and gone to live at grandma's, which is the bad news, but that means we can get the dog back."

Poor, Leo. Delighted though he was to get Tigger back, he hadn't wanted his mother to go.

"She's only at your grandma's, you'll still be able to see her," I said, with a sense of déjà vu.

"But it's not the same," he said, reinforcing that sense.

The next night, after a sleep-over at Leo's, Josh came back and said, "Mam, you know Arnie? Well he's a really good bloke. You could do a lot worse than him I can tell you. I'm not kidding, Mam, he makes a great Pot Noodle with Butterscotch Angel Delight for afters, much better than the rubbish you make; broccoli and cabbage and stuff. 'Get that down ya, kidda,' Arnie said, 'and don't let anybody tell you Arnie Stoker can't cook!'"

"What do you mean, I could do a lot worse than Arnie?"

"Well you know, you two could get together, innit. Dad's not here now and Mandy's done a runner."

"Don't even think about that, Josh, it's not going to happen. Pot Noodles or no Pot Noodles."

The kids were once again writing and performing their raps and I was once again their audience:

*Join the army*
*Are you BARMY?*
*Do the garden,*
*I beg your PARDON.*
*Help your dad*
*You must be MAD?*
*Wash that dish*
*You WISH.*
*Clean up that sick*
*You're taking the MICK.*
*Make a meal*
*Are you for REAL?*
*Earn some pay*
*No way HO-SAY*

*Get out of bed*
*You're off your HEAD.*
*Get in the bath*
*You're having a LAUGH*
*Go to school*
*Do I look like a FOOL?*
*Put out the trash*
*Where's the CASH...*

Instead of dreading my hospital visits, I now looked forward to them. It was great to see my mother getting better day by day. I thought she'd be itching to get home, but she wasn't, she seemed quite happy to stay where she was, for the time being anyway.

Then one day, while Sadie and I were visiting, one of the nurses came in with a posy of flowers, little pink rosebuds mingled with Gypsophillia, and a card which said, 'These roses reminded me of the colour in your cheeks, but there were no flowers in the shop that could match the blue of your eyes. Hope you like them and my very best wishes for a speedy recovery. Your friend, Ian McAllister.'

Ian McAllister! My horrible, foul-mouthed boss! Why would he send my mother flowers with a message which brought even more colour to her cheeks! What was going on there?

I told my mother I'd be back shortly and I went outside to ring Ian 'perv' McAllister.

"My mother, Ian, has just been given a posy of flowers, from you, with, it has to be said, a pretty personal message attached. What's that about?" I asked, accusingly.

He sounded offended. "Honest, Jo, there was nothing sinister about it. I was really pleased when you said your mother was recovering and I sent the flowers to cheer her up. That's all. You see, about a year or so ago, your mother called into the office and gave me loads of dry cleaning vouchers which had been given out at an Age Concern do. Your mother said it was ridiculous giving pensioners dry cleaning vouchers, they'd never use them and she had gathered them up and brought them in for me because she knew I always wore suits and she said it must cost me a fortune in dry cleaning bills. Honest Jo, that was the most thoughtful thing anybody has ever done for me and I never forgot it."

*That* was the most thoughtful thing anyone had ever done for Ian? Poor Ian.

"Sorry, Ian," I said, contritely, "I'm a bit all over the place at the minute what with one thing and another. My mother loved the flowers, thank you. They're lovely and they have cheered her up loads."

The next few days were spent arranging visitors for my mother so as not to have too many at any one time. Father McCaffrey kept popping in and Sadie was there at some point most days and of course Lucy and Josh wanted to see their Gran and she wanted to see them. Alison managed a couple of quick visits and there were my mother's friends from Age Concern and Autumn Leaves and her neighbours.

Then one day my mother had a surprise visitor. He bowled in on his bandy legs clutching a box of Milk Tray and a bunch of freesia.

"Gwendoline Griffiths! You look as pretty as a picture sitting up in that bed. And with those roses in your cheeks and those bluebells in your eyes you put all of these flowers to shame," he said, sweeping his arm in the direction of the vases around the bed.

I had to hand it to Sam Pickles, for an old sea-dog, that was some chat-up line.

He said he had come as soon as he had heard she was in hospital. He'd been out of the loop for a while (his phrase, not mine) as he hadn't been well himself: a touch of Bronchitis.

He leaned over, kissed my mother on the cheek and whispered something in her ear, which made her blush.

"Get away with you, Sam Pickles," she said, laughing, "you could charm the birds from the trees, you could."

My mother became a girl again when Sam was around. Even I had to admit that. Before he left, my mother took his hand and said, "Please call again, Sam. I can't tell you how nice it has been to see you."

So it seems Sam was back on the scene.

Each day, around eleven, after the doctor had finished his rounds, I went in to see my mother and to take clean stuff in and bring used stuff out. I also made sure she had supplies of the things she liked: 4711 cologne in a push-up ice stick for rubbing onto her temples to cool her when she was feeling hot which was like gold dust to come by, the little old fashioned chemist on Sycamore Street being the only place who seemed to stock it, Lavender Radox bath salts; Johnson's baby talc; Oil of Olay face cream; bath sponges with exfoliating scrub on the back; lemon juice to dilute with hot water and coconut macaroons.

Then one afternoon as I was driving home from the hospital, past the library, I noticed a woman and a boy sitting on the seat just before the turning into our road. I got closer and saw it was Leo. I assumed the woman must be Mandy, his mother. She was wiping her eyes with a tissue and he had his arm around her. I drove past.

Two days later, the woman was on the seat again, but this time she was on her own. Her hands were folded in her lap and she looked a bit forlorn, as if she'd been stood up. I slowed down and pulled in. I decided to go back and introduce myself, after all I knew Leo and his dad, so we had something in common. I parked the car and got out and walked back to where she was sitting.

"Hi," I said, cheerily, "I'm Jo Charlton, Leo's friend's mam. I saw you here with Leo the other day. I'm assuming you must be Mandy."

She looked up, "That's right," she said.

I sat down, "Leo not with you today then?"

"No, he hasn't come. I think he was a bit upset last time."

"He really misses you."

She became tearful. "And I really miss him. I want to come home, but they'd rather have that horrible dog than me. I asked Arnie to choose between me and the dog, and it took him at least five minutes to decide! Five minutes!"

"Well if it's any consolation, Arnie said he only hesitated because he knew what not having the dog meant to Leo."

"And what did he think not having *me* meant to Leo?"

She had a point.

"It's a pity he can't have both you and the dog."

"But it stinks, that dog. You can smell it all over the house."

"At least Tigger is calm. I was lumbered with a dog when my husband left- Millie, she's not only smelly she's also bonkers. Yet, somehow she seems to have slotted into the family. Perhaps I should have rephrased that." I smiled.

But Mandy wasn't amused.

I prattled on regardless, "Millie's always around the kids in the thick of things and she manages to get on all the photos and she's generally a damned nuisance but I suppose if it hadn't been for walking their dogs on the green, Leo and Josh wouldn't have become friends, so every cloud, eh?"

"Suppose," she sniffed.

"Anyway," I said, "I'd better be going. I might see you around. Bye then."

"Bye," she said, without looking up.

# 29

## SETTLING IN

The doctor pulled the curtain round my mother's bed. "I'm glad I've caught you here with your mother, Mrs Charlton. There's nothing to worry about, your mother is doing fine. The thing is, Mrs Morrison, you have been really quite poorly and rather than send you home when you are discharged from here tomorrow, I think you would benefit greatly from a period of respite care. We have an excellent new facility attached to the hospital for patients such as yourself. Perhaps ten days would be sufficient to see you properly back on your feet. I'll leave you to discuss it with your daughter and you can let the staff nurse know your decision."

I really wanted my mother home, but I also wanted to make sure she was absolutely ready to come home. I told her I didn't think another ten days or so would do any harm and if the extra care was available then she should take advantage of it. She agreed and so the decision was made, my mother was to spend some time in The Laurels, the new annex built especially for the convalescing elderly.

"But I don't want a wheelchair, Joanne," said my mother, lowering her voice, "It will make me look like an invalid."

"But you are an invalid, Mam."

We were waiting to be shown around. Apparently The Laurels had been opened by the wife of one of the Queen's cousins two years ago. This had impressed my mother.

"But I can walk a bit now."

"Yes, but not enough to be able to walk around this place, it's huge. It's going to take me all my time to manage it."

"Hello, I'm Nurse Ali," said a pretty, smiling, middle-aged lady who came walking towards us from the main doors, "you must be Gwendoline and...?"

"Joanne," I said, "this is my mother."

She shook my mother's hand and smiled. "Well, it's my job to welcome you to The Laurels, Gwendoline, and to hope you have a very pleasant stay."

Nurse Ali and I helped my mother climb, albeit reluctantly, into the wheelchair. I secured her straps, released the brake and after a bit of a stuttering stop and start we were off. We passed the reception desk and a shop.

"It's a nice building," said my mother as sunlight streamed through the windows lighting up the walkways and walls.

I'd like my house to look like this, I thought to myself, pondering the tasteful sage green walls on which were hung black and white abstract prints in silver frames.

The corridor was straight and long with a series of doors on each side.

"These doors we're passing now are usually kept locked, medicinal supplies, linen, etc. We'll soon be coming to the communal areas," said Nurse Ali, as we turned left and onto a square bit of passageway.

"And here we are, Gwendoline, these are the communal areas. I'll show you into these so you can become familiar with them before I take you to your room in the ladies quarters. The communal areas divide the living areas of the men and women, although try telling that to the patients. Some of them will just not abide by the rules and do their utmost to get some hanky-panky in before they leave to go home." She smiled, shaking her head in a resigned, after all they might be getting on a bit but they're only human, fashion.

Bloody hell! We had passed a couple of the patients on the way here. Enough said!

"This is the television room." The expensive-looking carpet, the dark brown leather armchairs and sofas, the Indian wood magazine tables and tall plants gave the room an extravagant, modern look, something out of a 'Homes' magazine and definitely out of place in here, it seemed to me. I wanted this look in my house. I mean at the risk of sounded ageist, the folk in here were getting on a bit, surely they'd be more at home with chintz covers and china cabinets stuffed with souvenirs from Blackpool and a horse brass or two on the walls.

"It's all very nice, Joanne, but I can't help thinking it looks a bit too modern, bare somehow, as if there's something missing," whispered my mother. "It would look much cosier with some nice frilled cushions and a china cabinet or two displaying a pretty willow pattern tea set. That would set the room off a treat."

"Just what I was thinking, Mam," I whispered back.

Situated one at each end of the room, were two large, flat screen televisions. Two men in cardigans and slippers sitting side by side on one of the sofas were glued to 'Springwatch', neither looked up as we went in. But then an arm shot in the air from somewhere behind them and a man's voice called out.

"Nurse, nurse."

We waited while he padded a tartan slipper shuffle across the room.

"Yes, Albert. What is it?" Nurse Ali, sighed. "It's not about the smoking ban again, surely? We've gone over that so many times."

It was.

"It's like being in bloody prison in here," he said, "except when I was in bloody prison I could smoke to my heart's content."

"But as you well know, Albert, it's now against the law to smoke in a public place. There's a perfectly nice shelter outside on the patio which you can use."

"Oh aye, and catch me bloody death in the process," he grumbled, "there's no bloody consideration given to auld folk these days, not like in my day."

"If you don't shut yer gob, I'll come over there and shut it fo' ya," a voice threatened from deep down in one of chairs. It was a woman. She was minuscule and she was wearing brown so she wasn't that easy to spot. "Yer nowt but a winging auld bugger and if it was that good in prison, get yersell back there why don't ya, yer'll be no miss here."

"Aye, I might just do that," said Albert, "and if I do it'll be cos I've throttled you, yer miserable auld bag."

Hmmm, hanky-panky? I think not.

"Now, now, you two, that's enough of that," said Nurse Ali, sounding more like me than me.

Next door to the television room was the library/reading/computer room. Perched on modern, veneered desks were four desk-top computers each with flat screen monitors and with the internet installed and running. There were bookshelves lined with books, but the room was empty of people.

At the opposite side of the corridor was the theatre. It was in darkness so Nurse Ali switched on a light as we went in, it only being used when necessary. There was a piano against one wall opposite an elaborately curtained stage, something in the style of an old-time music hall, and to the side of the stage were tables holding lighting and sound equipment.

"If you play the piano, Gwendoline, you must feel free to come in here and play this one whenever you feel like it. One of our residents played all the time but that gentleman has left us so the piano is a bit neglected now I'm afraid."

"I did play a little, but that was years ago so I won't bother, but thank you for asking," said my mother.

Further down the corridor was the dining room and next to that the kitchen. The round tables in the dining room were set for lunch, with four place settings to each table. Immaculate white cloths were set with brown place mats, red serviettes and a red ceramic posy bowl centre piece. The kitchen was well equipped, the stainless steel appliances spotless and gleaming.

The hairdressing salon was empty, the hairdresser being only available Monday and Wednesday mornings.

We looked into the various treatment rooms: aromatherapy, which smelled gorgeous and in which a lady was enjoying an Indian head massage; chiropody, which smelled of antiseptic and where a man was having his feet treated; and then to the physiotherapy room, which was empty. We were then introduced to Doctor Singh, who was very tiny, very beautiful and very friendly and who would be looking after my mother during her stay. She shook my mother's hand and said she hoped she would enjoy her time there and that she would see her in a day or two after she'd had time to settle in.

We looked into the little chapel with its light wood fittings, its red carpet up the central aisle, its fresh flower displays on the altar and its one inhabitant bend in pray. From the chapel we bypassed the corridor which led to the men's living quarters and walked further on and to the right where the female rooms were allocated. There were six rooms with four occupants to each room. We were introduced into five of them where we were either ignored, nodded to, stared at indifferently or eyed with varying degrees of suspicion or interest.

Nurse Ali suggested we might like to sit outside on the veranda for a while, in the sunshine, before going to the room which was to be my mother's. The veranda was square and nicely paved with wooden bench seats and potted plants on three of its sides. The other side opened onto a built up pond in which swam Koi Carp and floated lily-pads. Trickling into the pond from a slight slope at the back and between rocks surrounded by Azaleas, Japanese Maples and Bamboo structures was a small waterfall.

Nurse Ali came back. "Well how do you like our Japanese garden, Gwendoline? It's especially pretty at dusk when the solar lights glow."

"I think it's lovely. Water is so relaxing," said my mother.

"Most of our residents seem to like it, but Mr Wainwright says expecting to like anything to do with the Japanese is an insult to the men who died building the bridge over the river Kwai. Some people still have bad memories. Still, you can't please everyone. Would you like me to show you where to find the drinks vending machine, Joanne?"

I followed Nurse Ali to the machine, got two cups of drinking chocolate and went back to my mother. Nurse Ali left us to our drinks saying she'd be back shortly.

"Well if I don't get better in here, Joanne, I don't deserve to," said my mother, somewhat overwhelmed by it all, "did she say the Queen opened it?"

"No, it was the wife of a relation of the Queen."

"Oh," my mother was disappointed, "I thought she said it was the Queen. I hope it wasn't that Princess Michael, they say she's a Nazi. Still, you can't believe all you hear. Mrs Kruger who lives in Pine Street married a German. Herman the German we called him. He was a prisoner of war and she was a land girl and they worked on the same farm. He stayed on after the war and they got married. Poor soul was badly beaten up though, on account of his being a German. Nice looking lad he was."

We sat for a while and finished our drinks, then, when Nurse Ali returned, we followed her to the room which was to be my mother's and where we were introduced to Nell, Ruth and Bella who were to be her roommates. Then we were left to our own devices in order to get my mother settled in.

Healthy, shiny leafed plants stood out against the pale, sand coloured walls, giving the room a light, bright and airy feel. Each occupant has a well-equipped ensuite, a bed, a dressing table, a chest of drawers, a wall mounted TV, an easy chair, a dining chair and a small table. A folded bamboo screen pushed against the wall can be opened out and used for privacy and all of the furniture is light oak, modern and well made.

Bella is directly opposite my mother with Ruth to Bella's right and to my mother's left is Nell.

"Excuse me, miss," called Bella, "don't suppose you could pass me that glass, could you? Just it's got me teeth in and I'll be needing them shortly for when they bring the tea and biscuits round."

I looked around. Did she mean me?

"Yes, it's you I'm talking to," she said.

I went over and handed her the glass.

"You couldn't take them out for me, could you luv? And give them a bit of a wipe. There's some tissues on the table over there. I have to keep taking them out see, cos they make more noise than I do if I try to say owt. Clattering about like they do. They used to be a decent fit once but now they're neither fit nor nowt else. The doctor says it's cos I've lost that much weight. Well anybody would lose weight if they'd had half their insides taken out. He says I should get some new teeth fitted. I might someday. Guess what weight I used to be, bet you can't."

I shrugged. "Twelve stone?" I said, distractedly, concentrating as I was on wiping her teeth without gagging and wondering how on earth nurses do this kind of stuff.

She opened her mouth and laughed like a drain, "More like sixteen. And now I'm six and a half stone and that's wet through. I was always a big lass. Bonny mind. I had all the lads running after me, I did."

"Aye, and now she has everybody else running after her!" laughed Ruth.

Bella beckoned to me to come closer, "I hope your mam has something to keep her mind occupied," she said, "else a person could go stir crazy in here. Nell over there has her crochet, Ruth likes watching all the old films on daytime telly in the television room and I think up fictional book titles and authors. I've a list of them here." She reached over and opened one of the drawers in her cabinet; "Cat Training by Claude Balls, Clinging On by Virginia Creeper, Showing Off by Ivor Biggin… you know the kind of thing… Speaking Correctly by Ella Cution, Premature Ejaculation by I.M Cummin, it's a bit naughty that last one, but I like to slip it in, if you see what I mean," she said, winking mischievously while trying me out for size.

"Oh, put a sock in it, Bella, the poor lass'll think she's come to a loony bin," said Ruth.

Bella laughed. "Mind you, loony bin isn't far off the mark," she said, "there are some in here as mad as ships cats. Wild Bill for instance, keeps a kids holster and gun under his pillow for pretend gun-fights and then there's squawking Dan, the parrot man. You just couldn't make it up!"

I looked over at Nell. She was smiling over her crochet, but not joining in. I went back to my mother. "Well, Mam," I said quietly, "it certainly seems lively enough, don't think you'll be bored in here."

"Lively! You ain't seen nuthin yet, has she Ruth?" said Bella, proving that whatever else she was short of, it wasn't hearing, "Just you wait till Mr Hedley-Smythe puts in an appearance. That always livens things up."

"Yes, such is life in the big city," said Ruth, for some reason I couldn't fathom.

"Mr Hedley-Smythe? He must be a doctor with a name like that, don't you think so, Joanne?" said my mother.

Hmmm. Something told me the jury was still out on that one… something about the way they were laughing.

# 30

## NEANDERTHAL MAN

Arnie came to the door.

"Is Leo here, Jo, just I've had his tea ready for ages?"

"He's upstairs with my two, I'll give him a shout."

"Before you do, Jo. A quick word. I think Mandy might be coming back. I haven't said anything to Leo yet in case she changes her mind cos she's one fickle dame, that one. She rang last night crying her eyes out, saying how much she misses us. I said, well just get ya backside back here, woman, and stop ya snivelling. I know she wants to come back, but she's waiting for me to beg, but I don't do begging. I'll leave that to the dog."

"Well one of you should back down, Arnie. It's poor Leo who's in the middle of it. Did she mention anything about having to get rid of Tigger before she comes back?"

"No, not a dickey bird about, Tigger."

Leo heard his dad's voice and he came downstairs followed by Lucy.

"What-the-hell! Leo! "

"Don't say anything Dad, it's my life."

"But you've got nail varnish on, son! Black bl[ ]
varnish! And eyeliner for God's sake!"

"So?"

"Actually Arnie, it's *Guy*-liner, lots of guys wear it these days," Lucy said, Arnie being Neanderthal Man.

"Oooo, *guy*-liner is it! Well you've got some bottle, kidda, I'll give you that." Arnie rolled his eyes shook his head and handed Leo his crash hat. "Here spook, put that on and get on the back of that bike. See you, Jo. Bye, kids."

We watched from the kitchen window as they mounted Arnie's motorbike. Bulky Arnie, with his tattooed neck and his knee-high laced-up boots and worn leathers and his gentle, lanky, long-haired, eye-linered son, clinging onto his waist; secure.

"I might become a Goth," said Josh, seeming to be thinking out loud.

"Oh! Pleeese!" chimed in Lucy, "you'd be the most pathetic looking Goth. Leo looks awesome but you would just look too ri-dic-ul-ous!"

"Like you, you mean?"

And they were off.

# 31

## PROXY INTRODUCTIONS

"Have you seen the other in-mates, Joanne?" Bella chuckled, "Aren't they a gorgeous lot!? Especially that Blanche in Room 3, she could be a film star with a face like that. If they were filming the Siege of Stalingrad they could do worse than use Blanche for a peasant and then there's Greta Garbot who sits staring out of the window all day and who just 'vants to be alone'. I thought I was skin and bone but Greta's like a bag of sticks. She reckons she was a victim of domestic violence because she was given a three-year stretch for attacking her old man with a poker. You have to laugh. Then there's the two Susan's. The one with the orange hair and the long, black cat earrings is Spooky Susan – who, they reckon, dabbles a bit in the occult and I wouldn't put it past her, and the other one is Snooty Susan; more edge than a broken bottle, Lady Muck from Cowshit Hall, you know the type. And there's knitting Nora, just follow the clackety clack of the needles and you'll come across her. No conversation mind, she just mumbles under her breath, knit one, purl one, pass the slip stitch over. Oh, and if you value your sanity steer clear of little Rose with the glass eye, she can talk the hind legs off a donkey and it's all rubbish."

"You forgot to mention Flash Gordon, Bella," said Ruth.

"Oh, so I did," said Bella. "Well, Flash hangs out – so to speak – wherever he thinks he'll get the most exposure, if you see what I mean," she said, tapping the side of her nose and winking at Ruth.

Did she mean what I thought she meant?

"While you're here, Joanne, you couldn't just get my other slipper from under the bed, could you? It went a bit too far under, and what with me having had my insides depleted and my bad back..."

While I was crawling out from under the bed, she said, "What do you think of The Body in the Morgue by Mort Tician?"

"Or, Painting and Decorating by Matt Emulsion and Making Plant Pots by Terry Cotta," I said, handing her the slipper.

She put her hand on her chest. "Oh, a girl after my own heart!"

"Right that's it! I'm outta here," said Ruth, grabbing her cardigan and making for the door.

"Partners in crime, those two, Joanne," whispered my mother. "A man wandered in last night after you'd gone, slippers, no socks, jumper over his pyjamas and with a checked cap on his head. Said he was waiting for the number eleven bus to take him home – poor soul. Bella told him he'd just missed it, but if he waited a few minutes more the number twelve was due and he'd be able to get on that one. He must have stood, staring at the wall and not moving a muscle for some twenty minutes before one of the nurses came looking for him and took him back to his room. Those two just laughed their heads off when he'd gone. I said to Bella, that wasn't very nice, Bella, 'Oh,' she said, 'you have to get your kicks where you can in here, Gwen, else you'd die of boredom.'"

"They might be like a couple of naughty schoolgirls, Mam, but at least they're cheerful enough."

Nell was sitting quietly looking at some photos.

"I'll just say hello to Nell, Mam, I'll just be a few minutes."

I went over, "Hi, Nell," she looked up. I nodded in the direction of Bella and Ruth, "I expect there's never a dull moment in here with those two."

"Oh they don't mean any harm," she smiled.

"Do you mind if I sit down?"

"No, not at all. I'll pretend you're my visitor."

She had the sort of smile that lit up her face. "Is that your husband?"

She handed me the photo. "Yes, that's Joe. He passed away last August, nearly a year ago now and I miss him so much. We didn't have any family, there was always just the two of us. That's why I'm here really. You see, when I was feeling better from my last bout of pneumonia I was able to go home as Joe was there to look after me. This time though I haven't anybody at home so they suggested I spend some time in here."

Joe was standing on a pier with the sun behind him, holding a dog in his arms and smiling at the camera.

"She's gone as well, our Penny – the dog. She only lived for a few weeks after Joe. Broken heart I expect although she was getting on a bit, poor thing. I miss her almost as much as I miss Joe, they're a bit of company, dogs. Have you ever had a dog, Joanne?"

I told her about Millie, well the good bits, so it didn't take long.

"Do you have any photos of Millie?"

"Dozens, she manages to get on every one I take. Would you like me to bring some in?"

"That would be nice. Of course it's not like the real thing, is it? It's the enthusiasm of dogs I like. People who haven't kept a dog don't know what I mean by that, but I'm sure you do."

Yup. If there was one thing Millie had more than her share of it was enthusiasm.

Then Bella's voice rang out, "Oh, here he comes. Well you haven't had to wait long, Gwen. Meet, Mr Hedley-Smythe."

And in strode a man with a handlebar moustache, hair plastered down in the style of the great Gatsby and wearing a sports jacket, a shirt with cufflinks and a bow tie, albeit with pyjama bottoms and slippers.

"Well who's first today then, wenches?" he said, in a lecherous 'Lord-of-the-Manor' voice, while twiddling his moustache then pulling at his cuffs.

"Oh let it me be, sir," said, Bella.

"Now, Bella, don't be a greedy girl, you had a good pull of it last time. What about that pretty little wench over there. What's your name, wench?" he said, striding over to my mother in her easy chair.

My mother, slightly bewildered, not being used to such behaviour from a doctor, said feebly, "Gwen."

"Not a prude, are you, wench?"

"Not that I know of," she said.

"That's what I like to hear."

And he stretched his neck out, putting his elasticated bow-tie into my mother's hand whereupon she took it as if it was obligatory.

"That's the way, now give it a good yank. Oh I think you must have done this before, Gwen. Oh! Gwen you naughty, naughty girl."

I was just about to rescue my mother, when Nurse Khamal came in.

"Mr Hedley-Smythe, I might have known I'd find you in here tormenting these poor ladies. Back to your own quarters. Now, please, if you don't mind."

"Now, nurse, the gels were only pulling my little dickie. No harm done." He bowed low, "G'day ladies, until we meet again."

I stood up. "I'd better get back to my mother, Nell, she looks a bit shocked."

"Well dear me, Joanne, that's an odd way for a doctor to go on," my mother said.

# 32

## EVERY DOG HAS HIS DAY

When I got home, the kids had written another song. My lucky day!

"We'd like your opinion on this song, Mam. We want to know if you think it sounds like a Gothic type song," said Josh.

They over estimated me, my children. It was my own fault, the result of my over-the-top enthusiasm. What on earth did a Gothic type song sound like? And anyway, Emmerdale was on in ten minutes.

They weren't sure who should sing it. Perhaps Leo should as he had made up most of the lyrics. Leo said a definite no, Lucy couldn't sing it because it was about a boy singing to a girl but she could join in the chorus. But Lucy wasn't sure if she wanted to join in the chorus. She was to be the backing beat and she might miss a beat if she had to sing the chorus as well.

Five minutes to Emmerdale.

"Take it in turns?" I suggested, "Josh could start by singing the first verse, then Leo could come in with the second verse and so on and all three of you could sing the chorus."

"Leo won't want to do that, Mam, he can't rely on his voice, it's all over the place, innit, sometimes it's just a squeak," said Josh, innocently.

"Josh!" shrilled Leo.

"Sorry," said Josh, affably.

I sloshed some dishes about in the sink, pretending I hadn't heard in order to save Leo's blushes while hoping I'd had the foresight to pre-record Emmerdale.

Lucy was being given directions from Leo as to how she should perform the backing beat. She looked at him adoringly. He pretended he hadn't noticed, but he blushed all the same.

Eventually Josh started. He was still in Eminem mode, so I wasn't sure he had taken the concept of Goth on board.

*Didn't want no complications*
*Didn't want no serious relations*
*Just wanted someone to take to bed*
*Didn't want to live inside her head*
*But you waited till my back was turned*
*It was a lesson I should have learned*
*When I saw you there was no compromise*
*You must be Harry Potter in disguise*

*Chorus: You put a spell on me*
*Yeah, yeah, you put a spell on me.*

*Didn't want no ball and chain*
*Didn't want to have to explain*
*Just wanted to be free,*
*To live my life for only me*
*But you waved a magic wand over me*
*You gave me witches brew and you said it was tea*
*You look so beautiful standing there*
*But you must have a toad and a cloak somewhere.*

*Chorus: You put a spell on me*
*Yeah, yeah you put a spell on me.*

*You stirred up a love potion*
*It set my feelings into love motion*
*Hubble, bubble toil and trouble*
*If this is love, don't burst the bubble*
*Hocus Pocus, Ali Kazam*
*I'm so spell bound I don't know who I am.*

*Chorus: You put a spell on me*
*Yeah, yeah, you put a spell on me.*

They looked at me expectantly and I clapped enthusiastically.

"Well what can I say? That sounds like a really good type of Goth song to me. Of course I'm no expert, but yes, that sounded really good," I said, convinced I'd missed my calling, which was obviously the stage.

But, they were pleased with my praise which was all that mattered. The children had already eaten so I heated up some Cottage pie and green beans in the microwave, poured a glass of Chardonnay and checked the recorded list. Emmerdale had recorded.

I finished eating, drained my glass, lolled in the chair and thought, tomorrow I will have to tackle the bombsite that is this house. It can't be put it off any longer.

But where to start. An insurance claim was out of the question. If the insurers were to come out to check, it wouldn't take much for them to realise the damage had been self induced and that would void the claim and even if they didn't, where would I find the money to cover the £250 excess? Anyway, did I want anybody else to see that mirror? No I did not!

Then it dawned. Silly me. The problem of the mirror was down to George. After all, he had it installed and he had a building business. And that building business had expanded with the amalgamation of Fran and was doing very nicely, thank you, according to the grapevine. Well what was I waiting for? I'd lie. I'd tell George the mirror and half the ceiling had come crashing down – on its own, out of the blue – and if I'd been in bed instead of sitting in the corner at the dressing table, it's likely I could have been seriously hurt or even killed, and not just covered in plaster dust, which was how the bath came to be involved. And if all that wasn't bad enough, my poor mother had been desperately ill and would be coming out of hospital in a couple of weeks and would need home care and how was I expected to bring her here with the house in this mess?

George was still sunning himself in Florida when I rang his mobile.

"Whaa," he said, in disbelief.

"And, I need to know what you intend to do about it?" I demanded.

"Bloody hell, Jo. You sure you weren't hurt? God that's terrible. I feel like shit now. I'll ring the yard and get somebody over there pronto to survey the damage and rest assured, everything will be repaired – like new – better than new. Write down a list of the damage, give it to Dale when he comes round and he'll sort it all out. Just one thing, don't mention my name. You know what lads are like, I'd be a laughing stock if they found out. I'll send some of the new lads. Say your name is Henderson or something and that you inherited the mirror with the house, use your imagination. I'll sort out the receipts and invoices and stuff when I get back, in about a week or two. Sorry to hear about your mother. My love to her and the kids."

Well now, that worked a treat. What was it my mother used to say about every dog having its day?

O-kay. I'd need a new bed, that's for sure and a new mattress and new bedding. The carpet will need to be replaced by waxed oak planks and a rug. A nice rug, perhaps that cream, fringed one I'd seen in the window of John Lewis. The curtains will have to be replaced with wooden louvered blinds and the walls will need to be skimmed and painted, perhaps a pale Wedgwood blue with white paintwork. And Laura Ashley have just the light fitting, table lamps, bedding and French style bedroom furniture to compliment all of that very nicely, thank you. The bath will have to come out and be replaced with a new roll-top, complete with futuristic taps and showerhead and the floor and wall tiles re-done. White and slate grey might be nice. And of course the cistern which is hanging off the wall will need to be fixed back. Erm, silly me. The cistern will be included in the *complete* new bathroom suite. Course it will. Then, when all is complete and to my satisfaction, Fran's cleaning personnel, suspect though their status in the country may be, will, nevertheless, be gainfully employed cleaning my house from top to bottom.

There now, that's that sorted.

I had to hand it to George, he didn't hang about because within about thirty minutes of my phone call, dishy Dale knocked. The dog recognised him immediately, first by going slightly berserk then by lying on her back with her legs in the air in a 'take me now' fashion which was something I could empathise with. We went upstairs.

"So this is the reason you were covered in plaster dust when you came to collect the dog from the school on Sycamore Street? You were lucky not to have been hurt."

Then he mused, almost to himself, "I wouldn't have thought it possible for a bit of glass to have brought half a ceiling crashing down, the noggins seem sound enough. But hey, mine is not to reason why. Just as well I gave you the company card, isn't it? Don't worry, we'll have this lot cracked in no time," He smiled his Ronan Keating smile before pulling out and extending his measure.

Dale did what he needed to do then off he went promising to be back first thing in the morning, then I hit the shops.

# 33

## GRAB A GRANNY

"I had a visitor today, Joanne," my mother said, "came swishing in in a cloak type thing, said he was a priest. I thought, well he can't be a Roman Catholic priest, not in that get up, too flashy by half; must be a Mormon or some such thing. Well, he gushed over to me with his arms outstretched, 'Ah, Gwendoline', he said, as if I was some long-lost relation and I thought for a minute he was about to hug me. Call me old fashioned Joanne, but give me Father McCaffrey any day of the week. You know where you are with him. He might a bit threadbare and his glasses might be held together with Elastoplast, but his shoes are always nicely polished. Bella said the one before this flashy one was the image of Jack Palance. She said she expected him to pull out a gun instead of a prayer book. We laughed at that."

"Jack Palance, Mam?"

"Oh, I don't suppose you know Jack Palance, Joanne. He usually played the baddie in the pictures, or else a Red Indian, he had that sort of face. Nothing stays the same, if they don't go about looking like Jack Palance they wear earrings and those stripey running shoes and put their hands in the air and say high five."

"That wasn't the only visitor you had today though, was it, Gwen?" said Bella. "Sam-the-Sailor-Man came in bearing gifts. You couldn't have got a pinhead between them, Joanne, canoodling they were."

"We certainly were not, Bella! Take no notice, Joanne. Bella goes a bit far sometimes."

"Can't say I blame you though, Gwen, a good-looking fella like that. I'd shiver his timbers any day of the week."

My mother was horrified. "Sam called in for a chat that's all. Brought me a Women's Weekly and a Turkish delight. He's good like that."

"I say, Joanne, you couldn't pass me that cardy and put it over my shoulders could you? It's a bit chilly in here and I haven't got love keeping *me* warm." Bella was doing her best to wind my mother up.

"Where's Ruth off to?" I asked, changing the subject.

"Oh her!" said Bella, "She's off strutting her stuff. There's no holding her since that new hip kicked in properly. Talk about flighty! She's off flaunting herself in that pink flowery frock, the one she came in. She's after the new fella, Frank, says he looks like Burt Lancaster. Can't see it myself although I have to admit, he is a bit tasty. She keeps giving him the glad eye, he just turns a blind one. Still, I wouldn't mind putting some feelers out in his direction myself, if Ruth gives up on him."

"I thought it was that Jimmy who wears the flat cap you fancied, Bella," said Nell.

"Oh him, I'm too much woman for him, anyway it's pigeons he fancies. No, I might just keep an eye on that Frank fella. You have to admit, there's something about a man who can carry off a Trilby hat with Bart Simpson pyjamas. It's not easy though, not with Nurse Saheed pacing like she does. She should have been a prison warden that one. I mean it's not like we're smoking weed or having it off in the linen cupboard, is it? Just a bit of harmless fun."

My mother tut-tutted. "It's a regular little den of iniquity in here. Sometimes I think I'll be pleased to get home."

"I'm just waiting for Ramadan, Joanne," continued Bella, ignoring my mother, "when all the staff will be at the Mosque and we'll have the place to ourselves. Then it'll be like, what yer waiting for boys, grab a granny and let's get this party started!'"

We all laughed. She was incorrigible.

I told my mother I wasn't able to stay long as I had the builders in. That I'd had a few problems with plaster flaking off the bedroom ceiling, that sort of thing.

"Oh," she said, "well if you ask them nicely, they might screw the cistern back, it's dangerous the way it is."

"You're right, Mam, I'll do that."

On my way out, I noticed for the first time, a poster pinned on the wall beside the reception desk which said, 'Patting dogs welcome'. On the poster was a picture of a perfectly groomed, smiling lady in tweed skirt and jacket with an equally groomed, smiling dog at her feet. I thought of Nell and I vaguely wondered if Millie could be a patting dog, then I decided the idea was too ridiculous for words and promptly decided to forget it.

# 34

## HOT OR WHAT!

After only two days, the work on the house had come on in leaps and bounds. The ceiling had been repaired and re-plastered, the bedroom walls had been skimmed and the old bathroom suite was out. Dale suggested we should go together to choose the new suite and fittings for the bathroom as he would need to check the fixings. I suggested we also chose the flooring, the tiles and the blinds together as I hadn't a clue about quantities, sizes, fittings etc. And so it was agreed.

And I might tell you, Dale scrubbed up very nicely. Very nicely indeed. Female shoppers and assistants alike gave him more than a second look. And I was more than happy for them to think of us as a couple and how lucky was I? I decided to do some probing.

"How long have you worked for the company?" I asked.

"Not long. I was taken on as part of the new staff when the two companies merged."

"What are the bosses like?"

"Well, George seems a decent enough bloke, quiet, unassuming, but it's definitely Fran who wears the trousers. Bit of an ice maiden, stuck up, superficial, walks around as if she has a rod up her backside, has a calculator where her heart should be."

"So not your type then?"

He said no way! He couldn't image any bloke in his right mind fancying her, which seemed to sum George up perfectly. He said he liked his women looser, earthier and with a heart-beat. I wondered if there was any of that criteria I could fill. I had a heart-beat. Unfortunately, it beat in the body of a haggard and harassed mother of two who didn't know half the time whether she was coming or going. But even if I didn't consider myself to be a catch in Dale's eyes, he must have thought I was loaded. I chose exactly what I wanted with absolutely no regard as to the cost and it was FRAN-TASTIC. It was all going into the final settlement for the job being done for Mrs Joanne Henderson; so that was all right.

Lucy asked if she could bring Chloe round for tea after school as she wanted Chloe to see how hot Dale was. I was shocked. They weren't even fourteen yet. I could just imagine how poor Dale would feel having two teenage girls ogling him and the jibes he would get from the other men. I told Lucy that Chloe was welcome to come for tea anytime, but NOT to ogle Dale who was only here to do his job. She rolled her eyes. God, how boring were mothers?

# 35

## MILLIE THE PATTING DOG

Poor Nell. She tried to smile, join in and look cheerful but she couldn't seem to manage it. She just looked sad, sitting in her chair with her photos in her lap. She didn't have any visitors; didn't have any family, and my mother said that's all Nell did, looked at her photos in between doing bits of crocheting. Bella's only son lived with his family in Australia and that's why she didn't have visitors, but it didn't bother Bella being as gregarious as she was, but Nell was different. For some reason I thought again of Millie becoming a patting dog. Nell had loved the dog that had died, they were a bit of company, she had said.

I thought I'd run it past my mother.

"Millie! But I don't think they would want fleas in here, Joanne, they're fussy about that sort of thing."

"We got rid of those ages ago, Mam. You have to admit she's a friendly dog, albeit a bit mad, but she likes people and she's not as hyper as she was, Leo and Josh have been training her. So what do you think?"

"Well if you think it would cheer Nell up, you could ask Nurse Ali what she thinks."

Nurse Ali was all for it although, she said, obviously there would be some of the patients who wouldn't be so keen. But providing the situation was well under control she couldn't see a problem.

And so it was arranged. I was to bring Millie in for an initial ten-minute visit, to try her out.

# 36

## STEADY ON

Lucy had something on her mind, "Mam, you know how Leo with be fifteen in November and I'll be fourteen in September."

"Uh-huh," I said, wondering what this was leading to.

"Well, do you think that's too young for us to start going steady?"

My mind raced. Was going steady a euphemism these days for having sex? I hesitated.

"You do like Leo, don't you, Mam?"

"Yes, of course I do, Lucy. But you are both still very young and…"

"You're thinking about the sex thing aren't you, Mam?"

"Of course not Lucy, that's the last thing I was thinking about!" It was sooo not.

"Well if it is the sex thing that's bothering you, Leo and I have talked about it and we won't even think about that until I'm sixteen and when we do decide to do it, we'll be sensible and use precautions. I mean Leo wants to go to college to do his music and I want to work in a wildlife conservation, so we know we have to be sensible."

They'd been talking about having sex! I thought they were rapping.

"Well, what can I say, Lucy?"

"There's not a lot you can say really, Mam." The comment was flicked in my direction as she turned and made her way upstairs.

Josh was subdued. "Has she told you then, about her and Leo?" He wasn't happy. He obviously thought he would have his nose pushed out. I had to sound nonchalant, it was just a passing phase, not to be taken too seriously, "Oh that, yes she has."

"Bloody cheek. He's my friend, not hers."

I put my arm around him. "But just think, Josh, if Leo found himself a girlfriend other than Lucy, chances are he'd stop coming round so much, whereas with Lucy as his girlfriend, he'll just come round as usual, probably more," I said, while wondering if it were possible for him to come round more, given that he practically lives here anyway.

"Well they'd better not have their tongues down each other's throats in front of me or I'll puke."

# 37

## THE MERCY MISSION

I was jittery. It was more than possible the whole thing would turn into a complete, unmitigated disaster. Was I totally devoid of sense? I was promoting as a patting dog the scourge of my life; the idiot dog who swallowed Blu tack and tampons and who shredded every piece of post as it came through the door; promoting her as if she were normal.

I looked through the rear view mirror. She was strapped in the back seat, wiggling her backside and smiling through the window at passers-by. If she could give them a wave she would. She loved being in the car. Thought she on was her way to the park or the beach every time. She was even clownish going to the vet's. Most sensible dogs held back, needing to be lifted or coaxed out of the car, then once out they had to be dragged towards the doors with their tail between their legs and their ears flat against their head, as if they were going to the gallows. Not Millie. She had to be restrained, because at the vet's there were other dogs to annoy and cats in baskets to bark at and shelves full of goodies to demolish. Thermometer up her bum! Yeah baby! Bring-it-on! And when other dogs and their owners (sensible ones), happen to come up against Tyson, the Bull Mastiff who goes around with the boys from the high-rise flats, they, sensibly, either flatten themselves up against a wall hoping to appear invisible, or else they turn tail and run. Not Millie. She bounds up and prances around Tyson hoping for some roll-about fun. He once, when she was a puppy, took her head in his huge mouth and thrashed her about a bit. I screamed, I thought she was about to be decapitated. But he let her go and strutted off. It was a warning not to mess with him and now he just seems bewildered by her nerve and nudges her out of the way with his great paws. And the boys, dead-pan, ganglander-like, nod in her direction and mutter,"Yo Millie, ree-spect."

I pulled up, got out, got the parking ticket then braced myself. Getting Millie out of the car was always something to be faced with trepidation. Managing it with some degree of restraint on her part and a smidgen of dignity on mine; in case of onlookers, was no mean feat. I opened the door on her side by about three inches and sneaked my hand in. Grabbing her collar I hooked the lead onto it and although looking for all the world as though I had complete control of the situation, I held on for grim death because once she'd leapt out of the car I knew that that'd be it, she'd drag me through the car park, through the hospital doors and down the corridors because today, she was on a mission. She didn't know, nor did she care, what the mission was, she was just on it. She was too excited. I could tell. She would jump all over everyone taking me with her. It was going to be a disaster. These were elderly people for goodness sake, vulnerable. Decorum was the name of the game. The whole place would be in an uproar in seconds. Why did I think it would be any different? Had I been dropped on my head as a baby or what?

We whizzed past reception, past the picture of the smiling, patting dog, lying at the feet of the smiling, tweed clad lady. We whizzed past the woman with the trolley who was bringing round the afternoon tea. Then three or four metres on, we suddenly came to an abrupt halt. Millie sniffed the air: biscuits. In seconds, we were reeling in an about turn, back to the tea trolley whereupon she skidded on her backside to a stop. She sat there, her eyes pleading for the woman to take pity on her and give her a biscuit. My heart was going like the clappers.

"Aah, what does the doggy want? A biscy is it? A nice custard cream? Well sit nicely and Doreen will give you one. There, now give Doreen a kiss." Doreen bent over Millie which was not a good move, and she got her kiss, a bit more than she had expected. She straightened up, blinked then fumbled around on her trolley for some antiseptic which she sprayed onto a tissue with which to wipe her face.

But it worked. Millie was calmer, probably sensing that if she played her cards right, there might be more biscuits where that came from. We walked at a steady pace behind the trolley with Millie not diverting her eyes for a minute from the custard creams. I was beginning to feel hopeful, perhaps it might be possible my visit would not resemble a scene from a dog disaster movie after all. And so, with my newfound confidence we followed Doreen into the dayroom where some of the patients were gathered for afternoon tea.

"What the…" one of the men exclaimed, not expecting to see a dog arriving with the tea trolley.

All eyes were on us. "She's a patting dog," I said, by way of explanation in a voice so feeble it didn't even convince me.

"Well tell her to giz a pat then," the man sneered.

"You pat the dog, you daft bugger," the man beside him said.

"Why would I want to pat a bloody dog?" the first man said, "Bloody stupid."

Then they went back to watching the telly while they waited for Doreen to pour their tea.

"I've never heard of a patting dog," said another, "must be something new they've brou like a terrier?"

The other woman shrugged. She didn't kı another and what's more, she couldn't care less.

"It's not a breed," I said, "I've brought her in to see if anyone would like to give her a pat."

"Well that confirms it," the first man said, "the lunatics are tekken ower the bloody asylum."

"I'll pat her if you want?" a small voice chimed in, by way of doing me a favour. The woman belonging to the voice shuffled over and gave Millie a token pat. "Why do you want her to be patted?"

It was a perfectly sane question, it just turned everything on its head.

They were looking at me as if I had just been released into the community. "I'm not sure now. It seemed like a good idea at the time," I said, making for the door and more than sure it was not a good idea now.

Well that went down like a concrete parachute, I thought, as I made my way to the ladies' quarters to see my mother and Nell, and then, I decided, I'd take Millie home, with my tail between my legs, so to speak. So much for my good intentions.

I was walking in the direction of my mother's room, when a man in a white coat came along the corridor towards me. He looked vaguely familiar.

"Oh," he said, as he got nearer, "so you're the dog lady and this must be the dog. Nurse Ali told me you were planning a visit."

Dog lady!

He bent down and stroked Millie who, with her usual uninhibited gay abandon, lay on her back with her legs in the

.r. He laughed. "She's a little sweetie, my Barney would love her, so he would." He rubbed her belly then straightened up, "Well I might see you both again sometime. Bye then."

I hurried on. So I'm now the bloody dog lady!

Millie bounded onto my mother's knee, knocking her glasses off it. My mother had been dozing and was a bit stunned.

"Oops, sorry, Mam, she just took off when she saw it was you."

"That's all right, Joanne. I'm pleased to see her. It makes me realise how much I'm missing home."

Nell came over, sat on my mother's bed and fussed the dog. "Do you know, Joanne?" Nell said, "Millie is just like a dog I had when I was young, Mitzi her name was. I loved that dog, she meant the world to me. Will you bring Millie in again so that we can get better acquainted?"

"Course I will," I said, without any conviction whatsoever.

I called over to Bella, "Fancy giving Millie a pat while we're here, Bella?"

"I'll pass on that, Joanne, no offence, but me and dogs have a healthy respect for one another, we stay clear of each other."

Ruth was in the television room. Nell had cheered up no end, which had been the object of the exercise, and surprisingly, chaos hadn't reigned. My mother though, now looked a bit down in the dumps, as she said, she was missing home. I sat on her bed with Millie at my feet and poured some juice into a paper cup. I took my mother's hand and said, "It won't be long before we have you home, Mam."

"I do hope so, Joanne," she sighed.

"Well, hel-lo Sailor," said Bella, loudly and as salaciously as somebody with no teeth in; could. We turned, Sam Pickles, with his bandy legs and cheeky grin was striding over to us bearing a People's Friend and a Fry's Peppermint Cream.

"As you were, ladies. Don't mind me. Well, who have we here, then?" he said, bending down to stroke Millie. As Sam stroked the dog, Nell quietly made her way back to her own easy chair.

On seeing Sam, my mother cheered up. I was about to make my excuses and leave them when she beckoned me to come closer.

"Joanne," she whispered, "I've something important to tell you when you come in tomorrow." She gave Sam a secretive little smile.

# 38

## COMPLIMENTS AND COMPLICATIONS

It was still early in the afternoon when I got home, the kids not yet back from school. The men were clearing away their tools, finished for the day and Dale asked me if I would like to check the work they'd done. I had left them mid-morning drinking tea, playing loud music and shouting to each other from room to room, yet, as ever, their productivity was amazing. The bathroom suite was fitted and working and looking fabulous, the floor was laid in the bedroom, everything was ready for the decorators and tilers to start work the next day and then it would just be the cosmetic stuff and the cleaning to finish. I was thrilled. It was even better than I had imagined it would be. Dale was happy to see me so pleased.

The men had packed up said their good-byes and piled into the works van, yet Dale hung back, it seemed he had something on his mind.

"Jo," he said, tentatively, "you know you said your old man had gone off with somebody else years ago."

Uh-oh, he had discovered my old man was George and that I was a liar and a fraud.

He shuffled about a bit. "Well, that being the case and as you don't seem to have anybody else in your life at the moment, well not that I can tell anyway, I wondered if you might fancy going out with me?"

Huh! "B-but Dale," I stammered, "you're so good looking, you can't possibly want to go out with me! I mean with your looks you could have anybody; you could be in a boy-band... West Life... and you're so much younger than I am..."

He threw his head back and laughed. "A boy-band! West Life! As if!" He had a nice laugh, not a guffaw and not an over-the-top loud, blokey laugh, just nice. "You are so funny," he said eventually. "But hey, I'm not that much younger than you, I'll be twenty-seven next birthday, that's not so young. The thing is, when we were out shopping the other day, I noticed people looking at us as if we were a couple and I was really happy for them to think that. I think you're great. Okay, admittedly you're no Mary Poppins meets Pollyanna but that's what I like about you. I love the way you just get on with things in your own way. You look after the kids and your mother and the dog and you always look nice. I love your hair and," pointing to my mouth, he said, "I love the way that front tooth slightly overlaps the other one, you've got a helluva lot going for you, don't sell yourself short. That husband of yours must've been mad."

Crickey! I was more than flattered, but it was the mad husband that was the stumbling block. He had specifically asked me not to let on that I was his wife. If I agreed to go out with Dale, then it was bound to come out sooner or later and he would see me for the liar I was. But hell and damnation, he was soooo nice.

"Dale, I can't tell you how flattered I am that you would even consider asking me out," he seemed to move in for a kiss but I side-stepped him, "it's just I seem to have so much going on at the moment that having someone else in my life is not really an option – not yet anyway – sorry. Perhaps when things settle down a bit..." D-A-M-N!

He put up his hand to silence me. "Okay, Jo, a knock-back is a knock-back however it's dressed up. But I do think you're great." And he picked up what was left of his pride, stuffed it into his bag with his tools and slung them over his shoulder. "See you in the morning then, eight-thirty sharp." And he was out the door.

I had to sit down. Where the hell had that come from? And why was life so complicated? Why didn't I just throw caution to the four corners and go out with Dale and bugger the consequences. It wasn't as if he was proposing marriage, he just liked my hair and my crooked tooth, and it wasn't as though I had any allegiance to George. On the contrary, I was screwing him for all he was worth but things had started off all wrong. I hadn't just moved into the house and inherited the mirror. I wasn't Mrs Henderson and the mad husband who'd scarpered years ago, was Dale's employer who I'd been quizzing Dale about. And George and I weren't even properly divorced yet and George was responsible for the mirror and that was something he didn't want 'the lads' to know about and I couldn't risk rocking the boat, not now, not with everything still to be paid for – although it's possible George would still acquiesce (so to speak) on the strength of his continuing guilt-trip, but Fran sure as hell wouldn't, or to put it another way, if I was Fran, I sure as hell wouldn't…

But for Dale to have asked me out, well that was certainly something I could hang my hat on, and I WOULD.

I was still sitting there, when the door opened and Josh's bag came hurtling along the hall, followed by him and Lucy. They were surprised I was at home, they had gotten used to me being at the hospital when they came from school.

"How did it go with Millie, Mam? Did she behave? Did they like her?" Lucy wanted to know.

"Hmmm, well yes and no. She had a mixed reception, but I suppose it went okay. There was no harm done, no damage, for which I was grateful and she did seem to cheer Nell up, which was the object of the exercise, but I don't think I would do it again, my nerves couldn't take it. Why not go upstairs while I get on with the tea and see what the workmen have done. You can actually have a bath now, or a shower; no more having to go to Gran's."

Josh groaned. He hadn't been going to Gran's anyway. He'd had a couple of showers at school after PE, which he reckoned, was more than enough.

Lucy was ecstatic. "This has got to be the best bathroom ever!" she called down, over the sound of the running tap.

Later we sat down to tea. Well Lucy and I did, Josh was muttering and complaining about lamb cutlets and cauliflower cheese.

"You can count me out. No way am I eating that! It looks like dog vomit. I'll just have a crisp sandwich."

"If you think I've been cooking for the past hour for you to have a crisp sandwich, young man, you have another think coming."

"I might go round to Leo's. Arnie lets us have crisp sandwiches he says the potato could count as one of your five-a-day and if it's cheese and onion there's a bit of protein in there as well."

"He's having you on, Josh. Now sit down and eat your food."

Just then Leo knocked then came in smiling.

"You look pleased with yourself, Leo, have you had some good news?" I asked.

He had. His mother was back. But not before she had made up some rules about Tigger. He was to be allowed to stay but only on condition that he wasn't to go upstairs to sleep on the beds, he wasn't allowed to chew filthy, disgusting bones that had been dug up out of the garden on the fireside rug, and his bed was to be changed from the soft, smelly, comfortable sort to the hard, plastic, easy to clean sort. Arnie and Leo had agreed with the conditions for the sake of a quiet life, but Arnie said he didn't think the dog would want to stay now. He said he wouldn't if he was the dog.

"That looks nice," said Leo, looking over Josh's plate.

"There's plenty if you want some," I offered.

"Yes please," he said.

And he and Josh cleared their plates then both asked for seconds.

# 39

## NICKED

"Joanne," whispered my mother, conspiratorially, "I've found the perfect man for you. You'll need to move quickly though, because Gladys in room two has her eye on him for her daughter, Daphne. You'll have seen Daphne, a big girl, green mohair cardy, works in B&Q, comes in about three o'clock most afternoons, then goes out after about ten minutes for a smoke. Bella says she thinks Daphne is part lesbian. Ruth says it must be the part that drives the fork lift truck round in B&Q. He's lovely, his name is Nick. He's Irish. Comes in to exercise the old people, the ones that cannot get about. They say he has a lovely touch."

"Oh, tell you what, Mam, I'll just put a notice on my head shall I? 'Desperate – come and get it'. Or, what about, 'Been dumped – up for grabs'. Or even, 'If you're Irish come into the parlour, there's a welcome there for you'. How about that, eh?"

"Joanne!"

"And incidentally, Mam, although everyone seems to assume I must be desperate to have a man in my life, I have just turned down someone years younger than me and who is so hot he sizzles. Oh, and let's not forget you thought George was

217

a catch so how could I possibly question your intuition about this Nick!"

Ruth was out of the room as quickly as her new hip would allow. Bella and Nell looked shocked, as well they might. As soon as the words had left my mouth, I regretted them, my mother didn't deserve it. But, I still had Dale on my mind. I really didn't want him just to walk off into the sunset with his bag over his shoulder without a backward glance.

Then I was contrite, "Sorry, Mam, that was uncalled for." I took her hand and looked over to Bella and Nell. "Sorry Bella, Nell, I think I'm just a bit tired that's all. Oh, go on then, tell me about this Nick."

My mother smiled, she wasn't going to be phased. "Well Joanne, he's got this way about him and the people who know about these things, the people he has worked on that is, say he has a lovely touch and he has such a nice smile and – oh, speak of the devil, here he comes now."

It was the man in the white coat I'd met in the corridor yesterday.

"Well, hello there ladies. I was just passing and I thought I'd pop in for a few moments to see how everyone is getting along."

"All the better for seeing you, Nick," Bella, flirted.

Then he saw me. "Oh and it's the dog lady, is it not? And the dog, isn't she with you today?" His smile was as wide as his shoulders and his teeth were as white as his coat.

"No she isn't, and excuse me," I said haughtily, "but if you must refer to my bringing in my dog – on a mercy mission, I might add – then please refer to me as the lady with the dog. I take great exception to being defined as the *Dog Lady*." Then I turned my back on him.

That told him! But he was still infuriatingly familiar.

The room went silent. Not even Bella said anything.

"Yes, you're right, that wasn't very gentlemanly of me. Please accept my apologies."

"I'm going to the kiosk, Mam, do you want anything?" I said, ignoring him and his apologies.

"N-no thank you, Joanne."

"Kiosk. Anybody?"

"No thank you, Joanne," mumbled Bella and Nell.

I picked up my bag and strutted out with my nose in the air. I went to the kiosk and bought a magazine and a Kit-Kat. I decided to go outside, through the back doors onto the grassed area and take in some fresh air. I was tired, hormonal and in need of chocolate.

"It's a bit blowy out today," said a woman's voice from the first bench, probably hoping for a bit of company, but I wasn't in the mood.

"It certainly is," I said, continuing to walk. I had my sights set on the deserted middle bench in the half arc which surrounded the flower beds.

I sat down under the shade of a lilac tree and leaned back. The branches of the tree were heavily laden and overhanging with blossom and I looked through them and into the sun. The breeze was carrying with it the perfume from the lilac flowers, some of which were already tinged with brown. Soon they would all be brown and dry and shrivelled and blown away by some other breeze. Today though they swayed and danced promiscuously, beckoning the bees to gather their nectar while they could.

Dried tendrils from the tree fell onto my lap and skidded across the magazine pages which I tried to turn but they just blew in on themselves, so I gave up. It was too much effort. I unwrapped the Kit-Kat, broke off one of the fingers and put it half-way into my mouth to suck the chocolate slowly through to the wafer. I leaned back. My hair was loose and the wind was blowing through it. The sun was warm on my face. God, I was tired. The days of hospital visits, shopping for my mother's stuff and for food that the kids could manage to make for themselves, choosing tiles, flooring and paint samples, along with the nights of sleeping on the sofa, had all taken its toll. I tried to think about Dale and what I should do to stop him drifting off and out of my life, but he became a blur as I felt myself drifting off and into some wonderful, peaceful, warm place called sleep.

Until that is, a hand touched my shoulder.

"Are you okay?" The voice was gentle but even so I nearly jumped out of my skin while nearly choking on the half submerged finger of Kit-Kat. I'd dozed off while the other half was still sticking out of my mouth.

It was him. And he was smiling. The sense of familiarity I had had about him jumped out and kicked me up the backside. I pushed the rest of the kit-kat into my mouth in a self conscious attempt to get rid of it, before realising there was too much of it and my cheeks bulged like a chipmunk's. Not a good look. A smile, even if I had wanted to attempt one was out of the question, my mouth being too full and my teeth covered in chocolate. Neither could I say anything, not until I'd chewed and swallowed, yet what could I say? 'We'll have to stop meeting like this, my pride can't take it'!

He sat down. I didn't want him to. I wanted to push him off the bench and say GO AWAY, don't you recognise humiliation when you see it! LEAVE ME ALONE.

"I'm awfully sorry, I didn't mean to startle you. I seem to be making a habit of that, waking you when you've dozed off. I just thought I should give you a little nudge. You seemed to be in the middle of eating something and I didn't want you to choke."

He was smiling, good humouredly. But I sat as solemn as a stone.

"Sometimes when you close your eyes against the sun it just happens and you're off before you realise it. It's happened to me before and usually when I should have been somewhere or had something important to attend to."

I didn't want to hear him making excuses for me. I just wanted him off that bench and out of my life.

"And your point is?" I said.

"Well, it's just that we seem to have gotten off on the wrong foot and I wanted to apologise properly. Is it Joanne or do you prefer Jo?"

"Whatever." I shrugged, sounding more like Lucy than Lucy.

"I just wanted to say I thought it was noble of you to have brought Millie in to see Nell and the other patients. The dogs that are normally brought in are trained and are introduced gradually, but you just jumped straight in with Millie and I thought that was very brave of you."

"The word you're looking for is stupid."

"No, I said brave and I meant it."

"Yes, well if you'll excuse me, my mother will be wondering where I've got to." I made to get up.

"They're all having lunch back there and it's such a nice day, pity to waste the sunshine, won't you stay a little while longer? I could tell you about my dog, if you like."

For God's sake! So I have a dog. So what! It doesn't mean I want to hear about other people's bloody hounds.

I sighed, sat down again and half yawned, hoping he'd get the message. "What about it?"

"Well, his name is Barney, he's a retriever cross and I got him from an old lady who couldn't keep him anymore. He was too boisterous for her to handle and as she knew I'd been a dog trainer many moons ago she asked me if I wanted him. He's very handsome, full of fun, gentle and clever. But he's still in Ireland and I miss him."

He was a dog trainer!

He went on to say that he and his girlfriend Suze (Suzanne, that is) who he had been with for the best part of five years had split up and he had decided on a complete new start. A friend of his, already living in England, had told him about this job, he had applied for it, had had a couple of interviews, was successful, so here he was.

"And what is the job?" He wore a white coat but he couldn't have been a doctor. My mother wouldn't have called a doctor by his first name.

"Physiotherapist. I split my time working in two of the local hospitals. I'm usually here most weekends and a couple of days during the week. Came into the profession a bit late really. I played rugby for a few years, even had a trial for Ireland when I was in my teens, didn't make the grade though. But I played semi-professional and over the years I ended up with plenty of injuries and those injuries required plenty of physio. Somewhere along the line I decided to give up the game and concentrate instead on the treatments."

"My son, Josh, plays rugby. He's in the school team."

"Really! Well if I ever get to meet Josh, I'd be happy to teach him all I know about the game."

I was mellowing. It was his openness and his ready smile and those dark blue eyes. "And your dog?" It just came out.

"Oh, poor old Barney is still where I left him, being looked after by Suze. He had to have blood tests before I could bring him out of the country and the results take about four weeks. I'm due to collect him and bring him over in a few days' time. Tell you what would be great, if Barney could meet Millie when I finally get him here. We could take them for walks in the country and on the beach, Barney loves the water. I'm sure they'd be the best of pals. What do you say?"

"Erm…" Was he asking me out, or what?

Then his bleeper went. He clicked it off, "Oops, sorry Jo, duty calls. I have an appointment waiting. Catch up with you again sometime." He got up and started to walk away. Then he half turned and winked and said, "I meant it about those walks."

I suddenly didn't want him to go. My mother was right, there was definitely something about him. About the way he smiled his quick, unaffected, disarming smile. And the way the blueness of his eyes stood out against the black of his thick, straight lashes. Yet something indefinable was behind all of that. Something much more potent. Something had happened to me with that wink. A feeling. Vague, yet positive. It might have in my toes or my fingers or inside my chest or my head. I couldn't tell. Whatever it was, it was something I wanted to hold onto. Was it that chemical reaction thing they talk about? Could it be love? But I had never been in love so how would I recognise it? Perhaps the reason it hadn't happened before was because I hadn't met him yet. There had been an Irish Sea between us.

I had to get a grip. Let's face it, if it was love it would be unrequited. I mean how could he possibly feel the same about me? Why would he? If he felt anything at all, it was probably pity. There was every chance he thought I was on drugs or something. He had nudged me awake, twice. Once while sleeping on a hospital park bench with my head back and my mouth open – possibly, and I shudder to think of it – snoring, and then while sleeping on a different hospital park bench with half a finger of kit-kat sticking out of my mouth. That wasn't much to go on. It certainly could have gone better than that. It wasn't exactly the sort of scenario Barbara Cartland would have considered for the opening of a romantic novel; even an auspicious opening of a romantic novel.

I watched him walk away. I watched the way he had his hands in his trouser pockets allowing his coat to blow about behind him. I watched the swagger of his walk. Not arrogant, just purposeful, capable, dependable. The walk of a man a woman could rely on. The fact that his head was closely shaven and he was stockily built with fine black hairs poking through the neck of his tee shirt and on his arms and on the back of his hands and apart from a bit of a dark shadow he was clean shaven and not my type at all; just didn't matter.

But it wasn't supposed to happen like this. I was supposed to be getting out there, getting a life, getting in with the In-Crowd, going where the In-Crowd go. That's where this sort of thing was supposed to happen. Not in a respite care unit, among elderly people and my poorly mother.

I returned to the annex feeling floaty and light headed. Not at all the moody, hormonal, stroppy bitch that had left. I wanted to turn a corner and bump into him and get that tingling feeling again, just to make sure I hadn't dreamt it.

My mother could see I'd returned in a much better mood. "Can we go onto the veranda, Joanne, I've some news which I want to tell you in private?"

We walked slowly, with the aid of her Zimmer frame until she said, "I can't be doing with this thing, Joanne. It hunches me up and makes me feel like an old woman. Can't we just leave it somewhere and you can hold onto my arm, I'm sure I'll manage." We dumped the frame and with a bit of support she managed fine.

The veranda was a suntrap, walled as it was on three sides. I made my mother comfortable then I went to the vending machine for some drinks. Although a brisk breeze was still blowing, we hardly felt it seated as we were in a sheltered corner amongst the pots of Cordylines and Geraniums. Opposite, a man was smoking and muttering to himself, too pre-occupied with what was on his mind to take any notice of us.

"Come on then, Mam, what's with all this cloak and dagger stuff?"

"Well Joanne, Doctor Singh came round while you were away, and she told me that all being well I should be able to go home by the end of next week."

"Oh, Mam, that's great news. I'll have the spare bed brought downstairs and I've already made enquiries about the hospital hire equipment, we should have no problem hiring a commode, you can't possibly climb the stairs for the toilet, not just yet, and…"

She interrupted, "There's something else, Joanne. This is what I wanted to tell you in private. I'll be going home to the bungalow."

"But that's not possible, Mam. You'll never be able to manage on your own, not just yet. What if you were to take ill again…"

"Well that's what I wanted to tell you, Joanne, you see I won't be on my own, Sam and I have talked about it and he's going to move in until I'm properly on my feet."

"Oh."

"Then, all being well, rather than continue to co-habit, because you know what the gossips will say, Sam has asked me to marry him, and I've said yes."

"Marry him!"

"I know what you're thinking, Joanne."

She really didn't. I was thinking Bloody hell! Just my luck to end up with a dad with a pony tail and tattoos.

She went on, "But Sam says eighty-three is the new sixty -three and we're both free agents and we've lost so many years already we just want to make the most of the time we have left"

I stretched a smile. "Well Mam, what can I say? I hope you will both be very happy."

And she looked so flushed and content that when I hugged her, I suddenly realised I meant every word of that, with all my heart.

"Will you give me away, Joanne?"

Give her away! I'd only just got her back. I felt the tears welling. "Course I will."

# 40

## WHAT'S IN A NAME

The work on my house was complete, the cleaning had been done, everything was great and it was time for the workmen to pack up for the last time. They had been brilliant, nothing had been too much trouble, the finished job was fantastic and I said I would contact their boss to tell him that. They gathered up their tools while debating who was to drive the van, but again, Dale hung back. He was fishing about in his bag on some pretence of having mislaid something. But I kind of knew better. He let the others go and when we were on our own, he said, "Is there any point in asking you again, Jo, or will the answer be the same?"

There was no point in him asking again. Although I was struggling with the notion, I knew my heart had set its sights elsewhere.

I shook my head. "Sorry, Dale."

He handed me a company card. "My mobile number is on the back in case you change your mind." He gave me a sad little look and a quick kiss on the cheek, picked up his bag and left.

My insides were fluttering like a bird in its cage, because

sweet and dishy though Dale was, I now knew for certain it wasn't him I wanted.

My mother always said God works in mysterious ways. Her illness was connected to so many of the things that had happened to us lately. Me and Jesus becoming thick as thieves (so to speak), Josh having to walk the dog which had led to him meeting Leo and consequently Leo becoming the love (at the moment) of Lucy's life and all of us now involved in the lives of Mandy and Arnie. Ian McAllister being shown in a completely different light (which reminded me, I had to get back to work at some point; he wasn't that full of joie de vivre). Me being asked out by someone like Dale who I hadn't, in my wildest dreams, thought would have even given me a second glance and my mother getting together again with Sam Pickles, who was now my prospective dad! (*Must* try harder to drop the 'Pickles') and Millie becoming a patting dog, of sorts, which had led me to Nick King!

I played around with the name; Nicholas King – nice, Nick King – hmmm, sounds a bit like nicking. Joanne King, Jo King, 'You must be Jo King', Joking! Damn and blast, I knew there'd be a catch somewhere. I could hear Alison now, "Bloody hell, Jo, it could only happen to you."

# 41

## WITNESS THIS

Later that afternoon, Arnie and Mandy came round. They came in giggling like a pair of teenagers, Mandy pushing Arnie through the door first.

"Well you two look pleased with yourselves," I said, laughing with them.

"We are and we've something to ask you, Jo. A favour like," said Arnie.

I waited while they took it in turns to nudge each other.

"Well, ask her then," said Mandy.

"You ask her, it was your daft idea."

"It's not a daft idea, it's dead romantic."

"Well ask her then."

"Ask me what?" I laughed. Their silliness was infectious.

Mandy took a deep breath. "We've decided to renew our marriage vows and we wondered if you would stand as witness."

Arnie held up his hands. "Her idea Jo, nowt to do with me."

Mandy punched him playfully. "That's not what you said in bed last night."

"Whoa, too much information," said Arnie, blushing.

"I think that's a lovely idea, Mandy. It *is* dead romantic and I would love to, when?"

"We haven't arranged anything for definite yet, but possibly sometime in September."

I was happy for them. Love was in the air. Was it possible I might breath some of it?

# 42

## PARTY PREPARATIONS

The next day, Sadie was telling my mother that Percy, from two doors down, had noticed through the garden railings that my mother's Alchemilla Mollis, was spreading like a Chinese whisper among the cracks in her crazy paving, and he wondered, while she was incapacitated, if he should use a spot of weed killer in the cracks, just to curb its enthusiasm. My mother was all for it. "It's a nice enough plant, Alchemilla Mollis," she said, "but give it an inch and it'll take a mile."

Christ! I thought. I should be out there doing Salsa or Zumba or getting that Life I promised myself instead of in here listening to this stuff.

There was an old lady, Maud, who was to have her ninetieth birthday in The Laurels the day before my mother was to leave. The theatre and the dining room were being festooned with balloons and bunting. The plan was to have a tea party in the dining room then music and dancing (although dancing could be stretching that concept a bit), in the theatre. Everyone was looking forward to it. Even the grumpy old men seemed tolerably pleased with the idea, in their own grudging way.

"It'll mek a change, if nowt else," I'd heard one of them say.

"Suppose it's summat to do afore we're boxed up and carted off to the crem," another one said.

Nurse Khamal came in asking if anybody had any special requests for music.

"Well, 'O-Sole-Mia', by Mario Lanza, has always been a great favourite of mine," said my mother.

"Anything by Elvis will do me," said Bella. "Preferably, 'One Night With You', it's so sexy, gets me going every time that does. Just make sure it's not that soppy Wooden Heart rubbish."

'Whatever Will be Will be', by Doris Day, was Nell's choice.

"And you Ruth?" Ruth was thinking about it.

"Well, I've always liked, 'The Windmill in old Amsterdam', by Max Bygraves."

"You what!!" said Bella, "That's for kids!"

"No it isn't, we always sing it when we go on the bus trip to Morecombe with the Perennials, that and, 'Didn't we have a lovely time the day we went to Bangor.'"

"A word of advice, Ruth. When you get out of here you really need to ditch them Perennials," Bella said, shaking her head.

"Thank you, ladies, I've made a note of your requests," said Nurse Khamal, "we'll see what we can do."

"Would you put us a bit of make-up on for the party, Joanne?" asked Bella. "I would do it myself but with my eyes the way they are, I'd probably end up looking like Bette Davis in 'Whatever happened to Baby Jane', or else poor old Nora Batty from along the corridor in room two. Poor soul had some lipstick on the other day, all over the place it was. She thought she looked the business what with that lipstick and her stockings wrinkled round her ankles, fluttering her lashes and eyeing up the men; but there were no takers. Old Bill thought she'd been eating beetroot and had missed her mouth. He went to the kitchens demanding to know why he hadn't been offered beetroot. Honestly, you have to laugh."

"Course I will, Bella. Anybody else want to be made up for the party?"

"I might think about that, Joanne," Ruth said, "but what I would prefer, if you don't mind, is to have some curlers put in. The hairdresser will probably be too busy for an appointment because such is life in the big city."

"I won't bother if you don't mind, Joanne," said Nell. "I've used nothing more than a bit of powder and a wet finger over my eyebrows since Joe passed away. It does me."

My mother said she would make do with her usual touch of lipstick and pat of pressed powder, but she would also like her hair done if she couldn't get an appointment with the hairdresser.

Bella produced the blue top she had worn when she'd come into hospital and asked if I thought it would do for the party?

"It's been around the block a few times with me in it and it's a bit on the big side now but it's comfortable, Joanne. You cannot beat a nice bit of Crimplene and I've always suited this shade of blue." She held it up to her face. I said I thought it would be fine for the party.

My mother asked me to bring in her pink blouse with the mother of pearl buttons and her string of pearls and matching earrings.

The excitement was mounting. I had my work cut out. But at the front of my mind was Nick. My mother would be leaving the day after the party and that would be that. No more tingling, no more living for that chance meeting around a corridor, just a distance memory of something that didn't quite happen.

# 43

## WEDDING BELLES

That night, Alison rang. She had been on an IT course in Manchester for four days; the company she worked for were upgrading their systems. She wondered how my mother was doing and if the builders were finished and if I had any news. I told her I had a bedroom and bathroom to die for; pity they showed the rest of the house up. I said my mother was doing fine and that all being well she would be coming home on Friday but I kept quiet about my mother's impending state of dissoluteness (as in living in sin with Sam Pickles). That was a revelation I was still getting used to myself (*must* learn to drop the Pickles). I told her about Dale. She thought I was mad. And I told her about Nick, she thought I was even more mad. She said a bird in the hand was worth two in the bush. I said perhaps she needed to rephrase that and we laughed. She said men! They're just like the buses, none for ages then along comes two together. But then she had some surprising news herself.

"Guess what?"

"What?"

"Guess!"

"You've won a prize for a night on the tiles with David Beckham."

"I wish."

"You're pregnant."

"Not yet."

"Huh!" I was joking. This was Alison, baby-phobic Alison, "I give in."

"Okay. Well what will you be doing the week before Christmas?"

"Hmmm let me think. Running round like a headless chicken, wishing Christmas could be done away with, panicking like mad about the state of my credit card, you know, the usual stuff."

"Just if you've nothing better to do, I'd like you to be my maid of honour."

"Sorry!"

"And I'd like Lucy to be bridesmaid. We'll all be in sumptuous velvet in gorgeous colours with fur trimmed capes, imitation of course. I'll be in royal purple, like the Queen. You'll be in emerald green; green being your colour. Lucy will be in rustic red and little Sophie, Nigel's niece will be in midnight blue. We'll have holly and ivy headdresses and we'll carry holly and ivy bouquets, imitation holly naturally, because of the thorns. All very Christmassy. So what do you say?"

I yelled something like, "Alison. My God! What can I say? Congratulations. When did all this happen? And why aren't you here so I can give you a hug?"

She apologised for telling me all this over the phone, but she couldn't keep it to herself any longer. She said Nigel had proposed – again – and this time she had accepted because after all she was pushing forty – well thirty-nine anyway, – they had been together for four years and she couldn't imagine life without him. She'd binned his cycle shorts and bum-bag and anyway it was possible he might be Prime Minister one day and she might be the next Cherie Blair – albeit with a better smile and more style – and last but not least, she loved him and her biological clock was ticking.

Hel-lo, Alison's biological clock ticking! My world was in a constant state of turmoil.

"Tell you what," she said, "as you're home now I'll pop round for a cuppa and you can give me that hug. Be about an hour."

Lucy was thrilled to be bridesmaid, although she had reservations about rustic red.

"I'm sure to blush, Mam, and if I do, I'll be the same colour as the dress. Do you think I could swop colours with Sophie?"

"Alison's coming round, you can ask her."

Alison looked radiant and happy and flashing a not insignificant three-stone diamond engagement ring. She had no problems with Lucy swapping colours with Sophie as Sophie hadn't been consulted yet and we all hugged and laughed and discussed the impending wedding.

# 44

## A FLASH IN THE PAN

Upon visiting my mother next day, I was alarmed to see the bamboo screen pulled across her corner of the room with, it seemed, my mother behind it. Bella saw I was concerned and she beckoned me over.

"It's nothing to worry about, Joanne, your mam's fine. Just there's been a bit of bother. Old Aggie Oliver died during the night and as they think Flash Gordon had something to do with it, they're interviewing all the women. It's so silly. I mean Aggie had had heart problems for years and was recovering from pneumonia so it was probably that that put an end to her, not Flash's shenanigans which nobody took any notice of anyway. Still, I suppose they have to go through the ropes. They've already asked me. Was it flaccid or erectile they said. I said it looked nothing like a plastic reptile. Did I need counselling, they said? What for? I said. For the trauma. Trauma! I said it made my day. I sometimes gave it a little flick on passing and that made Flash's day. After all, we're not dead yet, I told them. So they ticked the no box. Anyway, it seems Flash has been sent packing and as they're concerned in case somebody else might drop down dead, they're offering this counselling malarkey."

Just then the screen went back and Nurse Ali emerged, along with a lady in a suit holding a clipboard and pen. My mother was in her easy chair. She smiled when she saw me and didn't seem at all put out.

I waited until Nurse Ali and the clipboard lady went out, "Are you okay, Mam? Bella has told me all about it."

"Yes, Joanne, I'm fine. A storm in a teacup that's all. Shame about poor Aggie, but after all she was eighty seven and it seems she was never in the best of health. I told them Mr Gordon always seemed to me to be the perfect gentleman. He always stood to attention and saluted when I passed him in the corridor. Of course, I didn't always wear my glasses so it's possible I might have missed something, but there we are."

"It was the standing to attention they think hastened poor Aggie's demise," said Bella, sardonically.

Ruth wasn't bothered by any of it. She was too excited. She was to go home the same day as my mother, her daughter was coming up from Yorkshire to take Ruth to live with her.

Bella was worried in case they told her the same. She didn't want to go home. "What good is an empty flat to me, Joanne?" she said, "I need people around me, I like life in the fast lane, I'll die of boredom if they send me out of here."

Life in the fast lane seemed somewhat of an exaggeration but I sympathized, "Well there's nothing to stop us from meeting up again when you're home, Bella. We can all go out for a spot of lunch now and then. We'll go somewhere nice when you're both properly on your feet and feeling better."

"I'll hold you to that," she said.

"You too, Nell?" I asked.

Nell shrugged, she didn't seem bothered one way or the other.

Apart from being desperate to see the elusive Nick, I really wanted my mother home. I was becoming part of the fittings in The Laurels and I needed to get on with my life. But where was he? Perhaps he'd gone back to Ireland to get the dog. I'd made a few discreet inquiries, but nobody seemed to know anything. Some said perhaps he had just spent longer than usual at the other hospital. But I didn't want to leave without seeing him even if it was for the last time. Perhaps I needed to face facts. He had probably thought better of those walks on the beach, decided there was more to life than arranging a playmate for his dog and gone back to Ireland, made it up with Suze and decided to stay there. Damn! WHERE.WAS.HE!!

Just then Ruth came rushing in, rushing that is, with a small 'r', to say that hostilities had broken out in the men's quarters.

Bella said, not to worry, she was sure they'd have a cream for it.

Ruth said the men were up in arms over Flash Gordon. They said poor old Flash had been a victim of the nanny state, that he had been convicted of the death of Aggie Oliver before being given a fair trial. And in protest, a unanimous decision had been taken: they were to boycott Maud's party the following day.

Bella said, "So what. It's not as though Maud would be bothered. Poor soul doesn't know what day it is never mind that she's having a party."

All the same the excitement died down. The women weren't quite as enthusiastic about having their hair and make-up done and everything seemed a bit flat.

Until, that is, the morning of the party when everything changed again. As the caterers brought in and arranged the food trays in the dining hall, word soon went round about the delicious looking pies and quiches and cakes and trifles etc. that the men would be missing out on. And with all that lovely food, came a change of heart. Why, they began to ask themselves should they cut off their noses to spite their faces? After all, what was Flash but an old perv who deserved all he got. He was actually bloody lucky to have escaped jail. If he'd been on the outside and not in here, under the protection of the NHS chances are he would have been beaten up.

So, with Flash's fate sealed, normal service was resumed. I put make-up on the ladies and curled their hair and in the case of Bella, painted her finger and toe nails bright red to go with her lipstick. I stood back and admired them and prepared to stand in the wings while they enjoyed the party.

# 45

## IN THE NICK OF TIME

At lunchtime, amid exaggerated cheers from the staff, Maud was wheeled into the dining hall.

She'd had some beads put round her neck and some rouge on her cheeks. A stroke she'd had at some point had caused her mouth to droop and she drooled a bit but even so, she smiled happily when the candles on her cake were lit; two of them, a nine and a nought and, with help from the others, they were blown out. 'Happy birthday to you' and 'For she's a jolly good fellow' was sung heartily, mostly in broken English by the nursing staff and mumbled along to by the party guests. While the party food was being served I decided I'd have my lunch outside and enjoy some peace and quiet.

Strangely enough, even though I was sitting in the sunshine, on a hospital park bench, I managed to stay awake and I thought of Nick. I tried to put my finger on what it was about him that I couldn't get out of my head. It's not as though he ticked all the boxes, he didn't. So what was it? Yet, whatever it was, it mattered. But the day after tomorrow I'd walk out of here and chances are I'd never set eyes on him again. Wherever he was he probably hadn't given me a second thought and why should he? I was deluding myself, as per, it was the dog he liked, not me. And how sad is that. Second fiddle to a dog! That is really sad.

I looked at my watch. The party animals would be making their way into the theatre just about now, perhaps I'd look in for a few minutes, wave goodbye to my mother, then make my way home. I pulled myself up, stretched, gathered up my rubbish, found a bin, then made my way to the main entrance where I caught a glimpse of a white coat disappearing round a corner. My heart thudded in my chest. Had that been him? I wanted to run to where the coat had disappeared, but I held back. What was wrong with me? It could have been anybody. Doctor Singh, anybody. My heart was pounding. I pressed my back against the nearest wall. If I didn't get a grip, at this rate I'd have a heart attack. I took some deep breaths, straightened up then continued to walk.

The door of the theatre was open and I looked in. There wasn't a lot of action, couldn't really say the joint was jumping. There was music playing and some of the party guests were stretching over seats, chatting to one another. I heard Bella telling Nurse Khamal that a babycham or two wouldn't have gone amiss. Nurse Khamal laughed. "Azeef." she said.

I saw my mother and waved to her then I looked for party girl, Maud. She was parked in her wheelchair in front of the stage and kneeling in front of her, looking up into her face and talking to her, with his back to me was Nick. I nearly fainted. I don't know how I stayed upright. And just as I saw him, he turned and saw me and we looked at each other and he smiled. The tingling started, attacking every nerve in my body then finding its way to my brain. I leaned against the door hoping to look chilled but it was just to stop me falling over. He was back.

He stood up, took a portable CD player from his top pocket and inserted a disc. The music from it started up. Old, scratchy music. He put the disc player onto the floor of the stage then he took Maud's bony, wrinkled hands in his and gently lifted her from the chair. Holding her just above the floor and close to him like a piece of Dresden china, as the music played he carried her round, slowly, in time with the music.

… Moonlight becomes you…

It was scratchy and old fashioned but everyone knew it and they started swaying in their seats and humming along or mumbling the words they could remember.

*She leaned her head against his chest. It was her Tom, her young husband who didn't come back from the war. This had been their song, they had danced to it in the crowded ballrooms before he was sent abroad. She smelled the khaki serge of his uniform, felt the roughness of it against her cheeks, she felt the tears stinging her eyes. She didn't want him to go. She knew in her heart he wouldn't come back.*

The ladies in the room closed their eyes, some wiped away tears. They had their own memories. They all knew crowded ballrooms and young men who hadn't come back from the war.

The song finished. Nick took Maud back to her chair and gently sat her down. He took a tissue from a box on the piano and wiped her mouth then wiped the tears from her cheeks. He took the CD player from the floor of the stage and he gave it to her with the disc still in it, kissed her on the forehead and wished her a very happy birthday. I was fighting tears it was the most tender thing I'd ever witnessed.

I hadn't realised it, but Nurse Ali was behind me. "That was Maud's favourite song," she said, "Nick took the time to find that out, said he'd get a copy of the original in time for her birthday and he has. He always makes the ladies feel special. They all worship him. Must be that blarney stone the Irish have a habit of kissing."

Oh to be that blarney stone.

He walked towards me, well I was blocking the doorway and

he wanted to get out, so I suppose his options were limited. He nodded a greeting to Nurse Ali then he turned to me.

"Can I have a word, Jo?"

A WORD word word word.

"Oh, will it take long, just I was about to make my way home. I've been here all morning helping the ladies get ready for the party." Playing hard to get! Who was I kidding?

He took my arm and I very nearly passed out. We started walking down the corridor.

"It's just I've been over to Ireland and I've brought Barney back with me. I had to stay a bit longer than I had planned, there was some stuff to sort out, but I knew I had to get back today, before your mother left in case I didn't get to see you. I thought if you were up for it, we could have those walks on the beach – you know, with Barney and Millie – or else we could leave Barney and Millie and go ourselves, just the two of us – have lunch somewhere – we could always introduce the dogs to each other some other time and…"

"I'd love to. When?" So much for hard to get.

"You would!" he actually seemed surprised and moreover, pleased, "I know you'll be busy getting your mother home and settled in tomorrow, so how about the day after?"

We stopped walking, turned and looked into each other's eyes. This was the man I was going to marry. "The day after sounds just perfect," I said.

His bleeper bleeped, he clicked it off, "I'll ring you."

"You'd better have my number then." We laughed.

# 46

## AND WE ALL LIVED
## HAPPILY EVER AFTER

How did I get home? I vaguely remembered getting into the car in the hospital car park, then getting out again on my drive. There was a car parked just beyond my gates, but it didn't really register. I opened the front door and before I had time to close it behind me, George came through it.

"You ignored me," he said. His hair was longish, he was tanned, his teeth looked like they'd been in a bucket of bleach and he was wearing a thick gold chain round his neck (take away the chain and tone him down a bit and he was actually not bad looking. This was something I'd never noticed before).

"Did I?"

"I was parked outside and you walked straight past."

"Ooops."

"You seemed miles away."

"Did I?"

"Are the kids around."

"They're in school, won't be home for another hour. It's England."

He held up a plastic bag emblazed with the stars and stripes, "I've brought presents for them; a Baseball and a Mitt for Josh, some Cheer Leader batons for Lucy and bags of American candy."

"Wow, that'll make up for not bothering to ring them."

"You just can't help being facetious can you, Jo? Still, why break the habit of a lifetime."

"Was that an ef word, George? What *are* you getting like?"

"And as sarcastic as ever."

"Not in the mood, George."

"Well how are the kids and how's your mother?" He said that with more than a hint of an American accent.

"They're all fine, thank you for asking," said in the tone I would use to an enquiry from a comparative stranger.

"I can tell you're in one of your funny moods so I'll just look at the work you've had done. I've already seen the invoices. I hope they're justified. Fran thought you were taking the mick."

"Honestly! That Fran! As if! Feel free, it's not as though you don't know your way round." He went upstairs. I waited in the hall, leaning against the living room door with my arms folded.

He came downstairs. "Well you certainly went to town on that lot. Still they've made a good job, looks great. You do have good taste, I'll give you that. You didn't mention to the lads that we were... you know, connected?"

"You flatter yourself, George."

"You look good too, as it happens, Jo, lost a bit of weight, suits you. Not that you were ever fat..."

"You'd lose weight if you lived my life."

"You seem to have a kind of glow about you – sort of womanly."

"I am a woman."

"You know what I mean."

"You're not trying it on, are you, George?"

"Of course not, I'm just saying, that's all."

"I haven't changed a bit. The reason I look womanly is because you're used to looking at Fran."

"Oh a typical Joanne quip. I never could pay you a compliment."

"Yes, well. If there's nothing else, I was just about to Cillit-Bang the hob."

"The hell you were." He'd been watching too many John Wayne films. I could tell.

"There was something else. What was it? Oh yes, I thought I'd collect the dog while I was here. I've arranged for her to go into a pound. Fran can't stand dogs."

"A pound! Millie!"

"You said you wanted rid."

"That was then, this is now and we don't say pound in England, we say shelter, and keep your voice down, she's just in the kitchen, she'll hear. We've discussed shelters and she's fully conversant with that concept."

"But…"

"But nothing, George." I put my hand on his chest.

"Off you go and you awl have a nice day now, you hear," I said that in my best American accent as I pushed him backwards through the still open front door.

"Tell the kids I'll ring them."

"I don't lie to my children," I said, closing the door.

Millie was whimpering in the kitchen. I opened the door and she bounded out, tail banging, sniffing the air as though there had been something alien in the hall. I told her it had just been George with his Paco-Rabanne, a nasty man who wanted to take her away, but I wouldn't let him.

We sat in the hall, Millie and me, and as I stroked the hair out of her eyes, I told her that Nick used to be a dog trainer, so there was hope for her yet and that training the dog will soon be a tick on my 'goals to achieve' list and, with a bit of luck, I might also be able to tick off finding romance. I told her about Nick's dog Barney and how Nick had said Barney was very handsome but even if Barney tried it on, she wasn't to worry about getting pregnant because she'd had the operation. I told her how happy we would be when we were all living together; one big, happy family. How Lucy would be bridesmaid and Josh an usher at the wedding. How Nick would teach Josh his rugby tackles. I told her how special she was and how Leo, Arnie and Mandy had come into our lives through her, and how Josh and Leo now had rees-pect from the High Rise boys through association. I told her how she'd cheered Nell up by becoming a patting dog, of sorts – okay, not exactly a fully-fledged patting dog, but hey, near enough. Near enough to have interested Nick which was near enough for me.

She looked up at me and I looked down at her, at her stringy beard and her wet nose and her bright brown eyes with hair straggling over them. She was actually quite cute-looking for a dog and underneath that boisterous exterior she was really very gentle. As I stroked the hair out of her eyes she plonked her paw on my knee and we sat there, waiting for the phone to ring.

It did. "That'll be him," I told her.

It was.